Tongue in Chic

Books by Christina Dodd

Trouble in High Heels

Christina Dodd

Tongue in Chic

**Doubleday Large Print
Home Library Edition**

A SIGNET BOOK

SIGNET
Published by New American Library, a division of
Penguin Group (USA) Inc., 375 Hudson Street,
New York, New York 10014, USA
Penguin Group (Canada), 90 Eglinton Avenue East,
Suite 700, Toronto, Ontario M4P 2Y3, Canada
(a division of Pearson Penguin Canada Inc.)
Penguin Books Ltd., 80 Strand,
London WC2R 0RL, England
Penguin Ireland, 25 St. Stephen's Green, Dublin 2,
Ireland (a division of Penguin Books Ltd.)
Penguin Group (Australia), 250 Camberwell Road,
Camberwell, Victoria 3124, Australia
(a division of Pearson Australia Group Pty. Ltd.)
Penguin Books India Pvt. Ltd., 11 Community Centre,
Panchsheel Park, New Delhi - 110 017, India
Penguin Group (NZ), 67 Apollo Drive, Mairangi Bay,
Auckland 1310, New Zealand
(a division of Pearson New Zealand Ltd.)
Penguin Books (South Africa) (Pty.) Ltd.,
24 Sturdee Avenue, Rosebank, Johannesburg 2196,
South Africa

Penguin Books Ltd., Registered Offices:
80 Strand, London WC2R 0RL, England

First published by Signet, an imprint of New American Library, a division of Penguin Group (USA) Inc.

ISBN 978-0-7394-7881-3

Printed in the United States of America

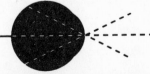

**This Large Print Book carries the
Seal of Approval of N.A.V.H.**

For my wonderful editor, Kara Cesare,
who suggests and titles
and revises with tact and genius.
Here's to a long and fruitful relationship!

ACKNOWLEDGMENTS

Thank you to Kara Welsh for a fabulous promotion and publishing schedule, and to Anthony Ramondo and the NAL art department for gorgeous covers that fly off the shelves.

And as always, thanks to the Squawkers, friends, booksellers, and fans who make writing and life in general such a pleasure. All my love.

Prologue

March 1951
Late Afternoon
On the South Carolina Coast

In the fourth-floor studio in the majestic Waldemar House, Isabelle Benjamin finished the last painting she would ever do there. Over the past week, the light had been good, the humidity oppressive but manageable, and the temperature had never topped eighty degrees. Now, when she stood back and studied the canvas, she nodded in satisfaction.

This was, without a doubt, her best work to date.

Taking a thin brush, she dipped it in black paint and, with a flourish, she signed her name.

She covered the pots of paint and cleaned her palette. She wiped her brushes on a rag, washed them in the sink, and carefully arranged them on the table. Untying her apron, she hung it on the hook.

She didn't know why she bothered. When she was gone, Bradley would throw everything that reminded him of her into the garbage. But she was betting—betting her daughter's future, in fact—on the probability that he couldn't stand to throw away her painting. If she was wrong . . . well, it would be a loss to the art world.

But then, no one would ever know.

She picked up the canvas. It was large and awkward and still too wet; nevertheless, she carefully maneuvered it into the heavy gilt frame. She tapped at the nails that would keep it in place, then turned the whole thing around and studied it. Her fingers had smeared a little of the detail along the edges, but she'd figured on that and created an unfocused background that hid the damage. The paint would seal the canvas into the frame; no one would try to separate the two. Certainly not Bradley . . . A bitter smile twisted her lips, and a single tear escaped and trickled down her cheek.

But she dashed it away. Enough of that. She'd cried too much over the last two years.

Her marriage was over now, and past time, too.

Picking up the painting in both hands, she carried it down to the third-floor nursery.

The room was absolutely perfect. Pink ruffled curtains hung in starched splendor at the long, old-fashioned windows. A colorful alphabet danced across the wall, and each teddy bear occupied its proper niche. The gleaming antique crib was fitted with white sheets over an appropriately firm mattress, and the sleeping three-month-old inside was swaddled in a pink blanket, and rested on her stomach to discourage colic. Her sweet pink lips moved occasionally as she dreamed of milk, and Isabelle's heart broke again when she remembered how her husband and her mother-in-law had bullied her out of nursing her child.

But no more bullying for Isabelle. No more cold, hard, proper nursery for Sharon. They were escaping. Going free.

The sour-faced nanny sat in the rocker

reading a *Reader's Digest* condensed version of *Les Miserables.*

Isabelle appreciated the irony.

At Isabelle's entrance, Mrs. Graham stood as a gesture of courteous—and false—respect. "May I help you, madam?"

"I've come for Sharon. Would you carry her downstairs for me?"

"If madam would allow an experienced nurse to advise her, after a baby has been put down for the night it's not a good idea to disturb her. Such an action sets a bad precedent and leads to reprehensible habits later in life."

"According to you, so does holding her when she cries and feeding her when she's hungry."

Mrs. Graham stiffened in offended horror.

Isabelle had never spoken to her that way before. Before, she'd tried to make the best of a bad situation. Tried to compromise and create change from within.

But now she had a child to consider. She couldn't allow her baby to grow up loveless, stifled, fit into a box furnished with white lace gloves and hats held under the chin with an elastic band, friends picked by their income and family background, and a debutante ball at seventeen that led to another tearstained marriage, another loveless childhood.

"Please put the knit hat on Sharon, wrap her in her down blanket, and bring her to me. I'll be in the library," Isabelle instructed.

"As you wish, madam." Mrs. Graham bobbed a curtsy that mocked Isabelle and promised that another phone call would be made to Mrs. Benjamin.

Isabelle didn't care. Not even the threat of her mother-in-law's displeasure could dissuade her from her course.

She walked down the two flights to the library. The painting, held carefully away from her body, got heavy. Her arms grew tired. And this part . . . this part she dreaded more than any other. But when it was over . . . it was over forever. And she'd be relieved. So relieved.

She walked into the lofty room with its shelves packed with leather-bound books, its massive desk and old-fashioned chair, and the alcove where two snarling lions guarded a marble fireplace.

As she expected, she found Bradley in his easy chair, his bourbon on the table beside him, his smoking cigar between his fingers.

He was a handsome man with a shock of

dark brown hair. When she first met him, his appearance had been what turned Isabelle's head. That, and the flattering experience of having a wealthy older man paying court to her. He'd said all the right things. He'd enjoyed her conversation. He'd been indifferent to her poverty.

Most important, he'd admired her art. For the first time in her whole life, someone who'd visited the Louvre and Florence and the Taj Mahal had seen in her paintings enough promise to call in the foremost art expert in the world.

Bjorn Kelly had been half Scandinavian, half Irish, with an eye patch, a limp, and an incredible charisma that mesmerized and enticed. He also had no patience with being dragged halfway across the world by the infatuated Bradley to look at a stupid woman's paintings—until he'd seen them. Then he'd yelled at her for bad technique and no vision, told her to stop drawing like a girl, and given Bradley the names of two American art teachers worthy of her genius.

That was the term Bjorn used—*genius.*

When Isabelle remembered that moment and how her love for Bradley had swept through her heart, she wanted to break the painting she held over his stubborn, handsome head.

Instead she walked with firm footsteps across the library—no more tiptoeing around—and leaned the painting against the fireplace facing him.

As if stung, he half rose from his chair. "What the hell is that? Some kind of cruel going-away present?"

"It's a gesture of my appreciation, Bradley. Without you, I would never have been able to create a painting like this." She dragged the wooden chair away from the desk and over to the fireplace.

"Without me—and that damned Kelly." Bradley's lips were so stiff they hardly moved as he spoke.

"Yes. Damned Kelly helped me, too."

"Don't be smart with me," Bradley snapped.

Isabelle looked him right in the eyes. "Or what?"

The silence between them grew and seethed until Mrs. Graham bustled in, breaking the spell.

"Sharon is still asleep," she said, her tone making it clear that she didn't expect the condition to continue, and that it was all Isabelle's fault. Mrs. Graham was an officious, judgmental woman who for thirty years had served the best Southern familes and fancied herself above Bradley Benjamin's upstart wife. Mrs. Graham would be delighted to see the back of Isabelle.

She wouldn't be quite so delighted to see her employment disappear at the same time.

"Wait there," Isabelle told her. "I'll take the baby when I'm done." She stood on the seat and lifted the old painting off the hook. She stepped down, walked over to the bookshelves, and placed it there. Picking up her painting, she stepped on the chair again. It rocked under the weight of her and the heavy canvas.

Bradley surged to his feet, caught her waist, and balanced her.

The two of them stood motionless, joined by the sensation of touch and all the old feelings: lust, fury, pain . . . so much pain.

Then Bradley stepped away and wiped his palms on his pants.

The insult broke what was left of her heart, and she almost doubled over.

But she couldn't lie to herself. She had known what would happen when he accused and she acceded.

Her hands trembled as she placed the wire over the hooks. She straightened the painting as well as she could, then asked, "Is it level?"

"Yes." His voice was gruff.

"I'm leaving you my best work."

"You're a damned whore." He rejected her with his voice, with his words, with his stance and his accusing gaze.

Mrs. Graham inhaled with shock.

"I know." Isabelle looked down at him. "But I won't contest a divorce or ask for support. I won't take anything of yours. You're free to find the woman of your dreams." She stepped off the chair and dragged it back to the desk. Going to Mrs. Graham, she took Sharon and hugged her close to her heart.

The baby stretched and wiggled, opened her eyes and closed them again. "Do you want to say good-bye to her?" Isabelle asked Bradley.

"Why?" He seated himself in his easy chair and picked up his bourbon. "She's nothing to me."

Any man who could say that about the infant he had cradled had ice in his veins.

Isabelle was doing the best thing for herself and her child. "You're right." She nodded and walked to the door.

When she turned back to look at him one more time, he was sitting in his easy chair, staring at the painting over the top of the fireplace.

One

The Present Day
Midnight
On the South Carolina Coast

Lightning flashed. Shadows of bare limbs clawed the tangled path, and the lithe, black-clad trespasser stumbled. Paused. Shuddered. Then continued toward the Victorian house set high above the ocean. The roar of thunder shook the ground, and the next flash of lightning followed hard on its heels, blistering the massive structure with harsh white light. The spires on the fourth-story cupola stabbed at the roiling clouds, the wind gauge spun wildly, and on the beach the waves growled and pounded. The posts on the second-story balcony stretched and twisted, and a hard gust of wind drove the first burst of rain up on the porch.

The figure ran lightly up the steps and toward the imposing double doors. The large silver key slid neatly into the lock. It turned easily and was quickly pocketed. One black-glove-encased hand rested on the beveled glass, then pressed, and without a sound the door swung open.

No lamp lit the interior, but the intruder confidently strode into the foyer.

Then the lightning struck again, blasting away the shadows. Thunder boomed. The figure halted and spun in a circle.

The wide hall soared two stories above the floor. Gold blazed off every picture frame, every finial, off the coved ceiling. Stern eyes watched from nineteenth-century portraits, and wide stairs stretched up and out of sight. The blast of thunder made the crystal chandelier shimmer, and the prisms sent colored light shivering across the walls.

Then the lightning was gone. Silence settled like dust in the house.

Shoulders hunched, the intruder crept

toward the second entrance on the left. The beam of a tiny flashlight slid around the room, touching briefly on shelves crowded with leather-bound books, the massive carved desk, the incongruously modern office chair. In an alcove in one corner of the room, two overstuffed chairs faced a tall fireplace finished with marble and flanked by two snarling stone lions.

The flashlight blinked out, but stayed in the intruder's hand. Each step fell soft and sure on the wide, custom-woven rug, headed in a straight line for the cozy sitting area.

The figure halted behind one of the chairs and stared up at the painting over the fireplace. The flashlight flicked on again and scanned the wall, once, twice. The picture there, that of a stodgy twentieth-century businessman and his dog, drove the intruder to cast the light around the room in an increasing frenzy. "Oh, Grandmother. You promised. You *promised.* Where . . . ?"

The overhead light flared.

A man's deep Southern voice demanded, "What are you doing here?"

The intruder half turned. One gloved hand flew up to protect against the brightness.

A tall, dark-haired man stood in the doorway, his hand on the light switch, his face craggy, tanned, and harsh.

He was the most striking, arrogant, handsome man Natalie Meadow Szarvas had ever seen.

The lightning flashed so fiercely static electricity skittered across the floor. In the yard something broke with a loud crack. The thunder roared and the windows shook.

She'd descended into hell.

She tried to run.

Her feet tangled in the fringe of the rug.

She tripped.

She grabbed for support. Missed. Hit the floor—hard.

Her head and the lion's head collided.

The lion won.

When the stars had ceased sparking behind her closed eyelids, she took a long, trembling breath. Her bones ached from hitting the floor. The fringed rug smelled good, like citrus and sandalwood. Her head . . . her head really hurt. She lifted her hand to touch the pain at her temple.

Someone caught her wrist. "Don't. It's bleeding."

The man. The one with the contemptuous brown eyes. How had he managed to get from the door to her side?

The explanation was easy. She'd been unconscious. But she didn't remember being unconscious. She remembered only . . . she remembered seeing *him*.

"Sir, should I call the police?" Another man. Eager. Quiet. Efficient.

"Call the doctor," Mr. Arrogant said.

"Then the police?"

"Just the doctor."

"Yes, sir." The other sounded disapproving—and obedient. His footsteps retreated.

Mr. Arrogant pressed something soft to her forehead.

She winced and tried to flinch away.

"Leave it," he instructed. "You're bleeding on the rug."

"Okay," she muttered. *Wouldn't want to bleed on the freaking expensive rug.*

"Open your eyes," he said.

She must be mistaken. This couldn't be the handsome one. A guy who used a tone that rude to a girl sprawled bleeding on his floor couldn't be attractive.

She opened her eyes. She looked up at him.

He looked back at her, a cool, assessing stare.

Her heart stopped. Her breath stopped. She was immobile.

Because she was right about one thing: He wasn't handsome—he was harsh, breathtaking, his glance striking like lightning and leaving her dead.

And what a way to go. If this was her punishment for trying to steal a priceless painting, then burglary had just become her way of life. "Wow," she said again.

Mr. Arrogant sat on his heels beside her. He wore a crumpled, starched white shirt with the cuffs rolled up.

Nice arms.

And a pair of blue jeans that caressed his thighs.

He held Meadow's wrist in one hand, and pressed a swathe of white to her forehead with the other, framing her in his arms, sheltering her with his shoulders.

Her heart jumped into a frenzy of action.

"Who are you?" he asked.

"Um . . ."

Apparently she wasn't fast enough with a

reply, because he shot a second question at her. "What are you doing here?"

"Here?" She lifted her head and tried to look around. The instantaneous headache and nausea made her relax back against the floor, close her eyes, and mutter, "I'm going to barf."

Gently he placed her hand on the cloth on her head. She heard sounds—him standing, moving away, coming back. "If you must, here's a basin."

She opened her eyes the smallest chink and looked.

He held an etched glass vase with gold decoration, absolutely exquisite, done in the Regeletto design.

Aghast, she asked, "Are you insane? That's a Honesdale vase, an original. I can't barf in that!"

For a second, the merest twitch of an eye, she thought she saw amusement.

But no. Mr. Arrogant was as forbidding as ever when he said, "Of course. Pardon me. I lost my head." He glanced around him. "Can you barf in a Limoges punch bowl?"

"No problem. But"—she took long breaths—"I think I'm okay now. I just have to be careful and not sit up."

Christina Dodd

"You have a concussion."

His certainty made her faintly belligerent. "You're no doctor."

"No, of course not. I wouldn't have sent for one if I were."

"Ha." She'd met way too many doctors lately, and while he acted superior enough to be a physician, he was too intense to fit the medical profile.

He continued, "But it doesn't take a surgeon to see that you hit the lion hard enough to break his tooth."

Cautiously she checked out the lion. He still snarled, but lopsidedly. "I hope that's not an omen."

"If it is, I don't know how to read it."

The other guy, tall, bulky, with Asian eyes and a dark brown complexion, returned and hovered. "The doctor's on her way."

"Sam, make sure I'm not bothered."

Without a glance or any acknowledgment of her, Sam left, shutting the door behind him.

"So who are you?" Mr. Arrogant slid the clip off her head—and smiled as her hair tumbled free.

People, especially men, tended to smile when they saw the fall of shining copper curls. In fact, people, especially men, tended to smile at her all the time, no matter what.

Not this stern-faced, hawk-nosed inter-rogator. His smile vanished at once, like a mistake he wished to call back.

She had more composure now, no desire to explain her mission, and a few questions of her own. "Who are *you?*"

"I'm Devlin Fitzwilliam."

Which told her absolutely nothing. "And you're here because . . . ?"

"I live here."

She stared.

"I own this house," he said helpfully. "The one you broke into. The one with the Honesdale vase and the now snaggletoothed lion."

"You own Waldemar?" She struggled to comprehend the incomprehensible. "What about the other guy . . . ? The one who used to own it?"

"Bradley Benjamin? Is that who you're asking about?" Devlin picked up her wrist again. He stripped off her black leather glove. He kissed . . . *Oh, my.* He kissed her fingertips. "Which Bradley Benjamin? The third or the fourth?"

"I, um, don't know." She hadn't prepared

for this conversation. She had planned to break in, grab the painting, and depart, not talk to a guy whose ruthless eyes demanded the truth and whose lips carried on a dialogue all their own.

"Bradley Benjamin the third sold me the house," Devlin said. "Bradley Benjamin the fourth—I call him *Four,* which irks him no end—likes to visit and whine."

"Oh." Grandmother was wrong. So wrong. Bradley Benjamin *had* sold the house. This stranger *did* live here. The painting was *not* in its place.

And Meadow was in deep, deep trouble.

"Who do you think you are, breaking in here?"

"I'm . . . Meadow." Not Natalie Szarvas. That was her professional name, and if he knew that, she didn't stand a chance of getting out of this mess. "I don't . . . I can't . . ." How stupid was this? She should have considered that she might get caught. Prepared some kind of story.

But Grandmother had been so sure . . . and now some guy with cold eyes and warm lips kissed her fingers and cross-examined her, and soon she'd find herself on the way to jail. And how was she going to explain that to her parents living just outside the small town of Blythe in Washington State, when they thought she was teaching a glassblowing seminar in Atlanta?

"You don't remember?" Devlin kissed her wrist.

Nice. Very nice.

His lips, not his questions.

"That's right. I don't remember. Because I . . . I . . . I have amnesia!" *Good one, Meadow! That's thinking on your feet!*

Lightning struck nearby. Thunder boomed.

Meadow jumped. It was as if God Himself called her a liar.

And Devlin's mouth twisted. He didn't believe her.

Hastily she added, "I don't remember what I'm doing here. I've probably had some kind of mental breakdown." A pretty clever lie, because what was the worst that could happen? The police would send her to an asylum for a few days' evaluation; then she'd be out on her own and she could try again.

Or perhaps the Almighty would send a bolt of lightning to strike her dead.

"When you didn't recognize me at once, I was afraid of this." Devlin gazed into her eyes so soulfully she didn't dare blink. "My darling, somehow you managed to find your way back."

"Huh?" She had a bad feeling about this.

Tenderly he gathered her into his arms. "I know you don't remember—but you're my wife."

Two

"Are you crazy? We're not married!" Someone was shouting, and the noise made Meadow's head throb. Because, she realized, the shouting came from her own mouth.

"You poor thing. You don't remember, but we married eight months ago."

Lightning struck. Lights flickered.

"Right! That's why you welcomed me with open arms!"

"You left me. On one of the worst days of my life you disappeared, and I didn't know what happened to you. I've been worried to death, and when you showed up, hale and

hearty and pretending not to know me, I . . .
I just . . ." He did a good imitation of a man
choking on his emotions.

Except he wasn't choking on his emotions; he was trying to think of a new lie to
tell. She knew it—because she'd never met
him before. Ever. She would remember him.

Any woman would remember him. He had
the face of a dark angel and the eloquence
of Satan's right-hand man. The flashes from
outside danced across his craggy features
like stage lighting in hell.

"You just what?" she insisted.

"All the months of uncertainty, of not
knowing whether you were alive or dead. I
wanted to shake you. But your poor bruised
head saved you, and now I've got my senses
back and I can hold you. Hold you as I've
longed to."

Which was tightly and with an intimacy
that took the edge off her pain and made
her heart beat too fast. Of course, she'd
had a scare. Probably that was why her
heart thumped. It couldn't be the pleasure
of discovering that the scent of citrus and
sandalwood came from his skin, or that she
could see the shadow of his beard darken-
ing the cleft in his chin. Beneath his shirt,

his chest had that taut warmth that made her want to run her hand over his pecs and down his belly. . . . Without a doubt he worked out, and while she liked a guy who was, as her grandmother would have said, built like a brick shithouse, Meadow was perfectly happy to view the bricks from a distance. In her experience, men who kept themselves buff were self-absorbed, and a brick shithouse–worthy man who wasn't self-absorbed would be deadly to her peace of mind.

Especially if he smelled good.

Good heavens. Was her nose buried in his chest?

She pulled away.

He gathered her closer again. "What caused the amnesia, darling?" he asked solicitously. "Did you hit your head then, too?"

"I don't know. I don't remember ever being with you." *Pin him down.* "Where did you say we were married?"

"In Majorca."

"Majorca." *Majorca?*

"A beautiful island off the southeast coast of Spain."

"Right." She didn't feel sick anymore. More like . . . giddy.

"I have a home there."

"Well, of course you do."

"You don't believe me?"

"I believe you've got a home on Majorca."

"And you can take my word, my darling amnesiac, that we met and married there. After all, you don't remember anything different, do you?"

She looked at him . . . at his tanned, rugged face, his dark, rumpled hair, his brown eyes . . .

A man like this—a man whose perpetual expression was harsh intensity—made it difficult to imagine he could be amused. But he had to be . . . didn't he? Was he punishing her for breaking into his house by playing a practical joke? Did the absurdity of the situation make him want to laugh?

Did he ever laugh?

She got the feeling she would wait a long time before he grinned and admitted he was teasing.

Which left her where?

"My head hurts." From trying to figure a way out of this maze.

At the sound of voices in the foyer, he glanced around. "The doctor's here."

"Wow. You got a doctor to make a house

call? I thought they only did that on old re-runs." In her experience, doctors never did anything to make matters easy on the patient.

"I hired Dr. Apps to be on call for the hotel. You've given us the opportunity for a dry run. Keep your hand on my handkerchief." He pressed Meadow closer to his chest, slid his arm under her knees, and very slowly stood with her.

"A hotel? What hotel?" She grabbed the soft linen as it slipped.

"Good girl." He spoke to her as if she were an obedient dog. "This hotel. The Secret Garden."

"This is a hotel?" Maybe her brain *was* affected by her fall. Or hell had frozen over.

Devlin had a sure way of moving that minimized the dizziness and, yes, he probably did it so she didn't throw up on his rug, but he made her feel secure, the way a Honesdale bowl must feel when she cradled it.

"The grand opening is in three weeks," he told Meadow; then his attention left her, and he spoke to someone else. "Dr. Apps, thank you for coming." Placing Meadow on the couch, he went to intercept the doctor at the door. "Meadow fell. . . ."

As he gave Dr. Apps the details, Meadow carefully lifted her head and looked.

Dr. Apps looked back and smiled with that mechanical interest medical people showed when faced with an unspeakably boring case. She had nice teeth. Nice face with a minimum of makeup, and lipstick that was a nice shade of pink. Nice, well exercised, extremely tall body. Nice brown hair done up with a nice clip.

Talk about unspeakably boring.

With Devlin's attention and his scent and his body elsewhere, Meadow relaxed against the cushions and tried to organize her thoughts.

Bradley Benjamin had sold Waldemar.

Devlin Fitzwilliam had bought it and was turning it into a hotel.

Her beautiful plan was in tatters.

The paintings had probably all been moved according to some decorator's idea of where they would be most attractively placed. Or they'd been appraised and sold. . . . No, she would have heard about that.

So what to do?

Stay here and poke around, of course.

But Fitzwilliam claimed she was his wife,

and she didn't know why. Or what he wanted.

Of course, there was the usual thing a man wanted from a woman, but he wasn't a rapist. She snorted. More likely he had defend himself against hordes of pursuing women. And why bother with a concussed female when he could have someone like the doctor? The doctor whose voice she heard crooning at Devlin. The doctor who couldn't have made her interest more obvious if she'd wrapped herself in pearls and presented herself on a clamshell.

Meadow moaned softly.

No response. Her *husband* kept talking to her *doctor,* and neither one of them paid her a bit of attention.

She moaned louder.

"Darling!" Devlin returned to her side.

That's better.

"Let's have a look at her." The doctor nudged him aside.

He went easily.

"Hello . . . I'm sorry, I don't know your name."

Meadow had heard Devlin tell Dr. Apps her name, but she was willing to play along. "Meadow. I'm Meadow."

"Tell me what happened, Meadow," Dr. Apps invited. She wore a blue smock with big pockets loaded with all kinds of doctor stuff, and she listened to Meadow's heart, shone a light in Meadow's eyes, examined Meadow's bump on the head, and listened with seeming inattention while Meadow confessed to breaking in, falling down, and blacking out.

"How long were you out?" Dr. Apps asked.

"I don't know. Long enough for him to get to me." Devlin stood off to the side, and Meadow indicated him.

"How long?" Dr. Apps asked him.

"Less than a minute," he answered.

Dr. Apps nodded. "Pupils look good. Nice and even. Eyes are tracking well. Any loss of memory?"

Here it was. Meadow's chance to escape. "You bet. I have amnesia. I don't remember what I'm doing here."

"I thought you said you broke in?" Ruthlessly Dr. Apps cleaned the wound on Meadow's head.

"Sure! He said I did"—she indicated Devlin—"and I'm sure he's got the security cameras to prove it."

Devlin nodded.

Great. When he dragged her into court, they'd show the video and throw her in prison for the rest of her life. "But I don't remember that at all. I don't remember anything."

"But you told me your name." Dr. Apps didn't appear to believe her any more than Devlin did.

"That's the only thing I remember. I don't know my last name." Meadow was starting to feel like Klinger in *M*A*S*H*—trying desperately to convince the doctor that she was crazy. "I only know I woke up with my head bleeding."

"Hmm. How unusual." But Dr. Apps wasn't looking at her. She was staring at Devlin as if he'd said something. Which he hadn't. He was still standing there, impassive and waiting.

"Really." Desperate to get her attention, Meadow got up on her elbows. But that made her head throb, so she slid back down. "You ought to take me to the hospital for a mental evaluation."

Dr. Apps returned her attention to Meadow. "Any nausea?"

"Not anymore," Meadow said.

"She threatened to throw up in a Limoges punch bowl." Devlin perched on the arm of the couch.

"Oh, dear. Oh, no." Dr. Apps pursed those lovely, lipsticked lips in real distress. "Those bowls are exceedingly valuable, Meadow." Obviously the woman fancied herself a connoisseur and Meadow a Philistine.

Devlin made no move to correct her.

Meadow glared at them both. "So's the rug, and at least you can run a bowl through the dishwasher." She savored the sight of Dr. Apps's sputtering horror.

"Darling, stop teasing. You know what happened the last time you ran a Limoges bowl through the dishwasher. All the gilding washed off." Devlin dusted Meadow's forehead with his fingertips. "But I'm afraid she's telling the truth, Dr. Apps. She doesn't remember a thing. She doesn't even remember that she's my wife."

Dr. Apps looked at the two of them. Looked again. And laughed so heartily Meadow would have liked her if she weren't a doctor. "Devlin, you jerk. You set me up, didn't you? You wanted to see how well your emergency medical plan works, and you called me in on a fake case."

He shrugged as if admitting guilt, but answered, "I would hardly bash Meadow over the head to check out your response time."

"So one of your cleaning staff fell and you took advantage of the opportunity." Dr. Apps stuck her stethoscope and her eyeball light into her capacious pocket. She pulled gauze and tape out of her other pocket, and in swift motions and with no care for Meadow's discomfort, bandaged her with tape and gauze. "You would have suckered me completely if not for the story including breaking in *and* having amnesia *and* her being your wife. That last is a little too much to swallow." She patted Meadow on the arm. "Did you make all that up yourself?"

Devlin smirked. "Meadow, next time, stick to the script I give you so we can get through a practice run."

"I did! You're the one who said . . . I told the truth!" *Mostly.*

It would serve them both right if Meadow did barf in a Limoges punch bowl. Unfortunately her nausea had subsided under her indignation at being accused of lying.

Sure, she was committing perjury, but not for such a paltry reason as Dr. Apps imagined.

"She really did hit her head," Devlin pointed out.

"She's going to have a headache, maybe dizziness, maybe irritability. She might need bed rest for a day. Let her make the decision, but no heavy lifting or hard work tomorrow. I'll leave a prescription for pain relief. And tonight someone needs to wake her every hour to make sure she's conscious. Don't worry; she's going to be fine." Dr. Apps talked about Meadow as if she weren't even there, and as Devlin rose, she tucked her hand into his arm. "Now—how did I do on my dry run?"

"Very well. It took you less than ten minutes to arrive." He escorted her toward the door. "I was sorry to wake you, but it was too good an opportunity to miss."

"I understand. Don't hesitate to call whenever you need me."

The thunder cracked again, shaking the sofa and the floor. "Those storms won't stop coming," he said. "I'll send you home in one of my cars."

"It's less than a mile," the doctor protested, but she sounded pleased.

"And you'll get drenched." He sounded firm.

Their voices faded.

Outside, lightning struck and thunder cracked.

Inside, Meadow fumed. Not only did they both patronize her, but the doctor didn't believe she had amnesia. Of course, neither did Devlin, but if she denounced him for saying they were married, she'd have to confess that she didn't have amnesia—and he'd have her thrown in jail. She couldn't fool herself; he looked like the kind of man who would prosecute her to the full extent of the law. He'd probably set his snaggletoothed lion on her.

But if she didn't confess, she was stuck here.

Stuck. Here. At Waldemar. At her grandparents' home, looking for a painting she desperately needed, and which was nowhere in sight.

Her plan had been simple.

Break into Waldemar.

Steal the painting.

Get out of Waldemar.

Sell the painting for an absurd amount of money.

Use the money to pay for her mother's very expensive treatments.

She turned over to stare at the fireplace. That pompous old gentleman mocked her.

No matter how many times she stared at it in disbelief, it never changed. It was the wrong damned picture.

Three

How was that possible?

In Meadow's pocket, the key poked her in the hip. Pulling it out, she looked at the length of silver, the huge teeth, the ornate handle. This she should hide. She might need it again.

Hearing Devlin's footsteps, she hastily poked the key between the couch cushions and the back, down far enough that it wouldn't be easily discovered by the cleaners.

Lightning danced across the portrait, making the haughty gentleman's eyes glint with disapproval. She didn't care. Disapproval of any sort was of no importance to her. Finding the right painting was.

She reclined just as Devlin Fitzwilliam walked back into the room. She looked up at him.

He looked so . . . tall. And . . . austere. And . . . intent. On her.

If he gave a damn about Dr. Apps, he hid his interest well.

"Ready for bed?" Without waiting for an answer, he scooped her into his arms and headed toward the door. "Tell me if you feel sick."

"I'm fine." Except for the fact that he held her against him as comfortingly as a man might hold his beloved wife—and she liked it. She almost felt he wanted her here.

He climbed the long, elegant sweep of stairs. The place smelled of fresh paint and wallpaper glue, and everywhere she looked she saw antique lamps, gilt-framed mirrors, and designer touches that echoed an elegant age. Waldemar had been refurbished into a showcase of comfort and ease.

"It looks great," she mumbled.

"The house? Yes, it came out well." His gaze roamed the corridor, and he looked grimly pleased. "We have a saying in Charleston. 'Too poor to paint, too proud to whitewash.' Bradley Benjamin didn't have the money to maintain the old girl like she deserved. I did the house a favor when I bought it from him."

"And him? Did you do him a favor, too?" So that was why Bradley had sold the house? He was broke?

"No. Old Benjamin and I have a deal—I don't do him favors, and he doesn't call me a bastard. At least, not to my face. Not very often." He turned sideways as he went through a doorway. He carried her through a sitting room decorated with masculine furniture in claret tones. "Here we go."

She caught a glimpse of a huge, lush bedroom painted a warm gold and touched with claret highlights. They entered a huge en suite bathroom with swathes of black marble, a black tub, a sleek and gigantic glass shower done in claret tile, and fresh gold chrysanthemums in blue Chinese vases.

He placed her on the counter, her head against the wall, her feet in the sink. The cold from the marble leaked through her slacks, chilled her flesh, and brought her halfway to perkiness.

"I imagine you want to use the bathroom before you go to bed." He looked down, his eyes hooded and enigmatic, and he didn't take his arms away.

"Yeah." He was warm. Toasty.

"Can you manage on your own, or shall I . . . ?" He tugged at the hem of her black turtleneck T-shirt.

"Hey!" She caught at his hand. "I can do it!"

A lovely sort of half smile cocked his mouth. "Are you sure?"

She wouldn't have thought it, but this austere man looked almost . . . charming. "I can do it. You go out. If I need help, I'll call."

"Promise? I don't want you to hit your head again."

"None of us want that. I'll call you if I need to." She turned, dangled her feet off the counter, and watched as he strolled away.

"There are new toothbrushes and whatever else you need in the top drawer. There's a robe on the hook by the shower." He walked with a long-legged grace that made her fingertips tingle.

She would really enjoy touching his ass.

He turned at the door and lifted his eyebrows. "Are you sure you don't need me?"

Maybe. But not for the reason he was thinking.

She slid to her feet. "I'm not dizzy. I'm not sick."

"You just don't remember who you are."

"I certainly don't remember being your wife."

"I promise I'll do everything in my power to remind you." He studied her openmouthed consternation, then firmly shut the door behind him.

"Oh, no, you won't!" she said to the closed door.

It didn't answer.

She looked into the mirror at her pale, strained face, at the white bandage partially taped to her hair, at the faint smear of blood on her forehead.

She'd lived through the last two grueling years with her faith in good thoughts and good living intact. She'd faced the challenges with a smile, knowing she kept everyone's spirits up.

Now she looked like hell. She felt like hell. And she blamed Devlin Fitzwilliam.

Her mother would make the case that

Meadow was responsible for the events of the day.

In an excess of guilt, love, and determination, Meadow dropped her head into her hands. Her mother. If her mother knew where Meadow was and what she was doing . . . Meadow moaned at the thought.

"You need to go to bed and get a good night's sleep," she said to herself. "Tomorrow you'll know what to do." Because tonight she was so confused.

She had lied to Devlin about having amnesia. Did he believe her?

Of course not. He didn't, did he?

He'd lied about their being married. If he didn't believe she had amnesia, then he knew she knew they weren't married.

Possibly he was trying to wring a confession out of her. But it didn't feel that way. The way he acted, he wanted her here. And why? What was he up to?

Worried, she pulled off her sweater. On a good day, her boobs were an A cup, and this athletic bra mashed her flat. She didn't have much of a rear end, either, and her black leggings, the ones she wore to yoga, hugged her body. Devlin had seen the package, so clearly he wasn't after her voluptuous body.

She leaned on the counter and stared into the mirror.

Or her face, which at this moment looked singularly cheerless and unappealing. And unattractively pale and sweaty. And worried. Really worried.

So what was he after? What did he want? What was his plan—and *why*? Why was he doing this?

She opened the drawer and found every soap and lotion a woman could want, all in sample-size bottles. She brushed her hair back and washed her face, avoiding the bandage. She slipped out of her shoes, her pants, her socks, and dropped them in a heap on the floor. She put on the plush white bathrobe. Like all hotel robes, it was huge. The hem brushed her at midcalf, and she had to roll up the sleeves to see her hands. She tied the belt into a knot, then opened the door.

The bedroom was empty.

He hadn't gone far. He'd promised to come if she called, and she recognized a man who kept his word.

She climbed into the tall four-poster bed and sighed as the mattress, the pad, the cool, soft sheets enveloped her. She pulled the comforter up; it was light yet lavish. Nine feet above her, the ceiling glowed the same warm gold color as the wall, and the intricate cove molding was painted to look like cherrywood.

The artist in her admired the craftsmanship. The exhausted woman wanted nothing more than to close her eyes and go to sleep.

Except . . .

Did this guy want her here? A weird idea—but why else would he tell such a whopper of a lie? Why would he say she was his wife, and go through such incredible gyrations to keep her at . . . what did he call it? The Secret Garden?

She knew only one thing for sure—his reasons for trapping her here could not be good.

Meadow's beautiful blue eyes, the eyes that had betrayed her, were closed in slumber. Her copper-tinted hair glowed like a nimbus on the pillow around her face, and the flickering lightning caught each shining strand. Her skin was tinted like a peach and was—Devlin ran his fingertips over her cheek—just as soft. Her lower lip was rosy and slightly swollen—every time she told her silly lie, she bit into the tender skin.

The doctor's bandage was a large white blot on her forehead, and that, combined with the dark circles under her eyes, gave her a fragile appearance.

He suspected that was a mirage.

He knew so much about her already—and so little.

She had a name, Meadow. But he didn't know exactly who she was.

She was a thief, and here for a reason. But he didn't know what it was.

When it came to art, she had a discerning eye. But he didn't know what she did.

Yet he knew more than she could ever imagine. People in the South had embarrassingly long memories, especially when a scandal was involved, and Meadow's grandmother had been the biggest scandal in a generation. No one in Amelia Shores had ever stopped talking about Isabelle, or her affairs, or how thoroughly she had humbled the proud Bradley Benjamin.

Devlin had never met Isabelle, but he liked her.

For years, when he was young, Bradley Benjamin had made Devlin's life hell. The reasons were myriad and diverse—two hundred and fifty years of rivalry between the

Fitzwilliams and the Benjamins, Bradley Benjamin's old-fashioned dislike for successful women like Devlin's mother, and most of all, Bradley Benjamin's pure, unmitigated hatred for a child born out of wedlock. A bastard.

Like Devlin.

Bradley despised him. And why?

Because Devlin reminded Bradley of his own well-publicized failure, and the humiliation that had followed him ever since.

So when the opportunity for revenge presented itself, Devlin had seized Waldemar, storming the ancient bastion of Benjamin superiority. Even better—the sheer stupidity and incredible incompetence of Benjamin's own son had been the reason he'd been able to obtain their ancestral home as his own. And what a lovely, delicious dollop of warm pleasure on the cold dish of revenge—rather than living in the home, which Bradley would have hated and mocked, Devlin had turned the grand old mansion into a posh hotel.

That was what bastards did.

He smiled down at Meadow, an unpleasant curve of the lips.

Now, sleeping in his bed was the possibility of more and even better revenge.

Would Bradley Benjamin recognize Isabelle's granddaughter?

Probably.

Would he wait and cringe, fearing that moment when everyone in Amelia Shores identified her, and all the gossip started up again?

Definitely.

Would he give a damn that Devlin had married her?

Yes. Just . . . yes.

Bradley Benjamin hated Isabelle, but she had once been his, and if there was one trait Devlin shared with Bradley, it was their possessiveness about their property. He would hate to think of his former wife's granddaughter in the filthy clutches of the Fitzwilliam bastard.

Devlin touched Meadow's throat and noted the contrast between his tanned hand against her fair, freckled skin.

Bradley would hate to think of Devlin and Meadow thrashing together on a bed.

Best of all, the whole maneuver would cost Devlin nothing.

Well . . . except the investigation into Meadow's background.

He didn't know exactly who she was—

according to gossip, she didn't exist—but by the time his detective had finished with her, Devlin would know her age, her birth weight, and the names of every man she'd ever dated.

Taking Meadow's cell phone, he flipped it open.

It was searching for service.

Of course.

He searched for her call list.

Nothing.

He looked for the numbers she'd last dialed.

Nothing.

The smart girl had wiped the memory on her cell phone clean before she'd broken in.

Only she *hadn't* broken in. Somehow she'd unlocked the door and walked in. The cameras hadn't caught her sleight of hand, but something she'd done had overridden the security chip in the huge old-fashioned lock. Of course, the motion sensors had caught her as she walked through the foyer, setting off the silent alarms, but still, he wanted to know—his security man wanted to know—how she'd done it.

With a touch of uncharacteristic whimsy, he wondered if it could be something as simple as the house knowing she belonged here.

But he didn't care whether she belonged here and he didn't. He would solve all of her mysteries and in the process take a pound of flesh from Bradley Benjamin.

Devlin had always had the luck of the Irish.

Meadow proved he hadn't lost his touch.

Four

Meadow woke to sunshine pressing against her eyelids, a rebound of her optimism—and someone in bed with her. Behind her. Spoon fashion.

A man. Most definitely a man. Most definitely the man who'd been there to wake her up every hour all night long.

No wonder she was feeling optimistic.

She flipped over and found herself facing Devlin's rugged, handsome, unsmiling face. "Good morning, darling." His fingers caressed her cheek. His chocolate brown, dangerously intense eyes plumbed the depths of her soul.

Her soul, ridiculous thing, stretched and purred under the flattering attention.

"All right." She managed to sound stern. "What are you doing here?" Like she didn't know. He'd seen an opportunity and moved to take advantage.

"Where else would I be except in bed with my beloved wife?" He slid closer, his legs tangling with hers.

"I'm not your beloved wife!" *Oops*. Panic reaction. Because of his words. Because the robe she'd wisely slept in last night was open from the waist down and the waist up, and her bra and panties left her very bare. And because he wore only a soft cotton T-shirt and . . . well, she didn't know what he wore below the waist, because the blankets covered him, and she wasn't about to grope him to find out.

"Darling, of course you are. You just don't remember." His fingers wandered down the slope of her throat. "I'll help you."

"Stop that." She slapped at him and inched back.

"Does your head still hurt?"

"A little." A nagging headache behind her eyes. Certainly not enough to stop her from doing what she must.

"The doctor said you could stay in bed today."

"The doctor is an idiot. I'm fine." And thoroughly irritated that he should quote Dr. Apps to her while he was horizontal with *Meadow.*

"You're grouchy." He shook his head sadly, as if he actually knew what her moods were like, when he didn't have the foggiest idea. "You *should* stay in bed today."

"I am not grouchy. See?" She smiled, grinding her teeth all the while.

He smiled back, all allure, ease . . . and seduction. "I'll let you get up on one condition: You promise that if you feel faint or ill, you'll let me know."

"As if you really cared." Maybe she was a little grouchy.

He touched his lips to her forehead.

"What do you want?"

"I want you back. I want to be together like we were in Majorca. I want the romance, the talk, the passion. . . ."

She ought to say, *That never happened.* And *Tell me why you want me here.*

Maybe she would. Later. When her thigh wasn't trapped between two of his. "I don't remember."

"Then I'll make it happen again. We could go down to the beach and meet by accident—"

"We met by accident?"

"With Fate as our matchmaker. I was worn out from making the deal on this house, and bitter about the acridness of business. I'd lost my way, my pleasure in living, and I was leaning against a boulder, staring out at the sea. . . ."

The sun warmed his upturned face. The waves lapped at his feet, and the Mediterranean smelled briny, while a hint of lavender wafted through the air. This moment was perfect, a gem set in the restless flow of time . . . yet an unusual yearning tinged his soul with melancholy. All his life, he'd enjoyed his own company, cherished his solitude, his moments snatched away from the swift and cutthroat business of making deals, renovating warehouses into trendy apartments, constructing luxury boutique hotels on dilapidated properties.

But today didn't feel like solitude. Today he was alone. Very alone.

Out of the corner of his eye, he caught

a swift slash of color. He turned to see a woman, a tall woman with hair shining like a new copper penny—

Meadow interrupted. "I'm not tall. I'm only five-five."

Devlin placed his finger on her lips and reproved her with a shake of his head. "The flow of your sundress made you look tall, and your long, leisurely strides made me think of only one thing. . . ."

"Yeah, and I'll bet I know what it was."

He knew this was the woman for whom Fate had intended him.

"I would have lost that bet," she said.

She held her sandals in one hand. She kicked the sand while she walked, her gaze fixed to the horizon, where the blue sky blended with the blue sea. Her expression was far-off and wistful. He thought she looked as lonely as he felt, and when he stepped forward, her eyes were first startled, then wary, then . . . warm. Without a word, she took him in her arms and kissed him, and since that moment, nothing had been the same.

"Wow," Meadow whispered. He was good. She knew it was all garbage, but when he wove his story, he pulled her in and she almost believed it. Almost lived it with him.

"Maybe you don't recall me, but your body knows mine. Your body yearns for the pleasure I can show it." His voice sounded the way black velvet felt—soft, rich, seductive. His hand cupped her wrist and slid beneath the wide sleeve to the inner bend of her elbow. His thumb stroked back and forth on the tender skin. "We don't need warm white sand and Mediterranean breezes. We don't need palm trees and glass-bottomed boats. All we need is each other . . . and the world drifts away."

He wasn't so much encroaching on her body as he was seducing her with his words. Each phrase sank into her mind and sent a thrill down her spine to places that had nothing to do with marriage and everything to do with mating. His thigh rubbed hers over and over, and distractedly she tried to recall the last time she'd shaved her legs.

Then she decided she didn't care, because she wanted to rub herself against him. In fact, her hips were headed in his direction when some remnant of sense stopped her.

She wore almost nothing. He wore . . . who knew? Dangerous ground for a woman whose one fledgling affair had faded under the pressures of family illness.

She turned her head away from his fingers and her gaze away from his. "Don't."

He rose onto his elbow. "Look at me."

She did. She had to. She needed to observe his moves, try to keep ahead of him. If that meant she obeyed him, there was no help for it. If her gaze intertwined with his again, and those heated brown eyes stripped away her pretensions and left her bare to his scrutiny, there was no help for that, either. He had a way of making her feel helpless—and making her like it.

"We're lucky." He slipped his hand around her waist and splayed it in the small of her back. "Most couples have only one first kiss. We'll have two."

Her thoughts might be muddled, but her instincts were crystal clear. She should run. She should run *now.*

Instead she let him pull her closer, into the heat and the scent of him.

But it was okay. Because he was wearing boxers.

Specious reasoning, Meadow.

His head dropped toward hers. His breath whispered across her skin near her ear. "Sometimes when two people meet, they know that a touch would be enough to set off a wildfire, but they never have the chance to set the spark. We have the chance . . . and it would be a crime against nature not to find out. . . ."

She turned to look at him, to tell him to back off.

Somehow her lips met his—and the spark leaped into instant, glorious conflagration. Her eyes fluttered closed. The lightning from last night shivered between them, setting off flashes beneath her closed lids. Her hands rose and grasped him, one behind his neck, one against his shoulder, and the lightning crackled from her fingertips into his skin and back again, like magic performed by a cartoon magician.

What he did with his lips was wicked, an overload of temptation. His hands didn't wander; rather, they held her closely, and the heat that built seemed to ignite their scraps of clothing, leaving nothing but bare skin and the flare of desire.

Her breath came more and more quickly.

She was blind and deaf to anything but him: his breath in her mouth, his scent filling her nostrils, the fire he created as he rubbed his hips against hers.

She liked his tongue. She liked that he used it against her teeth and lips to taunt and touch. She liked that he gave up control when she wanted to explore his mouth. She savored the vibration of his moan as he rolled onto his back and pulled her with him.

He was solid beneath her, a great, strong beast of a man who radiated heat and moved her without effort. As she pressed him into the mattress, kissing him with growing intensity, he ceased holding her against him. Instead his hands wandered, pushing her robe aside so that only the tie remained between their bodies. His palms caressed her buttocks, cupping them, pressing her against his erection, and moving her in a pulsing rhythm.

Vaguely she knew things were moving too fast. She couldn't get intimate with a man who had lied to her. Not when she was lying to him, too. But on this sensual, physical, earthy level, they were far too attuned.

At least, she was attuned to him.

Maybe he was simply good at this stuff. She'd heard that some men worked miracles with a woman's anatomy, although she'd had little experience with that. But here and now, each shift of their bodies wrung another sensation from her taut nerves.

She searched out the hem of his T-shirt and slid her hands beneath it, climbing the ladder of his sculpted belly up to his ribs and then to his nipples. He stretched his arms above his head, inviting her—challenging her—to strip him.

As a girl, she'd once taken a dare to jump off the roof of the studio onto their trampoline. She'd broken her leg. While the doctor set it, he'd sternly warned her of the dangers of accepting dares.

Too bad Meadow's besetting sin was impetuousness.

Don't do this, Meadow.

Sitting up, she straddled Devlin.

You're going to be sorry, Meadow.

Peeling him out of his T-shirt, she tossed it aside.

Her conscience was wrong. She was *not* sorry.

Smooth muscles rippled beneath tanned skin. On his arms. On his chest. On his belly. She couldn't resist; she touched him with her fingertips, sliding up hills and down valleys, following his love arrow down his breast-bone, over his navel, to the waistband of his underwear. The contrast between her pink nails and his dark hair fascinated her, and she gloated over the strength and glory of his chest. "You're in great shape."

"After you left me, I had nothing worth-while to do except practice making love." He flexed his biceps. "By myself."

Damn the man! How did he know she was sucker for guys who made her laugh? "Practice makes perfect."

"Let's see." He slid his fingers under the waistband of her panties.

She had only one thought—*Take them off.*

She leaned forward.

He pushed them down her legs.

Stupid Meadow. Don't do this, Meadow.

She kicked them away.

His palms stroked the bare globes of her rear, raising the fine hairs all over her body. His fingertips skimmed the crack that led to the space deep into her body.

She tensed with anticipation.

He slid his thumbs over her clitoris.

She sank her nails into his skin.

He slipped—just barely—his finger into her body.

She gave a moan that revealed far too much.

"It was exactly like this in Majorca," he whispered in her ear. "You kissed me and we went up in flames."

A warning pealed loud and shrill in her head.

"Majorca?" He'd mentioned Majorca before, and it behooved her to remember— she'd never been to Majorca.

She wasn't starting out a relationship based on lies.

Devlin's lies.

Her lies.

"I'm out of here." She vaulted off the bed, one hand sinking into the mattress, the other mashing his stomach.

He *oofed* as she drove the air out of him.

It was farther to the floor than she expected. She stumbled when she landed, then stood with her back to him and took a long breath—a long breath that did nothing to restore her good sense.

Her brain clamored for her to get far away. Her body urged her to climb back on the mattress and make it rock.

And her common sense insisted on asking the logical question—had he mentioned Majorca on purpose? Had he wanted to stop them before they went too far? That suggested that a cool mind still operated beneath the heat of passion, and that one thought brought her temperature down to a reasonable simmer.

She pulled the robe closer around her, covering herself. She faced him.

He reclined on the bed, sheet to his waist, arms tucked under his head. Muscles bulged on his chest and pecs; hair dusted his armpits and breastbone. His hair glowed like a dark halo against the white pillowcase. His eyes smoldered with intensity.

He didn't look like a man in possession of a cool mind. Maybe he'd mentioned Majorca by mistake. "Are you always so reckless?"

"Never." He sat up on one elbow. "That's why I fell in love with you—you transform me from a dull businessman into a dashing beachcomber who knows what's important in life."

"What's that?"

"You."

She swayed toward the bed, pulled by the gravitational force of his desire.

Think, Meadow. Think!

She pulled back. "You're good." She'd always appreciated flattery as much as the next girl. Apparently she appreciated it a little too much.

"Let me put on my clothes. They're harder to get out of." She headed into the bathroom, sure she had seized control of her destiny again, and determined to ward off any more of his lightning-fast, underhanded, seductive maneuvers.

"I threw away your clothes."

Five

Meadow caught her breath in outrage. She stopped. She turned.

Devlin smiled a panty-dropper smile.

Too bad she wasn't wearing panties.

"Excuse me?" She stepped toward the bed, a half smile on her lips, fire in her eyes. "You threw away my *clothes*?"

"The shop downtown is sending out outfits appropriate for my wife." He sounded so . . . innocent. So reasonable.

"Outfits *appropriate* for your wife?" Her voice rose. "What does that mean?"

"It means I like the way you dressed in Majorca."

"And that would be?"

"In sundresses. With flowers in bright colors." He wiggled his fingers over his chest to indicate something. Bright-colored flowers, she guessed.

"Sundresses? With . . ." Normally she wore jeans and T-shirts. And Birkenstocks. With socks. "If I'm your wife, why don't you have my clothes from Majorca?"

Promptly, he said, "I left them there, hoping you would return."

The fresh-washed morning sunshine lit one half of his body and face, and left the other half in shadow. Who did he think he was? Some supervillain capable of lightning-fast changes designed to amaze and confuse her?

Because someone needed to bring him down to earth.

Like targets, his nipples drew her gaze. Grabbing one, she twisted. *Hard.*

"Ouch!" He grabbed himself. He looked down at the bruised nub. "What was that?"

"A purple-nirple." She watched in grim satisfaction as he rubbed the ache. "And no normal woman wears a flowered sundress for everyday. I wear jeans."

"You can't know that. You don't remember." Sarcasm. Definitely sarcasm.

"Are you trying to make me into a Stepford wife?" A spooky thought. Was that his intention? "I know what kind of woman I am. And I certainly know what I wear. What all women wear. You need to look around."

"I don't look at other women. I'm married."

She snorted. "I'll call and get you an eye appointment."

"That's a very wifely duty."

Conversation between them wasn't an exchange of ideas; it was a fencing match.

Worse, she was enjoying herself when she was actually angry at him. Very angry about . . . something . . . *Oh, yeah.* "Don't ever get high-handed and toss my clothes again."

"Of course not. I won't have to." He swung his legs out from under the sheets. "Not now. You're here with me, and I intend to keep you close."

Devlin was too tall. The way he loomed distracted Meadow, made her aware of his erection tenting his dark blue boxers, her bare feet on the cool hardwood floor, their recent and all too steamy intimacy. The things he said sounded less like banter and more like a threat, and when a woman had gone as far as she had—and that was far too far—she would be a fool to ignore her alarm. "Keep me close? What does that mean?"

"You're not well. You have a concussion—"

"Minor!"

"And you have amnesia about the most important moment of our lives."

She hated that he held that trump.

"More important, I'm opening a hotel here on the private, exclusive shores of South Carolina. It's the wave of the future; all of these old homes are falling to reduced incomes and increasing costs. But the wealthy here are still wealthy—and hostile to me, and there've already been incidents of sabotage."

"Oh," she said blankly. Such a scenario was so out of her league, she didn't know what to say. "Like what?"

"A few of the more important families made it clear that the merchants in town would find their mortgages inexplicably foreclosed on if they sold us anything. I'm trucking in groceries from Charleston."

"That's medieval!"

A smile quirked his mouth. "That's South

Carolina. It's one of the original thirteen colonies and still run by the same families."

"You're kidding." She was from the West. From the mountains of Washington and a family of bohemians, artists. Of course, her grandmother had told her about the old South Carolina family traditions that choked the life out of a person. But Isabelle had run away, and the stories she told sounded like fairy tales from long ago.

Now Devlin was saying nothing had changed? One look at his stern face convinced her he was serious. "What else have they done to the hotel?" Meadow asked.

"I built a cell tower behind the hotel. Someone knocked it down."

"Cell tower?" With a jolt she remembered. "My cell phone." She slapped her rear as if expecting to find a pocket. "Before you tossed my pants, did you retrieve my cell phone?"

"It's here on the nightstand." Sitting down on the bed, he extended his hand. "I have guards patrolling this place—"

"So how did I get in?" She didn't think he was lying about this.

"A guard who found shelter from the storm when he should have been making his rounds, combined with untested generators that allowed power outages. The problem will be fixed today."

"Fixed? You mean, the generators will be up and running?"

"And the guard replaced." His gaze grew cold.

She didn't like that expression. It reminded her of last night. It reminded her only too clearly that he had some ulterior motive for this farce he was playing, and if she didn't get that painting and get out of here fast, he was going to squash her like a bug. "Ah, come on. That was a heck of a storm!"

"I pay top dollar, and I expect the best."

"Yes, but . . . the poor guard! He's got no job."

She saw no visible softening on Devlin's face. "He should have thought of that before he signed the contract."

"I guess." Meadow honored her own contracts, but at the same time, her heart ached for the unknown man.

"Look. These people who want to stop me from opening are determined, and they've got the money to back that determination. I can't take the chance that someone will seize the opportunity to hurt my wife, and a sloppy guard would expose you to danger. You do understand, don't you?" Charm thawed his expression. With his dark hair disheveled from the night and that quirk of his lips, he looked almost . . . sincere. Intent. Interested in her. Only her.

Reluctantly she placed her hand in his. "Sure. Except . . . are you really going to tell people I'm your wife?"

"Of course." He rubbed his thumb back and forth across her palm.

It was on the tip of her tongue to ask what excuse he would make when she disappeared. But then he'd ask why his wife would disappear, and she'd be stammering around, trying to come up with a good lie. Her mother always said there was no such thing as a good lie, that the universe rewarded the truth and punished a falsehood.

Meadow's gaze fell on their joined hands, then on the bed. With last night's debacle and this morning's precipitate passion as cases in point, Meadow had to admit that her mother was right.

She could reveal the truth—she cast a glance at his harsh face—and be arrested for breaking and entering with intent to commit grand theft. *Good idea, Meadow.*

Devlin watched her flounder with the dilemmas of truth versus lie, him versus prison; and the way he smiled made her suspect he found her struggles all too amusing.

Jerking her hand from his grasp, she picked up her phone.

As she flipped it open, he said, "I looked for numbers, but the phone is blank." He strode across the room to the dresser and pulled a pair of jeans out of the drawer.

"You snooped in my phone?" He'd had the nerve!

"I thought it might reveal some names that would tell us where you've been." He pulled on the jeans.

"Oh. Yeah." Thank God Judith had thought to have Meadow wipe the memory or he'd be talking to her mother right now. Meadow could imagine how her mother would sound—as disappointed and upset as the time she'd caught the thirteen-year-old Meadow eating a hamburger—meat!—at her friend's.

What a horrible memory that was!

"So there's no cell service out here?" To avoid his gaze, she watched the little signal searcher do its gyrations.

"Until last year, the residents of Amelia

Shores hadn't allowed anything so crass as a cell tower to pollute the ambience of their elite village, and even now the signal doesn't reach out to the mansions."

"Medieval," she muttered again.

"I'm building another tower for the hotel's guests, but it isn't scheduled for assembly until the day before the grand opening. Then the frenzy of disapproval from the other mansions' residents will be at its height, and they won't even notice the tower going up behind the house."

"Yeah. Probably not." She snapped her phone closed. "I want a shower."

He opened his mouth.

"Alone."

He closed it.

"So where are these flowered sun-dresses?" She needed to search the house for the painting, and she needed to search fast.

"They're not here yet. I'll see what I can find you in the gift shop." He started for the door.

"Jeans. A T-shirt," she called after him.

"It's going to be eighty-five today."

"Shorts and a T-shirt, then."

He stopped and ran his unsmiling gaze over her.

"What?" She spread her hands.

"Five-five, one hundred and twenty-eight pounds, A cup, pants size six, shoes a size eight." Then he continued out, shutting the door behind him. He didn't ask if he was right.

"One hundred and twenty-*six* pounds. What's wrong with that?" A man with such acute powers of observation could probably read every thought before it crossed her mind—and she prided herself on keeping an open mind.

She was in such trouble.

She had to find that painting and get out of here. She wanted—desperately wanted—to go home to her parents with enough money to pay for her mother's medical treatment . . . and now Meadow had a second reason for haste.

She needed to get away from Devlin—before he lay further siege to her wary self, and ruined all of her well-made larcenous plans.

Six

Meadow dove for the corded hotel wall phone.

She dialed frantically, then slammed down the receiver. Would Mr. I've Got Security Everywhere know she was using the phone?

Probably.

But she felt pretty sure it was illegal to bug the phone lines in a hotel room, so her conversation should be private.

Besides . . . did she have a choice?

No.

Really, he probably hadn't had time to bug this phone.

And she had fallen over the edge into the pit of paranoia.

She dialed again, calling the one person who had listened to her rage and disappointment, encouraged her to look for a solution, helped her make her plans, and promised to be the contact in Blythe while Meadow was away.

Judith Smith had arrived on their doorstep when Meadow was fourteen, hungry to learn everything she could about art and painting. Before she was done with her apprenticeship, Judith had settled in as part of their family. She'd stayed for months, creating mediocre paintings, but the first time her art was rejected she had quit.

Privately, Sharon told her daughter that the only person who could declare an artist a failure was the artist herself, that Judith's demand for immediate success had put a stranglehold on her talent, a talent Judith refused to allow to mature.

So she'd quit and gone on to other careers—she didn't say what they were, but apparently she had money, for she came and went as she pleased. She'd helped Meadow get into the art program at Stanford and suggested she study abroad. Her mother, her father, and her grandmother had built Meadow's spirit and mentored her art, but when Meadow had left their mountain home and gone out into the world, Judith had been her real-life mentor.

Now Meadow held her breath, waiting for the first ring.

Judith answered before it was completed, her nasal voice tipped over the edge into panic. "Who is it?"

"It's me." Meadow hunched over the phone, keeping her voice low.

"Thank God. I've been so worried." Judith took a long breath. "Why aren't you answering your cell phone? What happened? Where are you?"

Meadow answered the questions in order. "Cell phone doesn't work out here. Got caught breaking in. At Waldemar."

"Oh, my God. Are you all right? Did you find the painting? Did you get hurt?"

"I got hurt a little. Nothing important. But the painting wasn't on the wall."

"I did try to tell you that was possible. People do rearrange their houses."

Judith sounded so calm, Meadow wanted to shriek at her. "Grandmother promised me it would be here."

Judith's voice sharpened. "Do you think she lied to you?"

"She didn't!"

"I'm so sorry. I didn't mean that. There's simply so much riding on this." Judith sounded contrite and embarrassed. "But you did say that sometimes there toward the end, she was a little confused."

"Yes. But the painting probably was there—once. The trouble is, people sell their houses." Meadow listened as Judith breathed hard.

"Waldemar is sold?" Sometimes, in moments of stress, Judith's voice sounded like pure New York. This was one of those moments.

"To a man named Devlin Fitzwilliam."

"Devlin Fitzwilliam," Judith said slowly. "Devlin . . . Oh, my God. *Devlin Fitzwilliam* caught you breaking in?"

"Yes, and he— Wait a minute." Judith's panic caught Meadow's attention. "Do you know him?"

"Everybody knows Fitzwilliam. He was the quarterback for Florida State."

"Quarterback. That's football, right?" The way he was built, that made sense.

"Yes, dear. That's football. The man's been

profiled in the *Harvard Business Review. Forbes. Entrepreneur.* He's one of the Fitzwilliams of Charleston, the son of Grace Fitzwilliam." Meadow could almost see Judith wringing her hands. "Do you recognize *that* name?"

"No. Not really." Meadow put her back against the wall and slid down, sitting on the floor, knees up, eyes fixed on the door.

"You ought to watch TV every once in a while. Grace Fitzwilliam is a home decorator with a nationally syndicated show. She demonstrates how to turn your house into a traditional Southern paradise."

"Oh." Meadow liked television. So did her father. But her mother wouldn't allow a set in her house, and Meadow had been living with her parents for the last—difficult—year and a half. She was out of touch and knew it—and, much to her surprise, she was happier than when she had been at college and very much in touch.

Sharon was a smart cookie.

"Is it a reality show?"

"More like Martha Stewart. You do know who Martha Stewart is, don't you?" Judith was half laughing, half sarcastic.

"Yes. Judith, I can't talk for long." Meadow

needed to get off this phone before she was caught, but she couldn't resist hearing about Devlin. "Tell me what I need to know to manage *him*."

"Fitzwilliam is a genius at developing profitable properties."

"He's turning this into a hotel."

"I'll bet. He's got a reputation as a ruthless son of a bitch out to make his fortune bigger."

"Ruthless."

"He's nobody's fool, and everybody knows it—or finds out to their peril. He runs over anyone who stands in his way. He's the son of that billionaire, Nathan Manly, the one who bankrupted his company, stole all the money, and fled to South America about ten or fifteen years ago. Bet you never heard that story, either?"

"No." Nor did she care, except as it related to Devlin's personality—and remembering his comment last night about Bradley Benjamin calling him a bastard, it obviously did. "So Fitzwilliam wants to prove he's not like his father?"

"That, and Grace's family didn't take it well when she popped up pregnant. She wasn't married to Manly—in fact, he was married to someone else."

"Every child born is a new thought of God."

"The Fitzwilliams are against new thought."

Realization dawned. "They're one of the families he was talking about. The ones who still control everything."

"That's right. So he carries chips on his shoulder as big as epaulets, and rumor says he's a real asshole when someone tries to screw him over."

"Oh." And Meadow had sort of liked him. Found him enticing.

But maybe that was the hormones talking.

"So you have to be careful. Very careful." Meadow could hear the worry in Judith's voice. "Now, what's your next move?"

Meadow couldn't bring herself to confess her ridiculous amnesia lie or his absurd marriage lie. The whole thing sounded like a Shakespearean farce, and it played like one, too, except for those kisses . . . which played like porn. "I talked him into letting me stay."

Judith hesitated, and Meadow could almost hear her brain whirling. Judith was probably more intelligent than any person Meadow had ever known. Not more talented, but more intelligent, and although she tried to hide it, hungrier for fame. Mom had once quietly confessed to Meadow that she felt there were teeth in that hunger, but Judith had never shown them to Meadow. "Do you think it's wise to stay? Maybe there's another way."

"I think there's no choice. He's got guards and security all over the place. I won't get in again. And I have to have that painting." Unbidden, the picture of her mother with a handkerchief tied over her bald head rose in Meadow's mind. She swallowed sudden tears. "We haven't heard it's been discovered, and we would be the first to know. Gossip in the art community spreads like wildfire. So it's got to be here in the house somewhere. I only have to find it."

"Yes. You're right. But if he's got all that security . . . how?"

"I'm a smart girl. I can turn off the security for a while, then turn it back on again."

"Oh, my dear, I'm so worried about you!" Judith burst out.

"I know." Meadow took a breath. "How's it going at home? Do they really believe I'm in Atlanta at a retreat?" She felt awful lying to her parents, but if her mom knew Meadow was here and what she planned to do, she'd be disappointed, and her mother's disappointment was a crushing weight to bear.

So it was better for them both if Meadow lied. Any guilt her mom would have made Meadow feel about stealing a lousy picture was nothing compared to the guilt Meadow would feel if she could take action and didn't.

Not to mention the fact that Grandmother would come back and haunt her.

River was a gifted artist and a great father, but he was a disaster at making sure they had food in the fridge, talking to their agent, and paying the bills, so Meadow had made Judith promise to stay with her parents and handle the day-to-day stuff that her mother usually handled. Now Meadow tried hard to feel relief and instead suffered a clawing anxiety.

"Yes, don't worry! Just concentrate on your job. And don't call them—I told them your retreat won't allow cell phones."

"Oh, but . . . " She talked to her mother almost every day, touching base, needing to hear that familiar, warm voice and know her mom was still in the world.

"You're a lousy liar," Judith said with brutal frankness, "and if you call your mother, she's going to know you're up to something. You don't want to worry her."

"No. You're right."

But that brought Meadow right back to the problem of Devlin Fitzwilliam.

If she was such a lousy liar, why was he keeping her here?

Judith hung up the phone and looked around the piece-of-shit room she'd rented at the Amelia Shores Bide-a-Wee Motel.

She'd worked years to get to this moment—she shouldn't pull back now just because the big cockroaches kept pet cockroaches. Besides, she'd been here once before, eighteen years ago this September, and yes, it was seedier than it had been then, but she was so close to her goal, she could almost taste it.

In some ways she felt bad lying to that kid. She'd known her for years, and Meadow was as genuine and open as her parents.

On the other hand, Meadow was as talented as her parents, too, and that made Judith's gut burn. It wasn't fair—why some people were geniuses and others . . . others were just good. In the art world, *genius* won you international appreciation. *Good* won you a place in the traveling Starving Artists' Shows and a painting on a restaurant wall with a two-hundred-dollar price tag stapled on the frame.

That wasn't what Judith had wanted. All her life she had needed to *be* someone. She wanted people—critics—to notice her, praise her, recognize her. And twenty years ago, five years after getting out of college, she'd had to face harsh reality. She didn't have genius—so she went about getting her fame a different way.

She was going to find a lost masterpiece.

It wasn't hard. It could be done. It merely took a little research and the willingness to track down rumors to their source. Not all the rumors had panned out, of course, and she'd spent a lot of time viewing really lousy art masquerading as masterpieces.

After about a year she heard a rumor about famed artist Isabelle and the masterpiece she'd left behind. She'd heard another rumor, and another, and finally she'd bought enough drinks for the bitter old nursemaid, Mrs. Graham, to get confirmation. The masterpiece was real, and it was in the grand old mansion of Waldemar.

But Mrs. Graham was so deaf she shouted every word, and such a lush she'd give up her information to anybody with enough cash for a mimosa and some pretzels. Judith hadn't had a choice, and really, it wasn't hard to spike her twelfth glass of the evening with a little rat poison. When the police found her the next day in the alley outside the bar, they'd carted her away and listed her death as "natural causes."

Southerners had a real way with covering up the ugly side of life.

Judith's break-in at Waldemar had yielded no painting that fit the description. It had, however, yielded some dog-teeth marks on her ass and a perfect description of the thief by one furious Bradley Benjamin. For those reasons, she hadn't dared try again.

So she had gone about matters a different way. She'd gone looking for the papers of the famous—and infamous—artist Isabelle . . . and instead found Isabelle's *supposedly* dead daughter.

The whole setup was too perfect. The grand old artist Isabelle had announced her daughter had been killed in a car wreck in Ireland at the age of four. She'd "adopted" Sharon, then kept her out of the limelight, and ever since, Sharon had been hiding in plain sight, not avoiding the press, but not courting them, either.

After Sharon married River Szarvas, they'd used the money Isabelle had made from her art to establish an artists' colony, one dedicated to fostering talent and training the next generation of geniuses. They funded scholarships. They trained their successors, for shit's sake. They always had ragtag kids who imagined themselves artists hanging around, sleeping on their floors, eating their food, talking about their art with burning eyes. . . . It hadn't been hard to show up at the household in Blythe and move in as Judith, a woman seeking her muse.

And for a while, she'd thought she'd found it. She created the best paintings of her life while living there and breathing that rarified air. For a while, she'd forgotten the stupid lost masterpiece and painted at a fever pitch, sure she'd at last tapped her inner genius.

Then, when she had shown them to an art critic, he gave her the name of a restaurant willing to hang and sell paintings for a commission.

She wanted to put poison in *his* coffee.

Instead, she'd crawled back to the Szarvases', listened without interest to Sharon's pep talk, and volunteered to transcribe Isabelle's diaries into the computer. Sharon felt sorry enough for her to let Judith do it, and while Judith discovered eye-popping gossip and fascinating insights into the female artist's life, she'd found nothing about the masterpiece.

She had tactfully probed Sharon's memory, trying desperately to become the kind of confidante Sharon would trust in all things.

But Sharon had held back; her acute eyes had made Judith think that . . . well, they had made Judith think Sharon saw through her.

At last Judith took an interest in Isabelle's granddaughter, and hit gold.

Isabelle had told the child everything. *Everything.*

A quick trip to Amelia Shores had revealed that the painting was no longer hanging above the fireplace.

Of course not.

That would be too easy.

And she couldn't figure out how to stay there and search. Old man Benjamin was still alive. The police still had the description of her. She got in and out of town in a hurry.

Right about then, her money had run out. She put her father, the meanest son of a bitch who had ever lived, in an asylum, sold his home, and cashed in his assets. That gave her another two years.

Then she needed funding.

Mr. Hopkins made his offer so promptly, it was as if he had been observing her. Of course, knowing what she knew now, he had been.

She could have the fame.

He wanted the painting.

She'd never seen him. He'd been a voice on the phone, counseling her to be patient. She'd thought *she'd* been patient all the long years, but he defined staying power, and in the end . . . he was right. With his help, her moment had come.

The painting—and the glory—was within her grip. She would allow nothing to stand in her way.

Nothing—and nobody.

Seven

Gabriel Prescott stepped into Devlin's office.

"Hey, Gabe." Devlin didn't glance up. He didn't have to. He sat before the banks of video screens set into the handsome, old-fashioned bookshelves. He'd been watching, so he'd seen Gabriel come through the front door. He'd seen every step Gabriel made all the way to the office.

But he was still viewing the screens, a slight smile on his face.

"What are we doing?" Gabriel shut the door behind him.

"We're watching her."

Always interested in a *her* that put that

tone in Devlin's voice, Gabriel came to stand behind his shoulder. The monitor showed a woman wandering down one of the corridors—and she was gorgeous. Her red hair glowed like a candle flame about her pale skin. She had long legs and curvy hips and small, high breasts, all lovingly arranged by a master hand. She wore a pair of white shorts, a yellow tube top, some silly-ass flip-flops decorated with rhinestones, and over it all, a man's large white starched shirt with a knot tied in each front corner. She wore a yellow Band-Aid on her forehead—from here it looked as if it was decorated with happy faces—and she moseyed down the corridor, stopping at every other painting and staring.

Gabriel pulled up a chair and seated himself so he could see the screen, too. "Anytime you need help looking at her, I'm your man. Who is she?"

Devlin shot him an enigmatic look. "My wife."

"Your wife?" *Misstep!*

"Meadow."

It took Gabriel a moment to realize Devlin meant that was her name. "Really." He'd known Fitzwilliam for a long time, ever since his firm had first started installing the security on Devlin's projects, and never had Devlin mentioned a wife.

But then, they weren't friends. Devlin was a grim, secretive son of a bitch with no sense of humor and an adversarial way of making conversation. He was also damned possessive about his properties, and watching him watch Meadow made Gabriel feel sorry for the girl. She was in for a bumpy ride.

"What's she doing?" Gabriel asked.

"She's searching for something."

"A painting?"

"She could very well be." Devlin sounded satisfied.

Okay, fine. Devlin was feeling enigmatic today. Might as well get to business. "I hear there was a break-in last night."

"There was."

"And you caught him."

"Her." Devlin nodded at the screen as Meadow turned a corner and moved to a different monitor.

"Her?" Gabriel was getting confused. "Your wife broke into your hotel."

"Right."

"Why don't you tell me about it?" Because

Gabriel sure as hell couldn't think of any reasonable explanation.

"No, *you* tell *me.* How'd she get in without setting off the alarm on the front door?"

Gabriel's people had done their work before he got here, so he knew the answer. "She opened the door with a key."

Devlin swiveled to face Gabriel. "A key? Why wouldn't a key set off the alarm?"

"People still use keys, so as standard operating procedure we make sure a key will open a lock without setting off the alarm. That's been changed." And the guy who didn't ask what the owner preferred was kicking shit down the road right now. Gabriel operated the biggest security firm on the East Coast. He'd built it from the ground up. He didn't accept mistakes like that.

"So any key would have opened the door?" Devlin asked.

"Any key that fits that lock, and there aren't many that will. It's a Sargent and Greenleaf lock. They've been a solid, innovative firm for a hundred and fifty years. That lock was fitted on the door when it was put in place, the work of master craftsmen." Sargent and Greenleaf constructed the kind of lock that made work like Gabriel's easier.

"It's never easy to pick, and it wasn't picked this time. There weren't scratches inside or outside the lock. It wasn't forced. We found fresh metal residue inside a very old lock that had not been used for months, probably not since the former owner moved out." He sat forward, his arms on his knees. "More interesting, the metal was silver. That's an antique key, and even then it's rare—and it fit the lock."

Devlin stared at Gabriel long enough and with enough concentration to make the hairs stand up on the back of Gabriel's neck. Getting up, Devlin walked to the large desk and opened the belly drawer. He pulled out a key, a large, ornate silver key, and held it up. "Like this?"

"I would guess just like that." Gabriel examined it. "Fascinating. Does it open the front door?"

"No. Old Bradley Benjamin didn't give me the key to the front door. Claimed it was lost. But this was stuck in the back of this desk, so we went looking for the lock. Had a dickens of a time finding it—it opens a gate in the yard."

"What's on the other side of that gate that's worth a silver key?"

"A garden." Devlin's tone was flat and un-interested.

"A garden." Gabriel turned the key over in his hand. The silver glinted in the light. "Somebody must have loved that garden."

"Probably. The Benjamins are notorious for wasting their time with foolishness." Devlin dismissed both the Benjamins and their foolishness with a wave. "Where do you suppose Meadow got a rare silver key that fit the front door?"

"She's your wife. Why don't you ask her?" That seemed only logical, but the whole situation—a wife breaking into her own husband's house with a mysterious key—wasn't logical.

"I will." Devlin stood and clapped his hand on Gabriel's shoulder. "Thanks for coming in."

"I had to. It's not often someone breaches our security."

"I'd swear she didn't realize it when she did it." Devlin started for the door, then returned and shut off the monitor for the corridor where Meadow still wandered.

Yep. Possessive of his property.

"Have a cup of coffee," Devlin said. "Stay for dinner. The chef is trying out his new dishes in preparation for the grand opening. I've been eating like a king for two weeks."

"I'd love to, but I've got to catch a plane. There's a family gathering in Texas I want to attend. My youngest sister just had a baby, and we're getting together for the christening."

Devlin didn't understand how happy it made Gabriel to say that.

"Sure. Next time."

Gabriel sobered and got back to business. "I'll be here for the grand opening. I intend to see that nothing goes wrong with security. I hired someone new, a female with great references."

"Where'd she work before?"

"A guy in Atlanta by the name of Hopkins. Do you know him?"

"I've heard of him. Runs an import/export business." Devlin recalled another tidbit. "And lives on the shady side of the law?"

"A polite way of putting it." Gabe's mouth curled with distaste. "*Mr.* Hopkins, as he is always referred to, is never seen. No one knows where he lives. No police reports are ever made about him. Yet there are a lot of rumors circulating—that he rewards betrayal with a single gunshot to the back of the head. That he enforces his will with threats and torture. That he always keeps a few of Atlanta's politicians and judges in his pocket."

"Good God. Do we *want* his security?"

"Absolutely. Who has better security than a man who is never seen?"

"Right."

"Besides, female personnel are necessary for surveillance—guys can't watch the ladies' rooms in the public areas—yet damned hard to find. The weekend of the grand opening, there'll be no trouble at all." Gabe was a handsome guy, one of those blends of Hispanic and Anglo who had taken the best from both. He was tall, muscular, with black hair and green eyes that made women take a step back, then a step forward.

Devlin knew; he'd seen it happen. He liked Gabe. More important, he trusted him. "I know." His computer chimed. He had e-mail.

"I'm off to talk to my people." Gabe gave a wave and went out the door.

With anticipation, Devlin opened the e-mail—and frowned.

The report was short and decisive. *At the*

*age of four, while in the company of her
stepfather, Bjorn Kelly, Sharon Benjamin
was killed in a car accident in Ireland. Isabelle Benjamin had no other children.*

Bullshit, Devlin typed back. *Dig deeper.*

Eight

Meadow needed a floor plan. She'd left her room thinking she would look the hotel over, retrieve the house key from the couch, check out the paintings and find the one she came for.

Hey, she believed in positive thinking.

Besides, this time she had a lie ready—if caught, she'd claim she was lost.

But she became fascinated by the renovations that had turned a house called Waldemar into a hotel called the Secret Garden. The grand old house her grandmother had so carefully described had been changed.

Walls had been rearranged to create rooms where none had existed before. The long corridors were rabbit warrens bounded by closed and locked doors, and without windows of any kind. On the third floor, Meadow met a crew of a dozen maids pushing linen carts, running vacuum cleaners, and making beds. One guy was installing a Coca-Cola machine next to an ice maker.

She said hello to them.

They said hello to her.

She briefly considered asking if they'd seen the painting, but as soon as they spoke, they returned to work with a frenetic energy that told her more clearly than words how tight their schedule must be.

And asking about the painting wasn't clever; if Devlin was keeping an eye on her, as he'd practically threatened he would, he'd know who she talked to and perhaps question them later.

So she strolled along, looking at the art on the walls, but it was unremarkable—impressionistic landscape prints mixed with typical late-nineteenth- and early twenti-eth–century family portraits done by artists long forgotten. She glanced at the prints and dismissed them, but scrutinized the portraits, longing to catch a glimpse of a feature, a smile, a familiar posture. She'd gone up grand stairways and down elevators, but so far she'd had no luck.

Now her lie was the truth. She really was lost, and the corridors were eerily empty.

Maybe she didn't need a floor plan. Maybe she needed a compass.

She decided to head downstairs—as soon as she found more stairs or another elevator—in the hopes of finding the kitchen, where surely someone was cooking or getting ready to cook or something. At least, she hoped so. She was hungry.

Hearing voices somewhere—around the corner—she hurried forward.

"Why did the tree blow over?" It was Devlin's voice.

"Rotten to the core, sir." She recognized the voice of the guy who replied. It was Sam from last night, the man who had wanted to call the police on her.

"Must have been old Bradley's favorite tree. All right, I want it and the other one, the one struck by lightning, taken out today."

"I don't know if I can get the local guy out today."

"Then get someone in who'll do it."

She paused. Devlin sounded different than he had earlier. Harsh, driven, uninterested in excuses.

"I want the damned tree gone, the stump removed, and the landscaping done and growing before the grand opening." In fact, his tone and his words recalled last night before he'd declared she was his wife, and her first impression that he was cold, ruthless, and unfeeling.

"Yes, sir." Sam's submissive attitude only bolstered her feeling.

"What about the mattresses?" Devlin's attention whipped from one subject to another.

"They'll be here today. The company apologized for the mistake and offered to pay overtime to get them installed."

"Very sweet, but that's hardly enough to make up for the inconvenience."

"I know, so I told them to throw in mattress pads for each mattress. They did." Sam sounded pleased with himself.

"Excellent." Devlin gave brisk approval. "How are we doing at hiring more help before the opening?"

"I've got six new people starting today, and some woman who says she has experience in laundry called and is coming in for an interview. The trouble is, we've tapped out the number of people in town who are willing to take on the old guard."

"I hope those farts burn in hell." Devlin sounded vicious. Vindictive. Every emotion that was bad for his soul.

Before he could call down more bad karma, Meadow headed around the corner, talking as she went. "Whew! I'm so glad I found you guys. I've been lost for an hour!"

Devlin made the switch from hard-nosed businessman to smooth operator without a hitch. "We were about to send out a search party."

Sam started to move away, but she headed right for him, hand outstretched. "We didn't meet formally last night. I'm Meadow."

"Sam." He put his clipboard under his arm and briefly shook her hand.

"You must be part of the security team," she said. He was built like a linebacker, and Devlin's abrasiveness seemed to have scratched away any sense of humor.

"Actually, I'm Mr. Fitzwilliam's personal secretary," he said.

She laughed, then realized he was serious. "That's wonderful. What made you take a job usually considered the province of women?"

"Mr. Fitzwilliam pays well." He walked away.

She waited until he was out of earshot before turning to Devlin. "Did I hit a tender spot? I simply meant he's confident in his masculinity."

"Don't worry. You can't offend Sam. He's not much of a talker." He looked her over in a way that made it clear he'd dismissed Sam from his mind. "Is that my shirt?"

Recalled to a sense of grievance, she advanced on him while holding out the shirttails. "It sure is. I had to cover myself somehow. What made you think I would wander around this hotel in an outfit better suited to some prepubescent teenager than a—"

"Married woman?"

"Yes. No!" She narrowed her eyes at him. "Don't try to confuse me. I told you I don't remember getting married."

"You still don't remember anything?" Catching her hand, he tugged her closer.

"No." Inspiration struck. "But what do *you* know about me?"

"What do you mean?" He twirled a curl from her hair around his finger.

"We got married, and I must have told you about my life. Tell me about myself."

"I could." He drew out the pause while he leaned into her and took a long breath above her hair. "But I won't."

"Because . . . ?" She took a long breath, too, and his familiar scent started a chain reaction of longing, lust, and wariness. Because she did recognize his scent, and she'd slept in his arms, and come alive at his bidding.

He was a man to guard against.

"You have amnesia. It would be best if you discovered the truth on your own."

Damn, he was good! She couldn't catch him out no matter how hard she tried. "My amnesia seems to be spreading. I don't remember eating breakfast this morning."

"Hungry?" He spoke close to her ear, so close his next move would be to kiss her.

"Starving." She shoved his head aside.

"You could have called for room service." He placed his hand at the base of her spine and guided her down the corridor. "After all, you know where the phone is."

She braced herself, waiting to see if he recited parts of her conversation with Judith.

He didn't. He left the comment hanging, and said, "Come on; I'll show you where the kitchen is. We can beg something for you."

"I didn't know room service was working." As they walked, she leaned into him. She didn't know why. He simply felt as if he could support her—in every way.

If this farce continued for long, she was afraid she'd start to believe in him and his silly marriage story.

"The people working on the hotel need to eat," he said, "and the kitchen staff and service people need to practice. The Secret Garden's grand opening is in three weeks. So, yes. We have room service." He led her around a corner and there they were, face-to-face with an elevator. He pushed the down button.

"I came up on an elevator, but when I turned around it had disappeared." She glanced around. "And this doesn't look at all familiar. Do you think it wanders when no one's looking?"

"There are two elevators. You came up the other one."

"Oh." *Yep.* He'd been watching her.

"I have to get to a map," she said.

He showed her a speaker set into the wall. "Did you see any of these?"

"Yes. They're for music, right?"

He didn't laugh at her. She had to give

him that. "They're intercoms. See this button? Anytime you're lost, push it. Someone will direct you or, if you're really confused, come and get you."

She blushed. She couldn't help it. She'd seen intercoms at the university, but it hadn't occurred to her how useful they would be in a house as big as this. "I guess you think I'm a hick."

He ushered her inside the elevator. "I think you're delightful."

"I'd still like a map." Because she didn't want everyone to know where she was searching.

Well . . . apart from Devlin. And the security people. And anyone else watching the monitors.

"You can have whatever you want." He smiled whimsically, and that was an expression she would bet he didn't often wear. "Except . . ."

"Except what?"

"Except for your own bed at night."

As the doors closed he kissed her, a warm salute of appreciation, one so genuine she could almost taste the salt from the Mediterranean on his lips.

Nine

As the elevator slowed to a stop, Devlin lifted his head and examined Meadow's upturned face. Her flushed cheeks and supple lips showed a woman who had been thoroughly kissed, and when her eyes gradually blinked open, they were a soft, blurry blue.

Those eyes. Those beautiful, expressive, betraying eyes. "Let's get you that breakfast now," he said.

"Hmm?" She smiled at him, a smile of pure pleasure.

Then he saw her snap back into consciousness. He stepped out of the elevator and held the door.

"Hey. Wait a minute." She followed him out. "You never answered me about this outfit."

"I've never answered you about a lot of things." He viewed the kitchen with satisfaction.

Jordan Tapley ran a taut ship. The black granite countertops and black gas ranges shone brightly. The range hoods held nary a speck of dust or grease. The two cook's assistants chopped and rolled, their shoulders hunched, their faces unsmiling, and neither looked up, not even at Devlin's entrance.

Jordan himself had his head buried in the commercial-size refrigerator, flinging produce into the garbage with vicious abandon while demanding in a thick New Orleans accent, "Who is the idiot that okayed this asparagus? This celery? These tomatoes? None of this is fit for pigs. Do you hear me? Pigs!"

"Jordan. Come and meet my wife." Jordan had already tried to ban him from the kitchen, so when handling the temperamental cook, Devlin made it his practice to keep his voice low and his gaze level.

Jordan spun around, a graceful movement for a man with an immense girth and three chins. "Your wife? I didn't know you had a wife."

Nonsense, of course. Devlin knew that since last night word of his unexpected marriage had swept the hotel.

Slamming the refrigerator closed, Jordan minced over, his feet tiny compared to the immense bulk above. "Miz Fitzwilliam, it's good to meet you."

"I know you. You're the famous Jordan Tapley." Meadow went to meet him, arms outstretched wide. "I've got your cookbook!"

Before Devlin's astonished eyes, Meadow and Jordan hugged and kissed, both talking at the same time. His voice was loud and sounded like New Orleans. Hers was low and warm and without any hint of an accent. Yet the two of them were instant friends. Devlin heard indecipherable terms like *andouille sausage* and *garde-manger* flung about with abandon. For the first time ever, Devlin saw Jordan's teeth flashing, not in annoyance, but in an exultant smile.

As if waiting for an explosion, the two assistants watched the display warily and muttered to each other.

When Meadow and Jordan managed to untangle themselves, she bounded toward the assistants. "These must be your sous chefs!"

Jordan followed, beaming.

Devlin trailed behind, wondering how the quiet, chilly, professional kitchen had disintegrated to this boisterous cheer so quickly.

"They aren't all of my local staff, of course. I have three people coming for training this afternoon." Jordan waved a big hand at the thin, middle-aged, nervous-looking woman chopping onions. "This is Mia—she's very talented. In the fall, when we open the restaurant, I'm going to promote her to saucier."

Mia's mouth dropped open. "You *like* my sauces? Really?" At Jordan's outraged glare, she hastily turned her attention to Meadow. "I mean . . . good to meet you, Mrs. Fitzwilliam!" Wiping her hand on her apron, she offered it to Meadow.

Meadow hugged her around the shoulders. "Is that for dinner tonight? Then don't stop!"

"Thank you, ma'am." Mia had the softest, most timid voice, with an accent that sounded almost like Devlin's. Almost, but a little less educated and little more country.

"This is Christian. He's new. He has all his fingertips." Jordan dismissed Christian's inexperience with a snort.

"I hope he keeps all his fingertips and becomes your head sous chef!" Meadow hugged the pudgy young man, too.

"Thank you, Mrs. Fitzwilliam." Christian's accent sounded sort of Southern, sort of twangy.

"My head sous chef is coming from New Orleans a week before the grand opening," Jordan told her. "I'm training this boy as pastry chef."

"You are?" In astonishment, Christian looked at the piecrust he was rolling on the marble slab.

"Yes—if you remember to *keep a light hand*!" Jordan thwapped him on the back of the head.

At once Christian lifted the rolling pin. "Yes, sir! Good to meet you, Mrs. Fitzwilliam."

"Now." Jordan rubbed his hands together. "Miz Fitzwilliam, you look hungry. What can I get you for breakfast?" He glanced at the huge clock on the wall. "Or lunch?"

It was time for Devlin to remind them he was here. "We're going into town for lunch."

At the news, Jordan settled for an outraged glare at Devlin, then switched his attention to Meadow. "So . . . do you like blueberries?" Jordan rummaged in the bread box and filled a plate, then placed it on the counter beside her. He broke off a piece of scone and popped it in her mouth.

"That's wonderful!" she mumbled.

"Biscuits and homemade blackberry preserves?" A chunk of biscuit followed.

"Ummm." She closed her eyes and shivered with pleasure.

Devlin was getting hungry. For food. And for Meadow.

He wanted her to look at him with the same lust she showed for homemade blackberry preserves.

Why hadn't he turned her over to the police last night? If all he was interested in was humiliating Bradley Benjamin, he could have easily announced that he'd caught Isabelle's granddaughter breaking and entering, and the resultant scandal would have been a lovely taste of revenge.

But when Meadow had looked up at him with those big blue eyes and proclaimed she had amnesia, she'd been so sure she'd plucked a get-out-of-jail-free card. He saw her congratulating herself, and something in him—some previously unknown quirk in his character—rose to the challenge, and he'd declared she was his wife.

His wife. Of all the tales he could have invented, why had he made up that one?

"The cold quiche is delicious." Jordan's fork flashed. "Traditional. Bacon, eggs, cream, Swiss cheese, and Christian's pastry."

She held up a hand. "I'm a vegetarian."

Devlin could pretend he wouldn't be bested when it came to telling outrageous falsehoods.

But Devlin Fitzwilliam did not deceive himself.

When he held Meadow in his arms, when he breathed her scent and saw the shining tumble of her copper-colored hair, he felt as if a strong, fresh wind had blown into a life grown stale and grim.

And when she threatened to puke . . . he'd wanted to laugh.

He hadn't really laughed a real belly laugh in years. Maybe never.

"Of course you are a vegetarian. You are skinny." Jordan polished off the piece of quiche.

"I wish," she said.

"She's perfect," Devlin said.

Jordan and Meadow both flashed him a startled glance. Had they forgotten he stood here? Or did he so seldom give compliments?

"Of course she is perfect. Just too skinny." Jordan turned back to Meadow. "Vegan?"

"No." She shook her head. "No meat."

"Good! So much easier. So much tastier. So much better for you!" Jordan pinched her cheek. "Some iced tea? Today it is ginger-peach. Very good!"

"That would be great!"

Devlin had never imagined such a mutual admiration society would flourish between his cook and his . . . between his cook and Meadow. He didn't understand it, either. Jordan had been like Devlin's other employees— dour, hardworking, determined to take this opportunity to head a world-class hotel and restaurant. Now he was smiling, handing out compliments, and flirting with Devlin's wife.

And the other two cooks . . . they were smiling!

What the hell had happened? What kind of effect did Meadow have on people? Why didn't she ever beam that smile at him?

Sure, he was lying to her, and she was lying to him, and they both knew they were deeply involved in one hell of a game. But

they'd slept in the same bed. They'd exchanged the kind of kisses that branded a
man's soul.

And she couldn't spare him one of those
open, generous smiles?

Jordan bustled over to the bread box. His
knife darted, and before Meadow could respond she held a plate mounded with
golden pastries, a small bowl of unsalted
butter and one of jam, and a napkin in a silver ring. In the other hand she held a frosty
glass filled with sweet tea.

"Thank you!" She kissed Jordan on the
cheek. "I'll make sure we're here for dinner!"

"We were always going to be here for dinner." Devlin knew Sam had already informed
Jordan of that, because Sam always did his
duty.

Jordan ignored him. "Good! I'll fix something especially nice for your first night in
your new hotel."

"She was here last night." Concocting a
foolish story about having amnesia. Being
surprised when he concocted a story right
back.

If their perjuries were getting in the way of
her smiling at him, he'd do the right thing.
He'd give her a chance to tell him the truth.

She wouldn't do it, of course. Like every other person in the world, she'd tell herself a story to justify her larcenies and her lies. Nevertheless, he'd give her the chance.

"She came late, not in time for dinner." Jordan sounded impatient with Devlin.

Impatient. With Devlin!

Jordan shooed her toward the stairs. "It's a beautiful day. Go into the garden and eat."

"Come on," she said to Devlin. "We need to get out of Jordan's way. The man's an artist—he needs room to work."

"Could I have a glass of iced tea, too?" Devlin injected a note of polite sarcasm into his voice.

"Sure 'nuff, boss. Here you go!" Jordan answered with exactly the same note of polite sarcasm coupled with some mocking old-fashioned subservience.

Meadow laughed, a laugh so bright the air in the usually dour kitchen sparkled like champagne.

With unaccustomed surprise, Devlin realized he wasn't going to win this round.

What surprised him more was . . . he didn't mind.

No. He couldn't turn her over to the police. He would not let her go.

Not yet. Not until she smiled at him without wariness and with joy. Not until he had uncovered her mysteries. Not until he'd discovered why she made him feel . . . alive. Different. Newborn.

And not until he'd slept with her.

Especially not until he'd slept with her.

Ten

Devlin followed Meadow up the stairs and held the heavy utility door for her.

They stepped out into the sunshine. In the distance he could hear the chainsaw as someone removed the fallen tree. Nail guns whooshed as the carpenters erected the gazebo, and the trucks came and went, dumping loads of bark mulch for the gardeners. The estate sounded busy.

Good thing. They needed to clean up the havoc wrought by the storms and keep the schedule for the grand opening, or heads would roll.

"Isn't it a beautiful day?" she asked.

The humidity hovered at about eighty percent, the temperature at seventy degrees. He informed her, "This is average for this time of year."

"Average? There is nothing average about this day." She took a deep, long breath. "I love the way the salty scent of the sea and the spicy scent of the pines mingle. Don't you?"

He sniffed. To him it smelled of the sea, of the earth the gardeners had turned. It smelled of immense wealth and cruel snobbery brought down by inbreeding and stupidity—and his own ruthless intelligence.

It was a good smell.

"Look at the basil!"

He tried, but the tiny plants all looked the same to him, and he'd bet at least half of them were weeds. "This is the kitchen garden. The gardeners have been working getting the rest of the estate ready for the grand opening. They haven't touched it in here."

"So it's even better out there?" She walked toward the spring-hinged gate, hit it with her hip, and headed out into the estate.

Waldemar had been ramshackle when Devlin had gotten his hands on it. For all his pride, Bradley Benjamin hadn't been able to afford to maintain the gigantic house and immense grounds.

But Devlin had thrown his seasoned legion of interior decorators, cleaners, painters, and gardeners at the place, and now it boasted eight acres of seashore, forest, and lush gardens, with the freshly painted, newly cleaned, and redesigned house set high on the bluff overlooking the waves. An impressive iron gate announced the entrance to the estate, and from there the road wound past a carriage house—well maintained and serving as the eight-car garage—across the expanse of lawn and blooming wild roses.

This was what the estate was meant to be—and a slap in the face of Bradley Benjamin's overweening pride.

"This place is beautiful. Alluring." The tone of Meadow's voice changed from wonder to . . . thoughtfulness. "A woman could be seduced at the idea of owning this."

"Yes." He watched her and understood exactly what she was thinking. "Are you seduced?"

"What?" She blinked at him. "Oh. No. I've been taught better than that."

He knew why. He wondered if she did.

A crew of gardeners trudged into view,

shovels over their shoulders, pushing wheelbarrows full of soil and flowers. At the sight of Devlin and Meadow, they stopped and backed up.

"They don't have to leave. I don't want to get in the way of their work." Meadow started toward them.

Devlin caught her arm. "They've been instructed to stay out of sight of the guests. That's the rule. Let's not confuse them."

"I'm hardly a guest."

"You're much more important. You're the wife of the owner." He enjoyed saying that; enjoyed, too, her wide-eyed, blinking dismay. She didn't know how to handle him—and he suspected that was a unique situation for the nimble Meadow.

"Let's sit over there." He indicated the picnic table beneath a huge ancient live oak with moss in its crown, and branches so huge and outstretched they touched the ground.

"What a great old tree." As Meadow walked ahead of him, the sun shone through his white linen shirt, outlining her body, reminding him of the morning when he'd woken with her ass pressed against his crotch. He'd been lucky the night before when she had appeared at Waldemar; his luck had moved to a new level this morning when her eyes had widened at the sight of him and she'd caught fire in his arms.

Something about her chemical makeup responded to him.

If revenge was a coin, he held a rare gold antique.

She ate with a gusto that surprised him. No dainty picking at her food for Meadow—she consumed a scone and two biscuits with jam before wiping her lips with the napkin, sighing with satisfaction, and surveying the area. "Look at those rhodies!" she said. "Aren't they glorious?"

He glanced at the rhododendrons. They were blooming. They were pink. Wasn't that what they were supposed to do? "Glorious."

"Why do you call the hotel the Secret Garden?"

He loved it when she gave him an opening like that. "Don't you remember, love?"

She blinked uncertainly at him. "You love the Frances Hodgson Burnett book?"

"I'm not familiar with it."

"You're not familiar with *The Secret Garden*?" In an excess of horror, Meadow pressed her hand over her heart. "It's a wonderful book about a girl who's closed off from love, and a boy who thinks he's a cripple, and his father who's so bitter about his wife's death he won't love his own son, and this secret garden that heals them all."

"Sounds . . . mushy." A polite way of saying he didn't believe in such emotional revelations.

"No! It's inspiring."

She couldn't be so naive—could she?

No. Of course not. She'd broken into Waldemar in search of that painting. She'd been willing to steal from Bradley Benjamin— Devlin had no problem with that—but now she planned to steal from him. No one took anything that belonged to Devlin and got away with it. She'd find that out soon enough. No one, no matter how attractive, stole from him.

With ruthless intent, he smiled into her eyes and said, "I remember. . . ."

Hand in hand, they explored the island of Majorca and found a sun-drenched island of tourists, beaches, cliffs, scrub, and gardens. Wonderful, glorious gardens. Each day brought a new adventure, a sense of the world made new, for he saw it through her eyes. Then, high atop

a hill overlooking the sea, they discovered a small, forgotten patch of earth overgrown with weeds and brambles . . . and climbing roses and tiny crocuses thrusting out of the soil.

"You know what a crocus is?" she asked incredulously.

"I do now. You showed me."

She narrowed her eyes. "*I* know what a crocus is?"

He gestured around. "You know what a rhododendron is."

She nodded once, grudgingly. "Go on."

The garden had the remains of a house beside it, a place so old it had no roof and half the walls had tumbled down. She had screamed at the sight of a tiny mouse—

"I've really changed, then, because I'm not afraid of mice."

"Then maybe I screamed," he said impatiently. "Do you want to know about the Secret Garden or not?"

"Of course." She leaned her chin on her hand, and a smile lit her eyes.

The garden was enchanted. That was the only possible explanation he could imagine for the breeze that made the blossoms dance and the grass ripple.

The food in their hamper tasted of honey and love, and when they kissed, the world disappeared. Only the two of them remained, entwined on the blanket, while around them the garden sang around its siren song.

On that blanket, in that garden, was the first time they made love.

"So in honor of you, I bought an estate with a secret garden on its grounds." In honor of her, Devlin Fitzwilliam, a man whose life had been ruled by logic and profit, had woven fantasies guaranteed to charm her.

What spell had she cast on him, that he should be so adroit, so romantic?

"Here? At Waldemar? Has it got walls and a door?" Her blue eyes were bright and mesmerized.

"Walls of stone, and a door with a lock." He loved to look at her like this, her lips softly open as if he'd just seduced her.

"With winding paths and flowers of every fragrance and color?"

"And at its heart, an expanse of velvety blue grass where you can dance." He sat solidly on a bench in the middle of his yard, watching the breeze off the Atlantic made the blossoms bobble and the grass ripple . . . and tousled the bright strands of Meadow's hair.

And she watched him as if he were the embodiment of her every dream.

He had used his voice to enchant her. Now he found himself enchanted as well.

"Well." She tore her gaze away from his and patted her cheeks. "It's very warm here."

She was blushing. Blushing at the thought of making love to him in a garden.

"I thought the temperature was quite . . . comfortable." And she was quite adorable.

"Yes. I'm not used to the humidity."

He watched her face as they spoke, weighed which of her words were lies and which were truths, and wondered which truths he could use to discover everything about her. "It's not humid . . . where you came from?"

"I guess not." She didn't take the bait.

He was almost glad. He was doing what he should, of course. He'd given the house detective the number she'd called this morning and sent him to search Atlanta—the area code placed it in Atlanta—to see if he could find any information on whom she called. But Devlin didn't want this farce to end so soon. He was enjoying himself as he hadn't for years.

No. That wasn't true.

He was enjoying himself as he never had.

"Why did you come here now?" he was asking. He was coaxing. He, ruthless bastard Devlin Fitzwilliam, wanted to end the farce between them and start anew.

And he waited on tenterhooks, watching her eyes widen with uncertainty, inwardly urging her to trust him.

Instead, she bit her lower lip, then cleared her throat. "I'll get you a copy when we go into town."

"A copy?" He leaned back, all his cynicism confirmed. "A copy of what?"

"Of *The Secret Garden*."

He laughed, a brief bark of amusement. "I'm in the last stages of opening a hotel. I don't have time to read." Certainly not a sentimental bunch of drivel like *The Secret Garden*.

"I'll read it to you."

Long afternoons curled up on a hammock in the garden, just the two of them rocking as she read him a girlie story . . . why did that sound appealing?

But it did.

His little liar offered him a world he had previously scorned, and made him want it almost as much as he wanted her.

For the first time he realized she was more than a challenge and a distraction—she was dangerous.

A third voice intruded, a man's laughing, charming, aristocratic voice. "How touching. The sweet girl's going to read a children's book to the big, mean developer."

With a thump Devlin stepped ankle-deep into a pile of reality. He turned to find a blond, well-dressed, and far too familiar figure standing behind him, glass in hand. *Shit. Not him. Not now.* "Four. I told you to go away and stay away."

"So you did." Four swung his leg over the bench and sat next to Meadow.

"Then what are you doing here?"

"I live here."

Eleven

"Or I used to." Taking Meadow's hand, Four raised it to his lips. "I'm Bradley Benjamin the fourth. I'm handsome, kind, generous, trustworthy, and irresistible."

Meadow grinned at his insouciance. "I can see that."

"In other words, the exact opposite of stodgy old Devlin over there."

"Oh, I don't know." She was still half-aroused with the pleasure of Devlin's description of the Secret Garden. "I think Devlin's incredibly charming." Although he didn't look charming right now. He sat with his arms crossed over his chest. His mouth was grim, his teeth clenched.

"Devlin? Devlin Fitzwilliam?" Four stared at Devlin with bug-eyed disbelief. "Not this Devlin Fitzwilliam, the meanest son of a bitch—begging your pardon, ma'am—ever to walk the streets of Charleston?"

"The very one."

"You have a smiley-face bandage on your forehead." Four touched it lightly. "Tell me the truth. You fell and knocked all the sense out of yourself."

His guess was close enough to the actual events to frighten Meadow into flashing Devlin a questioning glance.

"Where did you hear that story?" Devlin asked.

"I didn't *hear* anything. But that's the only explanation I can imagine for her bad judgment." Four took a biscuit. "Never allow Devlin's temporary attempts at civilized behavior to fool you. The milk of human kindness has curdled in his veins."

She studied Four as he slathered the biscuit with butter and jam and ate it in two bites. He seemed sincere enough, but...

"Devlin seems indestructible."

Four snorted. "He hides everything. His feelings, his thoughts . . . then, wham! He hits you with a broadside and knocks you catawampus." He lifted the half-eaten biscuit. "But his cook is far superior to Father's."

"Yes." Devlin didn't waste time with graciousness.

"And your liquor cabinet is stocked with the best." Four saluted Devlin with his sweating glass.

"Help yourself." Like a stubborn case of athlete's foot, Four irritated Devlin.

Meadow could see why. Devlin appeared rugged, like a mountain man who had gotten lost and stumbled into this soft, warm, humid environment where the birds chirped and the sun trickled through the thick leaves.

Four was very different. He had a look about him, one she'd seen in her grandmother's black-and-white Fred Astaire movies—whipcord thin, world-weary, well dressed, and wealthy. Very, very wealthy. He wasn't tall, only about five-nine, but his blue polo shirt stretched across muscular shoulders, and his gray slacks were belted tightly around a trim waist. His hair was expertly cut—and thinning. She'd swear someone armed with an airbrush had sprayed on his tan. He smelled of stale cigarettes and expensive cologne, and he sounded eloquent and nobly Southern. But most important, he oozed charisma from every pore, a kind of jaded, old-world dissipation.

She didn't imagine he was anything like his father.

He took a drink from the glass he'd placed on the table. It was the same kind of glass from which she sipped iced tea. The liquid was brown like tea. But a few green leaves floated among the ice cubes, and the sweet odor of bourbon wafted through the air.

It was barely eleven in the morning. "I'm Meadow."

"Meadow. That's beautiful, and so appropriate. You're as fresh as a mountain meadow. But I didn't catch your last name." Four's hazel eyes danced with amusement as he observed Devlin's impatience.

"I didn't give it," she said.

At the same time, Devlin said, "Fitzwilliam."

"You're romancing your cousin?" Four guessed. "Isn't that a little traditionally Southern for you, Devlin?"

"She's not my cousin," Devlin said.

She studied her hands in her lap and

wished she could stuff her napkin down Devlin's throat.

Four studied them, then reached the inevitable conclusion. "She's not your . . . *wife?*" He choked on the liquor. He coughed until tears sprang to his eyes. Until she hit him on the back to clear his air passage. He waved her away and croaked at Devlin, "You're married? To her? You're pulling my leg. Since when? Don't tell me—you married in *Majorca!*"

So he'd heard at least some of the tale Devlin had spun for her. His eavesdropping made her uncomfortable and a little disgruntled. The fantasy was her story, a present from Devlin, and she didn't like sharing it with anyone. Most certainly she didn't want Four asking questions about a ceremony that had never occurred.

"Actually, Four, this is such bad timing." Devlin's sympathetic tone was at odds with his glee. "My wife and I are on our way into town. So go away."

"We are?" It was the first Meadow had heard of it.

"We need to pick up your prescription," Devlin said.

Her head ached, but not much, yet when

she started to say so she encountered a warning glance from Devlin.

All right. They were going to town. "We can pick up a copy of *The Secret Garden* while we're there."

"Another good reason to go into Amelia Shores," he said with almost indiscernible exasperation.

"Great!" Four said. "I'll go with you."

"No, you won't." Devlin was firm. "We're taking the Jeep. There's no room for you. There's no backseat."

"Devlin, that tone will never work! You can't tantalize with the news of your marriage, then get rid of me! I have a reputation as a gossipmonger to maintain. I drove out here. I'll drive back into town." Four laughed lightly and took another drink, more carefully this time. "While we're there, you can give me all the juicy details of the romance of the century."

"You don't take a hint, do you?" Meadow admired the man's impervious nature.

"My dear, if a person listened to all of Devlin's rejections he'd think he wasn't liked. In fact, I'm his best friend."

Devlin snorted.

"If I'm not, who is?" Four challenged him.

"My wife," Devlin said.

"That is so romantic," Four began.

But Meadow wasn't prepared to make up any stories about meeting on the beach and exchanging a kiss before they exchanged a word, and she certainly couldn't imagine expanding on the preposterous imagery of lying among the shrubs in a secret garden behind a crumbling house and making love . . . not until she was alone, anyway. "So your family used to own Waldemar."

"For over a hundred years." Four's pride unfurled like a flag. "It's the foremost estate near Amelia Shores, and Amelia Shores is the last and most important refuge for the hidebound and stinking rich of Charleston. My family—the most hidebound and stinking—held this place for a hundred years, through the Great Depression and every kind of tax. And we had to sell it to the most famous blue-blood bastard—pardon me, ma'am—illegitimate son who ever lived."

"It wasn't so much a sale"—Devlin locked gazes with Four—"as a surrender."

"Wow." Meadow looked between them, saw Four's clenched jaw and Devlin's insolent smile. Their malice acted like acid to corrode her pleasure in the morning.

But she was a fighter. If they were going to piss on each other's shoes, she was at least going to know why. "You guys get nasty fast. What happened? Did you have a fight in prep school?"

Four turned to her in surprise, then laughed and relaxed. "I'm older than he is, and too smart to pick a fight with little Devlin and his bony fists. He had a reputation for making the other guy bleed, no matter what the odds."

"Really?" That was the Devlin she saw in his unguarded moments—mean as a junkyard dog, overwhelming as an earthquake.

"But then, the whole Fitzwilliam family has been trying to destroy my family and its pride for two centuries." Four's grin turned malicious. "With no success."

"The problem is not your pride, but the lack of reason for it." While Four was growing angry, Devlin was growing cold.

Fascinated, she looked between the two of them. "Is this a real live family feud?"

"Rooted in tradition," Four said.

"For generations," Devlin added.

"What started it?" she asked.

Both men shrugged and looked away. They knew, but they weren't talking. Whatever rivalry prompted the sharp exchange was old and acrimonious.

"Slander?   Robbery?   Murder?"   She searched her mind for something that would really upset these guys so much. "Lynching?"

Four took a drink of his bourbon. "Broken betrothal," he muttered.

Meadow sat there, waiting for the rest of the story. When nothing more was forthcoming, she asked, "That's it? Your families have been fighting for . . . for—"

"Two hundred and fifty years," Devlin told her.

"Two hundred and fifty years over a *broken betrothal?*"

The two men nodded.

She burst into laughter. "How *girlie* of you!"

They were not amused.

"In early America, a broken betrothal was a huge point of honor," Four said stiffly. "When John Benjamin, who was a wealthy planter, did the honor of offering for the hand of Anne Fitzwilliam, who was his house-maid, she accepted, then decided she couldn't stand to marry him and left him at the altar."

"Thus showing that the Fitzwilliams have a long history of good sense," Devlin said.

"She was probably in love with someone else." Still smiling, Meadow watched the two men snipe over an old romance gone bad. A *really* old romance.

"She died a spinster," Four said.

"The ultimate insult." An offensive smile played around Devlin's mouth. "If she'd married someone else, the Benjamins could claim she'd lost her mind for love. Instead, she preferred to work as her brother's housekeeper—by all accounts, a thankless job—while he made his fortune shipping cotton to Britain."

"He made his fortune in trade," Four sneered.

"Yes, and the only difference between him and you is that he did it well."

Four stood up, knocking over his glass.

Ice clattered across the table. Brown liquid rushed toward Devlin.

Devlin scrambled to his feet, but not fast enough to avoid a lap full of bourbon.

Meadow would have sworn he was ready to leap across the table and beat Four.

Then Four laughed.

The sound of that insolent amusement acted on Devlin as the ice cubes had not. His flush faded and his expression cooled. "How clumsy of you, Four."

He wasn't talking about the spilled drink.

"Okay!" Meadow stood up, too.

Four ran his gaze up her legs. "Nice."

"Thank you." Exasperated at the way he used her to get at Devlin, she used Four's pride to get back at him. "And what a gentlemanly way of saying I look attractive."

He flushed. "Point taken."

"Make sure that it is."

Devlin slid his hand around Meadow's waist. "Let's go change now, darling, and we'll be on our way."

"Of course, darling." She fluttered her eyelashes at him. He didn't seem nearly as smug about her outrageous outfit now. Apparently it was one thing for him to appreciate her figure, and quite another for Four, with his lascivious smile and his handsome face, to enjoy it. "After we clean up this mess."

"I'll call for a crew." Devlin took the walkie-talkie off his belt.

"We can do it." Meadow stacked the glasses onto the plate.

Devlin ignored her, giving orders to the housekeeper on the other end. When he finished, he gestured at the wet spot on his pants and said to her, "Let's go."

"You don't need me to help you." She did not want to go into that bedroom with him again. Not while he removed his pants. As Sharon always said, it was easier to shun temptation than to fight it.

"He's not going to let you stay here alone with me. I might decide to avenge the insult to my ancestor by seducing Devlin's wife." Four thrust his hands in his pockets and grinned.

"What a jackass you are," she said cordially.

"What did I say?" Four glanced at Devlin in honest bewilderment.

Devlin's satisfaction couldn't be denied. "I believe my wife just said she wouldn't be seduced by a pretty face and a big ego."

"You almost got it right." Meadow pinched Devlin's chin and smiled deliberately into his face. "*I* won't be seduced *at all*."

Devlin understood. He understood very well, but he didn't accede. He stared back, answering her challenge.

Neither of them backed down. Nothing broke the silence.

Until the cleanup crew clattered out of the door and started toward them.

At the sign of discord between them, Four beamed. He opened his mouth to speak.

Meadow looked at him. Just looked at him.

He shut his mouth.

She approved Four's common sense with a simple, "Good man." To Devlin, she asked sarcastically, "Which of my flowered sundresses do you want me to wear?"

"Put on jeans," Devlin directed.

"Jeans. What a good idea." She'd won! She'd won! "I wish I'd thought of getting some jeans."

Or had she won? If jeans were already in her room, he'd ordered them when he'd thrown away her burglar outfit, and all that talk about only flowered sundresses was simply nonsense.

She didn't understand what drove Devlin—what he wanted with her, why he lied to Four, what he intended with his elaborate charade. She knew while she donned her outfit only that whatever it was she decided to wear, she would lock the door.

It was simply safer.

Twelve

Amelia Shores was a town of four thousand in the off-season and twelve thousand during the tourist season. Right now, in the spring, the bed-and-breakfasts had been freshly painted, Wendy's and McDonald's were hiring smiling faces, and the restaurants along Waterfront Row rolled out their striped canopies to cover their outdoor tables.

A few tourists were already there.

The hordes were coming.

As they wandered along the sidewalk, the Atlantic on one side and the street on the other, Four told Meadow, "The shops are gearing up for the high season, so before the tourists get here the regulars come down to D'Anna's for lunch and stay for a leisurely dessert, coffee, and gossip."

"Who are the regulars?" Her head swiveled between the beach and the shore. She'd never visited the East Coast, but no matter their location, coastal towns shared common sights and smells. Waves curled, and sunbathers wiped sand off their lotion-damp skin. Shops advertised with bright bikinis and intricate kites hung in the windows. Tourists traipsed along Waterfront Row in cover-ups donned too late to protect against the sunburn that seared their shoulders.

She didn't fit in; in a fit of rebellion against Devlin she had donned a silk flowered sundress and strappy yellow sandals, and now the breeze played with the edge of her skirt, and she had to use her hand to keep her wide-brimmed straw hat on her head.

"The regulars are people who live here." Four waved at a shopkeeper. "The people who work here."

"The regulars are the old farts who used to own the whole town and still control the city council." Devlin walked behind them, and his words were so at odds with his unemotional tone that Meadow turned and walked backward to stare at him.

He wore faded jeans and a white shirt with the sleeves rolled up to his elbows. He looked like a construction worker—except for his darkly sardonic eyes, which watched her with such intensity.

Could he see through her sundress? But no; the halter and skirt were lined, the hem reached midcalf, and he might not have been happy that she defied his instructions about the jeans, but he openly appreciated the smooth line of her shoulders and throat.

"You don't like the old farts," she said.

"They want to halt the march of time," he answered.

"And you *are* the march of time," she guessed.

"He's like an army battalion tromping through a flower garden. He leaves nothing in his path." She heard a sour note in Four's voice. "You're going to trip." Four caught her arm and turned her forward.

"If you didn't want to sell Waldemar to Devlin, why did you do it?" she asked.

Four did trip on a crack on the sidewalk,

and when he righted himself she saw that some of his charm had eroded like gold vermeil off well-worn silver.

"Four didn't sell the house to me," Devlin said. "His father did."

"Over my objections." Four looked toward the restaurant perched on the highest spot on the street. There uniformed waiters moved among the outdoor tables carrying bottles of sparkling water, and the fringe on the large round umbrellas fluttered in the breeze.

"He had no choice." Devlin continued his barrage on Four's dignity. "I made him an offer he couldn't refuse."

"Are you the Godfather?" Meadow laughed, then realized that Four's cheeks were ruddy with fury and Devlin was smiling that hateful smile. They were ready to come to blows again.

"He has aspirations," Four said grimly.

"Yet my ambitions are thoroughly crushed. The original Godfather of Amelia Shores isn't ready to step aside yet." Devlin indicated the group of gentlemen who sat along the metal railing, watching the street. "That's his father up there."

Meadow stopped still in the street and

looked up. From across and down the street, they looked too similar to tell apart—five older men dressed in tasteful, expensive leisure clothing and sipping aperitifs from tall glasses. "Which one is he?"

She tried not to sound too intense, too interested.

She doubted that she had succeeded.

Four stopped with her. "Left to right— Wilfred Kistard, toupee, and a crusty old gentleman with a kind heart. Penn Sample, bald, portly, ear hair, twinkling blue eyes that hide a shrewd brain. He's the one who thought of cutting Devlin's local supplies to the hotel."

"Did he?" Devlin didn't appear particularly worried.

But Meadow was learning a lot about Devlin, and she knew that as of this moment, if Penn Sample were drowning and going under for the last time, Devlin would throw him an anchor.

"H. Edwin Osgood. Never married, lives alone in his mansion—not a bit of trouble making his payments, I can tell you—and fancies himself quite the ladies' man. Hair color for men. Bow tie and thick glasses. He's my father's sycophant." Four grimaced.

"'Nuff said. Scrubby Gallagher, thinning white hair. He's my godfather, the oldest, and the only one of the bunch who's ever lived anywhere besides Charleston and here."

Meadow had been raised in her parents' art studio outside the small town of Blythe in the Cascade Mountains in Washington. She'd attended college at Stanford in California. She'd spent a semester in Rome taking classes and living with an Italian family. She was only twenty-two—and these old guys had never lived anywhere else? She couldn't imagine being so confined in her mind and heart. "Where did he live?"

"Atlanta."

She laughed briefly.

Four laughed with her. "Yes, quite a change of pace. His experience broadened his world scope—a profound character defect—and that's why the others pay him so little heed." He looked sideways at Devlin. "And it's the reason he's forward-thinking enough to invest in Devlin's hotel."

Devlin studied Four. "How did you know that?"

"I only suspected until this minute." Four

smirked so obnoxiously, Meadow wondered that Devlin didn't hit him.

Four was smart; he'd figured out something Meadow knew must be so secret only Devlin and Scrubby Gallagher knew. Yet so stupid; he had to taunt Devlin with his sly intelligence.

One of the gentlemen, the one with the whitest hair, waved.

She waved back.

Four didn't. "That's him. That's my father. He's only made two mistakes in his life—all the women he married, and all the children he fathered."

"Really?" Meadow considered Four. "How many wives and children has he had?"

"Four wives. One child. Me." Four pulled a cigarette from his shirt pocket and lit it with a match, protecting the flame from the ocean breeze with his body and his hand.

"Four wives." She had had no idea. "Did all the marriages end in divorce?"

"All," Four confirmed. "Three of them— number two, number three, and number four—cited mental cruelty. He's an indifferent old prick."

"And the first wife?" she asked.

"He divorced her, citing irreconcilable differences." Four chuckled, amused and ashamed by his amusement. "Actually, it was infidelity."

"Really?" She watched Four.

Devlin watched her.

"Mind you, this was before my time, but from what I've managed to gather, Isabelle was a beauty. Not appropriate, of course. Not one of our class."

"Shocking!" Meadow said.

"For my father it was. He must have been mad for her. She was fooling around with her art teacher, and when the old man confronted her, she admitted it without a bit of shame. He threw her out, of course, and the baby with her." Four shook his head. "Cold as ice. Apparently the kid was only a couple of months old, and Isabelle had no funds and nowhere to go."

"She had a baby?" Meadow's skin should have been warm in the sun. Instead a chill worked its way along her nerves.

"My closest shot at a sibling—except she was fathered by the lover." He flicked his ashes into the wind. "I wish she hadn't been. She might have taken some of the expectations off me."

"Not likely," Devlin said. "He doesn't expect much of a woman."

"He expects them to be decorative." Four's gaze swept Meadow, not insultingly as before, but appraisingly. "He'll approve of you."

"You can imagine my relief," she said coolly.

"He'll like that air, too. He detests a woman who's demonstrative about her feelings. In fact, he's not fond of feelings at all."

"Because the one time he gave in to his own, his wife betrayed him." Meadow looked between the two men's surprised faces. "Honestly, don't you guys ever think of this stuff?"

"Don't you gals ever think of anything else?" Devlin countered.

In a flash of irritation, she said, "On occasion, but we *gals* have our priorities right. Family and feelings first."

"Except Isabelle." Devlin lifted Meadow's hand to his mouth and kissed her fingers. "Isabelle didn't think of her family and their feelings when she had that affair."

Meadow snatched her hand from his. "I suppose that's right."

Four watched the interaction between

them curiously, as if he saw something askew.

He was correct, of course. She and Devlin were two actors in a nightmare play, performing onstage without knowing their next line, their next scene. And beneath the trappings of civilized manners and banter, dread and anticipation bubbled through her veins, caused not only by the fear that she would falter and betray her mission.

She also sensed that she was being stalked. Devlin was stalking her, maybe for sex, maybe for . . . she didn't know why.

She knew only that she, who was so good at reading people's motives, did not understand a single thing about Devlin. She knew only that when he watched her as he was watching her now, the blood flowed warm and thick in her veins and she wanted to go somewhere with him and be alone to kiss and touch . . . and mate.

"No photos of Isabelle exist in the family album," Four said thoughtfully. "Father tore them up. Is that why? Because he gave in to his feelings and she betrayed them?"

Meadow looked away from Devlin's mocking eyes, down at the ground, then out at the ocean. "Probably."

"How do you know he tore them up?" Devlin asked.

"One day I was digging through the boxes of his pictures and realized she was missing. I got curious, so I asked." Four took a long drag on his cigarette. "He about snapped my head off."

"He sounds delightful," Meadow said.

"He'd get worse when Isabelle's picture was in the paper. You see, his wife Isabelle, the one who made my father forever a cuckold in the eyes of his compatriots, went on to become a famous artist." Four clearly relished imparting the news.

"Really?" Meadow opened her eyes wide in astonishment.

"She was *the* Isabelle, acclaimed darling of the wilderness art world. Are you familiar with her?"

"Who isn't familiar with Isabelle?" It should have been a rhetorical question, but Devlin was looking at Meadow. Mocking Meadow.

And Meadow could scarcely keep from squirming in guilt.

"Her canvases command upward of a hundred thousand, and they're appreciating in value all the time," Four said.

"He must hate that." She hoped so.

"He really hated that whenever she took a lover, it was reported in the gossip columns. He got particularly nasty then." Devlin actually put his hand on Four's shoulder. "Do you recall when he reamed you out in front of the whole school?"

"You told him to stop, so, asshole that he is, he asked what last name you were going to give your children—and the other kids laughed."

"That was the first time he used that line," Devlin said.

"That was the first time she slept with a Kennedy." Four smirked.

Meadow looked between the two men and realized how much in common they shared. No wonder they were friends—or as much friends as Devlin would allow them to be. "Why would he say such a stupid, unreasoning thing?"

"He recites a chant over and over to remind him and the Amelia Shores Society of Old Farts of a world order that faded many years ago," Devlin said.

"It faded in most of America. But not here. Not in this tiny town, where the elders will kill to maintain their goddamn—pardon, ma'am—world order and their goddamn—pardon, ma'am—place of importance in it." Four took a long drag, then ground out the cigarette with his foot.

Meadow looked him right in the eye. "You pick that up."

He did.

"Good boy. Now, shall we go meet Bradley Benjamin?" While she was fortified by renewed indignation.

She started up the stairs to the restaurant.

As they approached, the old guys stood up. They were exactly as Four had described—and Bradley Benjamin was exactly as Meadow had imagined.

Of the old guys, he was the tallest. His posture was military, shoulders back, spine straight. His large, noble, aging nose drooped at the end. His shock of white hair was wavy and thick, his brows white and wild. His eyes were gray, cool and considering. He looked like an old-world aristocrat—and a surge of hatred caught Meadow by surprise.

This man had thrown her grandmother and mother into the street with no money, no support, and no remorse. He'd let Isabelle take her baby to Ireland to live with her art teacher, and when she sent word that Bjorn

Kelly wished to adopt Sharon, Bradley had signed the papers without hesitation. And when Bjorn had been killed and Isabelle had announced her daughter's death with him, Bradley had not sent a word of condolence.

Isabelle had insisted that he had emotions. That they were stunted and warped by his upbringing and his background, but that he had them.

If that was the truth, Meadow wondered what he would do when he discovered . . . what had really happened.

Thirteen

"Father." Four shook the old man's gnarled hand. "Good to see you."

Bradley Benjamin grunted and ignored his only son, as he'd been doing from the day he was born. His gaze went beyond Four to Devlin. "Fitzwilliam."

"Sir." Devlin offered his hand, too.

Bradley took it, shook it, and dropped it as if the contact would contaminate his skin. He scrutinized the pretty girl dressed in silk flowers, and his gaze warmed. "Who is this young lady?"

"This is Meadow Fitzwilliam," Devlin said.

She smiled at Bradley, that open, happy

smile that Devlin had come to realize characterized her personality. The one she so seldom wasted on him.

She might have secrets, but she didn't allow them to prey on her mind.

"Good to meet you, Bradley." She shook his hand heartily.

Bradley Benjamin stiffened.

She'd slipped in his assessment. This was the South, the Old South, and young ladies did not call their elders by their first name. In Benjamin's day, they didn't shake hands, either.

Then she smiled at Bradley again, and her sheer charm melted his reserve.

One at a time, Devlin introduced her to the old farts.

They twinkled. They beamed. Penn Simple even blushed and sucked in his stomach, and H. Edwin Osgood studied her with narrowed eyes, like man scoping out his next conquest. They all proved the truth of the adage, *No fool like an old fool.*

Damn the old fools.

She was like a weapon in Devlin's hands, to be used to get what he wanted, when he wanted, and all he had to do was sight down the barrel and squeeze the trigger.

Old Benjamin held her chair. "Won't you honor us with your presence?"

"Thank you." She seated herself and re-moved her hat, and the glow of her copper hair caught the gaze of every man in the place.

Devlin pulled up a chair without being asked and placed himself just behind and off to the side of her right shoulder. From here he could watch the door, watch the street, and, most important, watch the old farts, es-pecially Bradley Benjamin.

"Meadow is my wife."

The collective gasp was satisfying.

Benjamin's narrow-eyed outrage made Devlin want to laugh out loud. Devlin could almost hear him accusing Devlin of ruining a young woman's life, then of bringing a for-tune hunter into their midst, and finally of de-ceiving the old farts by presenting them with a woman of charm and not immediately iden-tifying her so they could snub her properly.

At last, predictably, Benjamin's attention turned to his son. "Devlin is married."

"I would be married, too, Father, if Devlin hadn't discovered the lovely Meadow first." Four performed a sitting bow in Meadow's direction.

"Congratulations, Devlin. I can already tell you don't deserve her," Penn Sample said.

"That's very true," Devlin answered easily. "No man alive deserves someone as delightful as Meadow—but I have her, and I will keep her."

She glanced over her shoulder at him, her eyes wide, and he realized how that must have sounded—and that, at this moment, he meant it.

"When and how did this marriage occur?" Benjamin asked.

"I went to my house in Majorca to vacation, and Meadow found me there," Devlin said.

"I wasn't asking you, young man," Benjamin snapped, "but your lovely wife."

Devlin didn't want her to say the wrong thing, but he shouldn't have worried.

"Let's just say—Devlin and I have had a tumultuous relationship, and leave it at that, shall we?" Meadow laughed. "Now all his lovely wife wants is a drink, and a chance to sit back and talk."

She handled the old farts so well. She only fumbled with Devlin, and that pleased him more than he could say.

He signaled for service.

The waiter appeared at Meadow's elbow. "Ma'am, what may I get you?"

She smiled at him, a zit-laden college kid, with exactly the same amount of pleasure she showed Benjamin and the other old farts. "Don't call me 'ma'am'! My name is Meadow. I would love a bottled water, and can I get a menu? I'm starving!"

"Yes, ma'am. Yes . . . Meadow." Dazzled, the waiter started to leave.

"Excuse me, Dave!" Four was half laughing and all annoyed. "I'd like something."

Dave came back, flustered. "Of course, sir. What will it be?"

"A mint julep for me, and for Devlin—"

"I'll take a bottled water, too," Devlin said.

"Have a julep," Four urged. "Daddy runs a tab."

"Water will be fine," Devlin told the waiter. "For all of us."

Four started to protest the edict, but Devlin subdued him with a glance.

Damn Four. He'd tricked Devlin into admitting Scrubby's investment in the Secret Garden. And not that Devlin thought Four would deliberately tell the other old farts, but when he got drunk, he said too much and acted like an ass.

Scrubby had risked his standing in his community to show faith in Devlin, and he deserved better than betrayal.

"Of course. Water is my favorite beverage." Four seated himself and lit a cigarette, as debonair, as privileged, and as annoying as ever.

"Mrs. Fitzwilliam, I know you're not from South Carolina, but I can't place your accent."

Trust old Benjamin to ask the questions Devlin needed answered.

"Now, how do you know I'm not from South Carolina?" With startling speed, she developed an accent.

"You have a good ear." Osgood spoke with a slight lisp, and his thick glasses distorted his watery brown eyes to an unnatural size. That, and the unskillful application of dark brown hair dye created a man better suited to a farce than to this elite group of privileged old men. "Usually when a Yankee tries to imitate us, the sound grinds like a chain saw."

"I do have a good ear." She sounded cockney, then smoothly switched to a Hispanic accent. "I tried drama in college, but I couldn't cut it as an actress."

Did she have an accent or didn't she? Devlin was suddenly unsure. Could she have fooled him from the moment she'd fallen on his stone lion?

He wanted to know her name. He had to discover her true identity. He needed to know everything there was to know about the mysterious Meadow . . . and before their affair was over, he would. He swore it.

"A lovely young woman like you? I would think you'd be a Hollywood star by now!" While Penn Sample pried, charm oozed from his pores like 3-IN-ONE oil.

"I cried when I played the sad parts and laughed at the funny ones." She laughed now. "As my coach said, that's not acting; that's audience participation."

Wilfred Kistard blotted his damp forehead with a snowy handkerchief, looked uncomfortable, and said, "Hot out here already."

Dave arrived with the waters. He twisted the top off one bottle and handed it to her, then delivered the menu with a flourish.

She glanced at the menu. "The house salad sounds marvelous! I'll have that with blue cheese dressing on the side, and the pasta primavera." She turned to Devlin. "Do you want anything?"

"Ham on rye, hold the mayo, deli mustard," Dave recited. "I remember."

"He is such a nice boy!" Meadow said as Dave left. Tilting up the bottle, she drank the whole thing, and each of the men around her watched her throat as she swallowed. She lowered the bottle and sighed with contentment. "That was wonderful! I was dehydrated."

"Another reason I know you're not from the area. You're more brash than a Southern lady, more forthcoming." Old Benjamin was not paying her a compliment.

"Thank you, Bradley. That is so sweet of you!" Devlin recognized the overly vehement note of pleasure in her voice, but no one else here knew her well enough to identify her annoyance.

Benjamin wasn't used to being misunderstood, and he visibly struggled against telling her what he had meant.

That gave Devlin the opportunity to say smoothly, "Yes, that was one of the many reasons Meadow succeeded where so many have failed. She's less stifled by tradition and the weight of expectations than the typical Southern lady."

Benjamin gladly turned his reeking frustration on Devlin. "We're all surprised, Devlin, that you've married at last."

"Thirty-two is hardly a great age, sir. After

all, I believe you were as old when you took your first wife." Devlin was pointed in his comment.

The other old men moved uneasily. The story of Isabelle and her infidelity always made them uncomfortable, recalling their own marital misadventures and the possibility—slight, in their minds, but always there—that not every female knew her place.

"Now, see, there's the difference between Devlin and me. He married me because I'm a child of freethinkers." Meadow grinned cockily. "I married him for his money."

The old farts sputtered with shocked laughter.

"And his good looks." Turning around, she looked mischievously into Devlin's eyes as she pinched his cheek.

All he had to do was sight down the barrel and squeeze the trigger. Too bad the damned weapon had a mind of her own.

And why in the hell did he enjoy having her make fun of him in front of the assemblage of old farts? If he wasn't careful, she would make him liked in this town.

"What did you say, young lady, when you discovered your husband was a bastard?"

Benjamin baldly asked the question, clearly hoping to catch Meadow by surprise, maybe tell her something Devlin hadn't had the nerve to tell her.

"Oh, Father." Four covered his eyes with his slender, uncalloused hand.

"Good shot," Osgood said.

It wasn't lack of nerve that had kept Devlin from informing her, but lack of time—they'd met only last night, and he seldom spoke of his fatherless state, certainly not within twenty-four hours of meeting a woman.

"What? Oh, I suppose he wants me to call him illegitimate." Benjamin challenged Devlin with his curling lip. "But I believe in calling a spade a spade."

Devlin waited, as curious about Meadow's reaction as the rest of the group.

"There's no excuse to call it a bloody damned shovel, at least not in polite society." Meadow's tone could have frozen pipes in August. "Perhaps when you wish to be rude, Mr. Benjamin, you should stick with calling me brash and hope I don't catch the slight."

Benjamin's gaze flew to hers, then dropped beneath the lash of her contempt.

"Brava!" Four clapped his hands softly. His eyes lit up, and he visibly admired Meadow.

Devlin schooled his face to impassivity, but marveled at Meadow's defense of him. He marveled, too, at how well Meadow read these men and used their weaknesses to manipulate them. She held her own formidable weapon—and Devlin needed to remember she held it.

"To answer your question, Mr. Benjamin, I have no interest in Devlin's parents except in the way they influenced his upbringing. It's the man himself who fascinates me." She turned her head toward Devlin and smiled. "I can hardly fault his charisma, his charm, or his kindness."

Either she was a better actress than she claimed, or she believed what she said— and Devlin didn't know which idea disturbed him more.

Benjamin recognized defeat when it stared him in the face, so he quit that battle and took up another. "So, young Devlin, what have you done with my house?"

"In three weeks, the Secret Garden will be an accredited five-star small hotel and receive its guests," Devlin said.

"Yet I hear you're having trouble getting goods from the local merchants." Wilfred Kistard leaned back in his chair and folded his hands across his round, sagging belly.

"The local merchants do what they must." Devlin had been pulled aside more than once while some storekeeper feverishly explained that his defection was temporary and if Mr. Fitzwilliam would simply have patience . . .

"You've had some accidents on the property." Scrubby tapped the table. "Any more problems?"

"Security has been tightened." Devlin met his anxious gaze and nodded.

"How bad is it if you don't get that five-star rating?" Penn Sample smacked his lips. "I'd say that would cause a significant loss of revenue."

"True. So true." Osgood's shoulders slumped as he looked toward Bradley for guidance.

"My hotels do not lose revenue." Devlin looked around the table. "The invitations to the grand opening will be going out in another week. Look for it in the mail. It will be the event of the season."

"Do you really imagine anyone will show

up to see you desecrate the sacred traditions of Amelia Shores?" Benjamin asked.

"You will. Your curiosity won't let you stay away." Devlin's certainty ran headlong into Benjamin's outrage.

Benjamin's wrath faltered. He would, indeed, be there.

Four ground out one cigarette, then lit another immediately and took a long draw like a man in need of a much stronger drug.

Bradley watched him with ill-concealed contempt. "You're too old to be smoking those things. Those are for adolescents. Try to be a man about one thing, at least."

"You want him to be a man about smoking?" Meadow asked. "How would he do that?"

"There's nothing like a cigar." Bradley held up his hand to forestall any comment from her. "I know some ladies don't like the smell, but there's nothing like the smooth, warm smoke of a good cigar."

Four must have really been irritated by his father's reprimand, especially in front of Meadow, for his voice ground with exasperation. "I don't like cigars, sir."

"I don't see why you value mouth cancer from a cigar more than lung cancer from a

cigarette. They both end in mutilating surger-
ies, awful bouts of chemotherapy, and
death." Meadow smiled, a slight upward tilt
of the lips and the least genuine smile Devlin
had ever had the privilege to view.

The contrast between that and her regular
smile was so great, every old fart there
looked taken aback, and Bradley har-
rumphed in perturbation. "Young lady, that's
a harsh view of a pleasant pastime. We raise
tobacco in this state, and we don't believe all
the propaganda about cancer-causing agents
and such."

"Mr. Benjamin, if you had ever once visited a cancer ward, you would believe." Taking the burning cigarette from between
Four's fingers, she stubbed it out in the ashtray. "Never mind the cigars," she said to him.
"Just give it up."

Bradley started to speak.

She looked at him straight-on, and did the
one thing Devlin thought was impossible:
She stared him down.

Bradley looked away. "Cheeky."

In the background, Devlin saw Scrubby
grin, and Kistard and Osgood leaned back in
their chairs, crossed their arms, and waited

for further entertainment. Bradley was well respected, but by no means popular.

A young mother came out onto the deck. She wore the tourist's usual uniform—flip-flops, a bathing suit, a cover-up, and drifts of sand. But she carried an extra decoration—a car seat hung over her arm. She looked hot and tired, and the baby wailed for attention.

"Oh, for God's sake!" Benjamin exploded with disgust. "Can't these people see this is a nice restaurant?"

The woman heard him. Of course she did. Her sunburned cheeks got redder, and her shocked, hurt eyes filled with tears.

Meadow was on her feet at once, arms extended. "Let me help you get settled so you can take care of the baby. Where would you like to sit? In the shade, I'll bet."

The mother shook her head and glanced anxiously at the table of old farts.

"Don't worry about him." Meadow's voice carried as clearly as had Benjamin's. "His arthritis is acting up." She found the woman a comfortable spot, sent Dave for water, and all the while chatted about vacations and seashells and eating carrots sticks with sand on them.

Slowly the mother relaxed and responded.

And all the while the old guys and Four and Devlin watched, because they couldn't take their eyes away from Meadow's gleaming copper hair.

Meadow lifted the three-month-old out of the car seat.

Out of the corner of his eye Devlin saw Bradley Benjamin start. Devlin looked over.

Benjamin stared at Meadow, frowning, puzzled.

She bounced it against her hip, smiling and talking in the low croon of an experienced caretaker.

Benjamin took a sharp breath. The color drained from his face. He grimaced and put his hand to his chest.

Devlin leaned back with a sigh of contentment. His plans were proceeding as he wished.

Bradley Benjamin had recognized Isabelle's granddaughter.

Fourteen

"Do you have a copy of *The Secret Garden*?" Meadow leaned across the counter toward the owner of the Amelia Shores Bookstore.

Mrs. Cognomi, middle-aged, stout, with a mustache and suspiciously black hair, glared as if she were offended. "Of course I have a copy. It's popular vacation reading for children. Hardcover or paperback?"

"Hardcover." As Mrs. Cognomi bustled off to fetch it, Meadow called, "I want it for Devlin." Without visible qualm, she indicated him.

Two other customers browsing the shelves turned to look at him, standing beside Meadow. One woman smirked at him. The other turned her back and silently laughed.

With one simple sentence, Meadow had ruined his reputation as the meanest son of a bitch in Amelia Shores.

Mrs. Cognomi fetched an oversize hardcover with an impressionistic painting of a young Victorian girl. She handed it to Meadow, who received it with soft, cooing noises.

Mrs. Cognomi straightened her black glasses and looked him over so critically she reminded him of his first grade teacher. "You know, Mr. Fitzwilliam, you should consider putting a copy in each room in your hotel."

"Yes! That's brilliant, Mrs. Cognomi." Meadow turned to Devlin. "That would be a nice touch."

"Who would care?" Devlin stood there stoically, his arms crossed across his chest.

"All the women who read *The Secret Garden* when they were young." Meadow confided to Mrs. Cognomi, "My husband has never read it."

Mrs. Cognomi *tsk*ed. "Yet it's a lovely story with lessons for us all. Would you like me to order the hardcover edition for the hotel?"

"I don't think—" Devlin said.

"No. People steal towels. Can you imagine how fast they'd snatch up a book like this?" Meadow slid it across the counter to Mrs. Cognomi. "Do you have it in trade paperback?"

"Yes, and a good choice indeed, Mrs. Fitzwilliam." Mrs. Cognomi approved of Meadow. Of course she approved of Meadow. Who didn't? "How many copies do you need?"

"Let's start with sixty," Meadow decided.

"There are only forty-five rooms," Devlin said.

"Yes, but we have to figure on loss during the grand opening," Meadow said sensibly. "So, Mrs. Cognomi, sixty copies to begin with, and we'll let you know when we need more."

"Lovely." Mrs. Cognomi pulled out her order pad and began filling it out. "How would you like to pay?"

"Devlin, give her your credit card," Meadow instructed.

Devlin couldn't believe he had suddenly accrued such an absurd expense. An expense that should be coming out of the corporation. But he knew his CFO. She questioned every receipt. And damned if he was going to try to explain why he had ordered sixty copies of a girlie children's book. As he flipped through his wallet, he asked Mrs. Cognomi, "If you do business with me, aren't you afraid Bradley Benjamin will foreclose on your store?"

"He doesn't own the mortgage on my store. Nor does he own the building my store is in." Mrs. Cognomi folded her arms across her belly and smirked with satisfaction. "I do."

Devlin developed a sudden liking for Mrs. Cognomi. "Better make it ninety copies."

"With the bulk discount, that'll be four hundred eighty dollars, plus tax. They'll be delivered here next Tuesday. I'll bring them out to you—I'd love to see the restoration work you've done." Taking Devlin's card, Mrs. Cognomi swiped it through the cash register. "Bradley Benjamin is the type of man who scorns fiction and reads newspapers and business journals."

"I don't understand that kind of joyless approach to life," Meadow said. "But let's not say anything disparaging about Mr. Benjamin. They just took him away in an ambulance suffering from angina."

Mrs. Cognomi looked unimpressed. "He's

gone to the hospital before. He always survives. Only the good die young."

"It sometimes seems that way, doesn't it?" For a telling moment, Meadow's lower lip trembled.

Devlin noted . . . and wondered.

Then she lifted her chin and smiled. "Don't forget to charge us for the hardcover copy! I'm going to read it to Devlin."

"Good for you." Mrs. Cognomi looked right at Devlin, her protuberant brown eyes enlarged by her lenses. "It would be too bad if Mr. Fitzwilliam became as joyless as Bradley Benjamin, wouldn't it?"

Devlin scowled with so much annoyance, Meadow knew she could get away with murder right now. Good thing she wanted so much less. "Mrs. Cognomi, can I use your restroom?"

"Of course, dear. They're through the swinging doors to your right."

"I'll be in the Jeep," Devlin called.

Poor guy. He couldn't wait to get out of here.

Meadow slid into the tiny ladies' room, flipped open her cell phone, called Judith—and groaned when her call went right to voice mail. In a low voice, she said, "I'm in

Amelia Shores, I'm going back out to Waldemar, and so far—except for a confrontation with Isabelle's husband, who almost had a heart attack afterward—everything's okay. But how's Mom, and where are you?" She hung up and leaned against the cool door.

Half an hour ago she'd been livid with Bradley Benjamin. She didn't care if he offended her, but to be cruel to Devlin about his illegitimacy had not been acceptable behavior, and his rudeness to that poor single mother had made Meadow want to smack him. She'd gone to help the mother just to keep her own hands off Bradley—and then he'd suffered that attack.

Four had had to give him the nitro he kept in his pocket. Dave had rushed over with water. The old guys flapped around like a bunch of excited peahens, except for H. Edwin Osgood, who kept his head and dialed 911. And when Devlin had offered his assistance, Bradley had shouted at him to go away. The ambulance had drawn up to the restaurant, and when she'd tried to wish Bradley well, he'd pretended to be unconscious. Pretended to be—she'd seen his eyelids fluttering.

Now she felt guilty for being so irked with

Bradley, and even guiltier for wanting him to live so she could use him. Nothing was turning out as she'd planned, and now she had to go back to Waldemar with Devlin. Devlin, who watched her like a cat at a mouse hole.

Unfortunately, the cheese he used to bait his trap was truly tempting.

She splashed water on her cheeks and wished she'd brought those pills the doctor had given her, because she had a whopper of a headache.

She wasn't going to admit it to Devlin, but maybe she'd overdone it on her first day with a concussion. She needed to go back to the hotel, crawl in bed, and take a nap.

She headed out through the restaurant and onto the street, where Devlin had parked the Jeep.

The top was off, and she could see Devlin seated behind the wheel.

Four stood facing him, his hand on the roll bar. "I make a pleasant dinner guest, and your chef needs practice. I'll ride out with you."

"You will do no such thing." Devlin's impatience couldn't be hidden.

"That's right. No backseat. So I'll drive myself," Four insisted.

"No." Devlin revved the motor and glanced

toward the bookstore. He caught sight of Meadow, and for an instant she thought his gaze warmed.

But she must be imagining what she wanted to see, for in the next moment he summoned her with a jerk of his head.

He *had* to be kidding.

She stopped walking. She jerked her head in imitation. She lifted her brows.

Four turned, watched the pantomime, and grinned.

Devlin looked as if he were about to choke with frustration, but his voice was warm and adoring when he called, "Darling, come on! Sam has already called from the hotel. The tree movers dropped the blasted trunk on the brand-new gazebo before the paint was even dry."

She resumed walking.

Four helped her into the Jeep, murmuring in a voice just loud enough for Devlin to hear, "He's a beast who's far too used to getting his own way, but you're training him, and he does take instruction well."

"Which is more than I can say for you." Devlin drove off so quickly Four leaped backward to avoid being run over.

Meadow scrambled for her seat belt. "Devlin! That wasn't nice."

"Don't worry about Four and his hurt feelings. They've been subdued by a large infusion of bourbon over ice. *My* bourbon over *my* ice." Devlin shook his head, but Meadow thought she discerned a faint fondness for the only Benjamin son. "He's almost certainly skipping toward his stupid little car right now, ready to drive out to the hotel."

"You're probably right. Four seems remarkably resilient, especially for a man with a father like Bradley Benjamin." She removed her hat and gathered a handful of her hair into a band at the base of her neck.

"When I was a boy, I used to long for a father like the other kids had. Then I'd meet old Benjamin and watch him abuse Four and count my blessings."

She hesitated, torn between so many questions that needed asking. Finally she settled on, "Bradley doesn't seem too fond of you, either."

"You heard him. I'm a bastard, and he reserves his most vitriolic abuse for me."

"Because you remind him of his wife's infidelity and the child he lost to it." She pulled on her hat and tied her scarf around it to keep it on her head.

"That's a new theory."

How could he be so obtuse? "There has to be a reason for him to care so much, and by all accounts he loved Isabelle; he just didn't know how to open his soul to her."

"You got that from what Four said?" The wind whipped past as Devlin cruised toward the edge of town and onto the southbound road toward the line of mansions.

She had to be more careful about revealing what she knew. "While you were talking to Sam on the phone, I talked to Scrubby." That was true. She had talked to Scrubby—just not about Bradley Benjamin's marriage.

"Did you two incredibly intuitive souls talk about me and my inner feelings, too?"

"No," she snapped. "We only talked about people we were interested in."

"Good."

He didn't say anything else, slowing where the pavement gave way to well-groomed gravel. He took the dip smoothly, then sped up again, not quite as fast this time.

She wished she hadn't succumbed to irritation. Because she wanted to know about his inner feelings. She always thought people were like pieces of art glass—strong enough to handle and use, delicate enough to shatter under a strong blow, and filled with swirls of color that fascinated the eye. But while most people—and most glass— allowed light through, she could discern nothing of Devlin's heart and soul through the smoke and mirrors he held before him.

And she was a curious girl. She loved people. She loved to ask them about themselves. Loved to listen to their stories. Flattered herself that she understood them . . . and she was lying to herself if she thought her curiosity about Devlin was anything similar to her curiosity about other people. With Devlin, she wanted to know everything about him. She urgently wanted to know what made him tick.

"Are you nervous?" He looked at her sideways. "I'm actually a very safe driver."

"What?" He drove so confidently she relaxed into the seat and watched the ocean. "No, I'm fine."

"You're tapping your foot."

"Oh. It's a nervous habit. When I'm thinking. So tell me about your childhood." *Smooth. Very smooth.*

He laughed. "I wondered how long you'd be able to keep your questions to yourself."

"How long did I?"

"Maybe a minute."

"It was longer than that."

"You're right." He waited two beats. "At least sixty-five seconds."

"That's better. So . . . your childhood."

"Comfortable. My grandparents were disappointed with my mother, but they didn't throw us out in the snow. We lived with them until I was five. At that point I got big enough to beat the tar out of my older cousins when they made fun of me and my mother. Mother had to move out to avoid blood on the antique rug in Grandmother's dining room, but by then she had her interior decorating shop established and her toe in the media. I went to an exclusive school—that's where I met Four—and before long I was beating the tar out of a variety of boys, some of whom were still my cousins."

"What is wrong with the people here?" Meadow burst out. "It's not the fifties! Women are allowed to have a baby with or without the option of marriage, and that child is valuable, a piece of God put on this earth."

"You're an innocent. People always love to

gossip, and children always love to be cruel to kids who are different. It's an eternal law, never to be changed." He sounded so sure.

How had he come from being that boy so free with his fists to a man closed to honest emotion?

"In addition to the onerous weight of human nature, I was born in Charleston. Charleston is old-fashioned. Then there was my mother's conviction that my father, Nathan Manly, was going to divorce his wife and marry her. So she lorded her conquest of him over her fellow debutantes—my mother is the slightest bit competitive."

Meadow heard a heavy dose of irony in his voice.

"Put all of those ingredients into the situation and you have a recipe for social . . ." He hesitated.

"Disaster?" She marveled that he was at last opening to her.

"Difficulties. Fortunately for my mother, her talent and ambition have allowed her to triumph over her former rivals, although not in the traditional way, with a rich husband and two socially correct children. And if challenges form character, then I have enough character to make up for Four's lack of it."

"I don't think it works that way. I think he'll have to develop his own. And what you need to develop is—" She stopped herself. She was thinking out loud again, and every time she did that, she got into trouble.

"What do I need to develop?"

Patience. Kindness. A belief, however unproven, that men are good at heart. Automatically, she said, "You're perfect as you are."

"A lovely thought. But you don't believe it."

"You're exactly who you should be at this point in your life." She knew the correct things to say.

He cast her a sardonic glance. "Where did you learn to babble such nonsense?"

"It's not nonsense!" She did believe it was true. The trouble was, she wanted to fix people. As her mother pointed out time and again, Meadow could only fix herself, and until the moment when she'd achieved nirvana, that should be her lifelong project.

But it was so easy to see what was wrong with other people and give them good advice.

"Right." The road wound away from the ocean, following a curving path into the woods filled with cedar and moss-draped live oaks. He pulled off to the side. Turning to face her, he put his arm across the back of her seat. His gaze captured hers. "I've confided in you. Now you tell me—when, my dear amnesiac, were you in a cancer ward?"

"A cancer ward?" she repeated. "What makes you think I was in a cancer ward?"

"When Bradley Benjamin instructed Four on smoking cigars, you ripped into him with a passion and a sarcasm reserved for serial killers." Shade dappled the Jeep and offered a false mellowness to his face.

She stared at Devlin, caught in the horror between a lie and the truth. Should she tell him?

My mother has cancer, she needs treatment, and if I don't get her a quarter of a million dollars fast, she might— probably will—slip out of remission and die.

Would he understand?

Maybe he would. But even if she found the painting, he wouldn't let her take it. He owned the house and all its contents. The painting, if it was still there, was his.

What was it Four had said? *The milk of human kindness has curdled in Devlin's veins.*

She believed it. She'd heard his hard-nosed handling of Sam, seen his impatience with Four, witnessed his satisfaction when Bradley Benjamin had suffered his attack. She couldn't take the chance and trust Devlin. Not with her mother's life at stake.

Devlin still sat there, waiting for his answer.

She looked away. "I know things. I know my first name. I know I don't like it when you summon me like I'm one of your maids, and you shouldn't treat any human being like that. I know what I think about life. I know what I think about smoking."

He leaned back. He looked her over, his eyes black with disappointment. "But you don't know anything about how your thinking got the way it is."

"No."

"Right." His arm slid away from her seat. "I give only so many chances, Meadow."

Her heart gave a hard, frightened thump. "What do you mean?"

"You know what I mean." He faced forward, put the car in gear, and got the Jeep up to speed. As he drove the narrow curves the tires spit gravel, and the silence felt like a weight on Meadow's guilt-ridden soul.

Maybe she should trust him. Her heart

said she should. It was her fears that held her back. "Devlin, listen—"

She didn't know exactly what she was going to say.

Then it didn't matter.

He tried to make the bend. The steering wheel balked. He swore. He hit the brakes. His arms strained as he fought the turn.

They weren't going to make it.

Fifteen

Fear and adrenaline surged through Devlin's veins. The steering was stiff—he'd lost it at the crucial moment in the curve. He worked the brakes, fought to control the skid on a damp gravel road.

The ditch was about a foot deep and full of last night's rain. The front tires smacked hard and deep. Water flew. Branches snapped as the Jeep ripped through them. The stand of cedars rushed toward them.

They hit a good-size tree head-on.

The air bags ripped the wheel out of his hand.

They skidded sideways. The side panel smacked another tree.

And they stopped.

The air bags deflated. The warm and comforting scent of cedar—no longer warm and comforting—filled the air.

In the sudden lack of motion, lack of sound, he could hear his heart thundering in his ears. Or was it Meadow's heart he heard?

She clutched her head.

Damn it. That concussion! "Meadow. Are you all right?"

She didn't answer. She was conscious, but she wasn't talking. And if Meadow wasn't talking, there was definitely something wrong.

He unhooked her seat belt. "Is anything broken? Can you move everything?" Two minutes ago he'd been furious with her. Twice today he'd given her the chance to tell him everything, and she'd refused. More than twice today she'd laughed with other men, charmed other men.

Then she'd had the nerve to look at him warily, as if he could be as dangerous and unforgiving as Bradley Benjamin and his cohorts.

A thought niggled at him—maybe he was more like them than he wished.

But he dismissed it when she said, "I'm fine." She wiggled various body parts to show him, but she kept her hand on her head.

He lifted her chin to look into her eyes. They were tear-filled. Pain-filled. "Meadow. Are you all right?" He enunciated each word slowly.

"I'm fine," she said again.

Yeah. Sure she was. She looked like hell. Her red freckles stuck out in stark relief to her white complexion. She closed her eyes, as if keeping them open were too great an effort, and leaned her head against the headrest.

He sure wasn't mad at her anymore.

"Damn it!" They were halfway between the Secret Garden and Amelia Shores. He pulled out his cell phone and looked. They had no service. They were alone out here with no protection. . . . His head whipped around.

A car was coming.

He leaned into the Jeep toward the pistol he kept locked in a box close at hand—and relaxed when Four's stupid damned MINI honked from the road.

"What happened?" Four climbed out, a long-legged clown out of an absurdly tiny car, and rushed toward them. "Did you miss the corner?"

"Yeah. I missed the corner." Devlin leaped out and hurried to Meadow. "Honey, I'm going to send you with Four." He slid his arms around her.

"I can walk," she said.

"But you don't have to." He headed for the MINI.

Four took one look at Meadow, then backed away as if he were afraid she'd hurl—and hurl on him. "Is she okay?"

"Take her to the hospital."

Four tiptoed after them and opened the passenger-side door.

"I'm fine. I'm just tired," she said, but she didn't open her eyes.

Last night she'd been lively even after hitting her head. Today she looked drawn, exhausted; and with a pang, Devlin realized he shouldn't have taken her to town, shouldn't have relied on her to tell him whether she was tired. Meadow didn't complain. Not while there was life to be lived.

Devlin slid her into the seat. "I want Dr. Apps to check her out. Don't take no for an answer." Taking Four's shoulder, Devlin looked him in the eyes. "Don't leave her alone, and don't let anything happen to her. Or I'll kill you."

"Right. I know. Don't blame you a bit. She's great." Four's breathless agreement could be anxiety for Meadow—or it could be guilt.

Had Four had a hand in this accident?

No. No, Four might be mad at Devlin, but he wasn't vicious. He never had been.

"What are you going to do?" Four asked.

"Call Frank Peterson," Devlin said tersely.

Four knew Frank, the mechanic and handyman. "I don't think he can fix *that* car."

"No. Probably not." But he could answer the question Devlin wanted answered.

Because this accident wasn't an accident.

Miss Louise "Weezy" Woodward, teenage volunteer at the Amelia Shores Regional Hospital, hustled out of the waiting room like her tail feathers had been scorched. She stopped by the nurses' station. "Mrs. Peterson, did you see that Devlin Fitzwilliam while his girlfriend was in having a CT scan? I offered him a cup of coffee and a smile, and he about ripped my throat out."

"Of course he did. He's madly in love with her. Haven't you heard?" Jazmin Peterson, nurse in command on this floor, grinned at the chance to impart the news and take pretty Weezy down a few notches. "That's his wife."

"His wife?" Weezy's cheeks turned as bright pink as her hospital jacket. "He's not married! He can't be. Who told you? When did he marry?"

Jazmin leaned on the counter and drawled every single syllable. "It is the most romantic thing. I heard all about it from my Frank, who's working out at the hotel doing odd jobs—and there are a lot of odd jobs to do, too, with stuff going wrong all the time, and half of it fishy stuff, if you know what I mean."

"I heard old Mr. Bradley Benjamin was so mad he swore to kill Mr. Fitzwilliam."

"I heard that, too. But Mr. Benjamin came through here not too long ago, and he's in no shape to kill anyone." Jazmin nodded wisely. "If he don't have a angiogram pretty soon, he'd better start preparing for the long journey home."

"Never mind him!" Weezy grabbed Jazmin's arm and shook it. "Tell me about

Mr. Fitzwilliam and how he got married without any of us knowing it."

"A long time ago, Mr. and Mrs. Fitzwilliam met and got married in Hawaii, then they had a big fight and she left him. That's why Mr. Devlin's been so ugly to everyone for so long."

"He was dying of frustrated desire," Weezy said.

"Yes, until she showed up on his doorstep last evening. They shared one night of passionate reunion; then he almost killed her by driving into a tree. That poor man. He's swimming in guilt."

"That is the most romantic thing I've ever heard." Weezy pressed her hand over her heart.

"And all true." Frank had said there'd been gossip that Mrs. Fitzwilliam broke into the house, but Jazmin figured that was just crazy talk, and she wasn't the kind of woman to spread crazy talk.

Weezy, who was Amelia Shores to the bone, asked, "Who is her family?"

"No one knows. She's some Yankee girl, but I'll tell you one thing for sure—she's not rich. I saw the calluses on her fingers myself." That had made Jazmin like her a lot.

"What's young Mr. Benjamin doing hanging around here?"

"I don't think but he's in love with her, too," Jazmin said wisely. "He's the one who brought her in, and you should have seen him. He was white-faced and shaking like a leaf."

"That is not fair. She can't have the two of them!" Young Weezy stomped her foot.

"I guess she can." Jazmin gestured down the corridor. "There they go now."

They watched the wheelchair roll toward the exit. Mr. Fitzwilliam walked beside the wheelchair, holding Mrs. Fitzwilliam's hand.

Four walked behind them, weaving slightly.

"Do you suppose he's been hitting the bottle again?" Weezy asked. "You know he always keeps that flask in his pocket."

"And fills it up at Waldemar, according to my Frank. He just hangs around out there like some sorrowful ghost. Rumor has it he's the reason Mr. Bradley Benjamin had to sell the house to Mr. Fitzwilliam."

"No! Why?"

"Young Mr. Benjamin's not got a head for business."

Dr. Apps stepped into the doorway of the

examining room and watched her patient leave.

Jazmin lowered her voice. "Dr. Apps must have agreed to send Mrs. Fitzwilliam home. She didn't want to—Mrs. Fitzwilliam was arguing like crazy—but Mr. Fitzwilliam said he would make sure his wife stayed in bed if he had to stay there with her. Dr. Apps looked as if he'd slapped her, and got real quiet."

"Dr. Apps had aspirations toward him."

"She wasn't the only one." Jazmin looked meaningfully at Weezy.

"Well, why not?" Weezy plumped her ample boobs with her hands. "I'm a good-looking girl, and there aren't that many handsome millionaires in this town."

They didn't call her Sleazy Weezy for nothing.

"Devlin Fitzwilliam is not a handsome millionaire." Jazmin chuckled. "He's a handsome billionaire—and honey, you are so out of luck."

Sixteen

Jordan hustled into the kitchen, and Mia flinched. She always flinched when he was around. He was so critical. He bellowed so loudly. And now that he'd said she was going to be his saucier, the stakes were higher. If she messed up he would throw her out, and she needed this job. The divorce had left her with nothing except bills and two teenagers who hated her because their no-good daddy had skipped town.

"Come on!" Jordan clapped his hands. "We're going up to stand on the porch and wait for Miz Fitzwilliam."

"They're not keeping her at the hospital?" Christian asked.

"Yes, but they're releasing her in the morning, so we'll stand there all night." Jordan rolled his eyes. "Of course they've released her. Now, *vite*! They've turned in the gate."

The two assistants took off their aprons and headed after their boss.

The sunshine made Mia blink, and so did the size of the crowd. She worked in the kitchen. She had no idea there were so many employees at the Secret Garden.

"There must be fifty people here," she whispered to Christian.

"Sixty-five, last I heard, and Mr. Fitzwilliam's secretary was hiring again today."

"I've lived here my whole life, and I don't know half these people." She hung back and let Jordan push his way toward the front. She hated crowds. She hated meeting new people. But she'd liked the new Mrs. Fitzwilliam, and she was glad Jordan had let them come up to offer their support on her return.

"Plenty of them heard there was work to be had and came in from other towns. Mr.

Fitzwilliam brought some in from Atlanta and such. And you know there's always some people who drift in for the summer because they want to live on the beach." Christian wasn't originally from Amelia Shores—in fact, he talked twangy, like a Texan—but he'd lived here long enough to think he was an expert. "It was probably one of them who nicked the steering fluid line with something sharp."

"No! On purpose?" She wrapped her hands around her waist.

Christian nodded. "Frank told Mr. Williams, who told Miz Burke, who told me that it happened while Mr. and Mrs. Fitzwilliam were in town with Mr. Four."

"Mr. Four didn't do it!" Mia liked Four.

Christian laughed. "Yeah, he is sort of a doof, isn't he? I heard it was his fault old Mr. Benjamin had to sell this place. I heard Four got into debt to Mr. Fitzwilliam, and this place was the only payment Mr. Fitzwilliam would take."

"How do you hear this?"

"I take my breaks in the break room instead of the kitchen. You should try it sometime."

Mia ignored that. "There they are," she said as the long limo pulled up to the steps.

Like a colorful aluminum can tied to the bumper of the real car, Mr. Benjamin's MINI followed.

"Mrs. Fitzwilliam is such a nice lady—and she's married to *him*." Christian shuddered. "I guess that proves any guy can get a wife if he's got enough money. Mr. Fitzwilliam scares me to death."

Mr. Fitzwilliam scared her, too. He was that kind of man. But he'd been kind to her, more than anyone else in Amelia Shores, giving her a job based on nothing except a stint as a cook at a long-vanished restaurant in town and presenting her to Jordan as a permanent employee. Her knees might quake when Mr. Fitzwilliam was around, but she was grateful to him. "I don't think he's that bad."

"Oh, yeah? Cecily said she got behind cleaning her rooms and he almost threw her out."

Mia gloated a little. She did have some gossip Christian didn't know. "Cecily didn't tell you everything. She got caught taking a nap on the bed she was supposed to be making, and the only reason she got a second chance was that she pleaded a dependent child. That, and the fact that Mr.

Fitzwilliam's having a hell of a time getting enough help, between the tourist season starting and old Mr. Benjamin dissing him all over town."

They watched as Devlin lifted Meadow from the backseat of the limo.

"Whew. Look at that. He's picking her up so carefully, like she's a diamond." Mia's heart trilled as it hadn't since the day she'd fallen in love with her louse of a husband. "And we didn't even know they were married."

"That's because it was a runaway marriage. Her folks are rich—"

"I thought they were poor!" Because Mrs. Fitzwilliam didn't seem like a rich girl. She was too nice.

"I heard they were rich."

"Does anybody really know?" Mia felt as if she were talking to one of her kids.

"C'mon, that makes sense, because her parents didn't want their little darling marrying that carpetbagger."

Sometimes Mia didn't much like Christian. "Mr. Fitzwilliam is not a carpetbagger. He's from Charleston!"

"He's buying up every piece of property he can get his hands on and make a profit with. What else does a carpetbagger do?"

She tried to object, but Christian talked over her. "Plus, he's a bastard, and the man who got his mother pregnant was a bigger scoundrel than Mr. Fitzwilliam any day."

"I heard that, too." Folks were stretching to touch Mrs. Fitzwilliam as Mr. Fitzwilliam carried her past.

Four followed them. He darted a look around and hunched his shoulders. He wiped his palms on his trousers.

Mia hated to admit it, but he looked guilty of *something.* She hoped not; he wasn't a good man, but he was a nice man.

"You can't blame her folks for not wanting that pretty girl to marry that mean son of a bitch." Like a boy caught tattling, Christian ducked when Mr. Fitzwilliam glanced his way.

As Mia said a silent prayer for Mrs. Fitzwilliam's recovery, she watched the way Mr. Fitzwilliam cradled his wife. The way he looked at her, and her all covered with white powder from the air bag, with dirty hair, and sporting a bruise on her cheek.

He was in thrall to her.

"Who knows what she has to put up with," Christian said.

"All . . . night . . . long."

"What?" Christian shook his head in confusion.

"That man has a look about him. He can go all night long," Mia drawled. "Trust me on this."

Christian looked as horrified as if his neutered spaniel had humped his leg.

Stupid boy. He thought that because she was twenty years older than him and didn't say much, she was a sexless nothing. She might be plain, and she might be divorced, and she might have been abused, but she recognized a man who knew his way around a bedroom. She added, "Besides, this morning it looked as if Mrs. Fitzwilliam had him wound around her little finger."

"Yeah, he isn't the only one." Christian nudged her and indicated their boss.

"My poor skinny little *poulet.*" As Mr. Fitzwilliam walked by with Mrs. Fitzwilliam, Jordan clasped his huge hands together under his chin, and his big brown eyes swam with tears. "I will make you a vegetable broth that will cure all your ills and bring roses to your cheeks again."

"Thank you, Jordan." Meadow would have said more, but Mr. Fitzwilliam didn't stop. He headed right for the open front door.

"She has to go to bed now," he said. "And she's not getting up for forty-eight hours."

"But I want to thank everyone for coming out to greet me," Mrs. Fitzwilliam wailed.

"In two days you can thank everyone. For now, you're going to bed." They disappeared into the house.

"See?" Christian whispered. "I told you he's scary."

Mia smiled at his naïveté. And sighed with gladness for Mrs. Fitzwilliam.

Maybe not tonight. Maybe not tomorrow night. But someday soon, Mrs. Fitzwilliam was going to be one very happy woman.

All . . . night . . . long.

Sam rushed ahead of Devlin into the bedroom and turned down the bed.

Tenderly Devlin laid Meadow down and covered her with the sheets. "How do you feel?"

"I'm fine." A line was etched between her brows.

"Lying will only get you into trouble." He watched her closely. "More trouble."

She jerked as if she'd been electrocuted. "I'm not lying!"

"You don't have to try to fool me." He

smoothed the hair back from her forehead. "You can trust me. I'll take care of you."

"Will you give me forty million dollars?" she asked truculently.

His hand stopped in midair. "Why do you need forty million dollars?"

"If you trusted me, you wouldn't care."

"Right." She was as cranky as a child. Dr. Apps had said she might be—Meadow had no serious injuries from the wreck, but she was exhausted and stressed. "You've got the worst damned headache you've ever had."

"I suppose," she said sulkily.

"And a sore wrist and a bruise on your cheek"—his thumb skimmed the black mark on her fair skin—"caused by the air bag slamming your hand into your face."

"I guess."

"So you can admit that you feel lousy."

"I don't feel lousy." She hesitated on the edge of major perjury, then gave in with a flounce and a wince. "I want a shower."

"Not right now. Sam, get some water." Devlin took the bottle of pills out of his pocket and shook one out.

Sam headed for the bathroom.

"I'm dirty. I've got that air bag powder on

me." She rubbed her arms and the powder came off in little pills.

"Tomorrow you can have a bath."

"I don't want a bath. I want a shower. And I want one now."

"As soon as the drug takes effect, you can get up and take a shower."

"Do you think I'm stupid? Do you think I don't know what that pill is supposed to do?"

"No. What?"

"Put me to sleep!"

"That is a problem, isn't it?" Devlin took the glass from Sam and offered her the pill. "But at least while you're asleep you won't think about being dusty."

She turned her head away. "I don't like drugs."

"You need to sleep."

"Then I'll drink some chamomile tea."

He handed Sam the pill and the glass. He seated himself on the bed beside her, taking care to put his hip against her hip. He put his hands on either side of her, leaned forward until their noses were almost touching, and said, "Darling, forty-eight hours from now you can go back to charming the staff, scolding old farts, and just generally being

Meadow. For now, you are going to do exactly as you are told."

"And how are you going to enforce that?" Her weary blue eyes shot lively sparks.

"To start with, you'll take this pill or I'll climb into bed and make love to you until you're so tired you'll fall asleep in my arms."

"Devlin!" Her horrified gaze flew past him. "Not in front of Sam!"

"Then you'd better take the pill." Devlin accepted the pill and the glass from his stoic secretary. He helped her sit up, watched her swallow the pill and drink the water, then slowly let her back down onto the pillow. "Now go to sleep. I'll be here if you need me."

She turned her back on him. "I won't need you."

"I'll be here anyway." He tucked her in and turned to Sam. "We'll work in the sitting room."

"Yes, sir." Sam headed toward the door.

"So much for being here," she muttered.

Devlin went into the bathroom, wet a washcloth, and returned to her. "Turn over," he instructed.

She did, and he wanted to laugh at the rebellious, sulky, wary expression on her powdery face. "Here." He smoothed the wet, cool cloth across her cheeks, her chin, her forehead.

Her eyes closed in pure bliss.

"Does that feel good?" he asked.

"Yes. Thank you." She rubbed the back of her hand against her nose. "I'm sorry I've been a snot."

"I wouldn't say a snot. More of a brat." He stroked the cloth across her mouth, then kissed her. Her lips were velvety and relaxed, but when he opened his mouth slightly, she responded. Reluctantly and just a little, but it seemed to him she couldn't help but answer him. "Go to sleep now."

She nodded, her eyelids drooping.

He stroked her hair one more time, tossed the washcloth in the bathroom, then walked out to the sitting room.

Sam sat at the desk, laptop open.

Devlin had found Sam eight months ago during a search for a temporary secretary. Sam had presented himself as a man who excelled at being an administrative assistant. He'd proved himself invaluable time and again—and never had he betrayed one bit of personal information about himself.

Devlin liked it that way.

Now Sam looked up, unsmiling. "The line was definitely cut. However, a sabotaged steering fluid line is not an attempt at murder."

"Yes, but there's always a chance of incompetence." Devlin seated himself in front of the desk. "Perhaps whoever it was, was trying to cut the brake line—and murder me."

Sam inclined his head. "True."

"Who would have the motive to kill me?"

"It would be a shorter list if we asked who doesn't have the motive to kill you." Sam wasn't being funny. In fact, as far as Devlin could ascertain, Sam didn't have a sense of humor.

"Don't sugarcoat it, Sam."

"How about Mr. Bradley Benjamin the fourth? Or more probably, Mr. Bradley Benjamin the third. Or someone in Amelia Shores who doesn't like the hotel. Or one of the people you've angered for one reason or another, and those are legion. Or a rival hotel owner. Or—"

"Okay, I get you. But I don't believe in coincidence, and the fact that Four showed up within five minutes of the accident doesn't play well with me." Neither did the fact that someone tried to hurt Devlin and had hurt Meadow instead.

In fact, that put him in a rage.

"I have been in contact with Gabriel Prescott. He's sending ten of his top men to patrol the Secret Garden inside and out."

"Good." He trusted Sam to handle the situation and give him reports as needed. "Tell me about the gazebo."

He listened to Sam describe the damage to the gazebo and how long it would take to fix, but all the while he was thinking that he'd pulled Meadow into this farce. He had figured he would use her and set her aside and hurt nothing more valuable than her feelings.

Instead, he'd almost gotten her killed.

She wasn't his wife, but she *was* his responsibility, and he was a man who took his responsibilities seriously.

So when he found the son of a bitch who had hurt her . . . he would kill him.

It was as simple as that.

Seventeen

The shrilling of the phone beside Four's bed made him groan and, without opening his eyes, grope for the receiver. "What do you mean, calling me at the outrageous hour of"—he cracked a lid and checked the clock—"nine o'clock in the morning?"

"Mr. Benjamin, how delightful to talk to you once more."

The smooth, warm, deep Southern tone shot Four into the sitting position. "Mr. Hopkins! How did you—"

"Get through to you? I have my ways. You ought to know that by now."

"Yes, sir. I do." The sunlight blinded Four.

His head throbbed. But he couldn't loll in bed while he talked to this son of a bitch.

He'd never actually seen Mr. Hopkins's face. Right before he'd been knocked unconscious, he'd caught a glimpse of silver hair and the shine of pale blue eyes. And vaguely, through the haze of pain, he recalled an impression of a sagging chin and bent shoulders.

But he recognized the voice. It was the voice of pure evil.

"How's the hunt going?" Mr. Hopkins asked.

"I . . . I haven't had much chance to look yet, but—"

"I'm not interested in excuses. I want what you promised me."

"I know. I know, but I just . . . are you sure it's here? Or even that it exists?"

"Are you trying to void our deal?" The voice didn't change. Mr. Hopkins sounded just as genial, just as kindly interested.

But Four had once made the mistake of underestimating Mr. Hopkins. He wouldn't do it again. "No. No! It's just that . . . I lived here for a lot of years. There are a lot of paintings, but I don't think I remember anything like you described."

"You're not there to think. You're there to search. Please remember, Mr. Benjamin, what happened last time you tried to weasel out of this deal."

Four ran his finger over the notch in his ear, and shuddered. "I remember," he said faintly.

"I could hold the rest of your ear in the palm of my hand. Or a finger. Or . . . I could hurt someone you care about."

Four found himself standing beside the bed, phone clutched to his ear. "What do you mean?"

"When a man's as amiable—and useless—as you are, it's hard not to care for people. Isn't it? A man like you makes friends, and that gives a man like me . . . leverage."

Four could almost hear the smile in Mr. Hopkins's voice, and his mind made the logical connection. "Did you cut that steering fluid line? *Did you*?"

"Just keep searching, Mr. Benjamin. Keep searching, and no one else will get hurt."

Four heard a soft click as the connection was cut. He stared at his hand holding the phone. If something happened to Devlin . . . Devlin despised him, but like a brother despised his weak-willed sibling. Yesterday in

Amelia Shores, Devlin had put his hand on Four's shoulder. For the first time since Four had screwed up so badly, Devlin had reminisced about the events that bound them in remembered hardship.

And Meadow . . . she was the most wonderful woman Four had ever met. Of course, she wouldn't bother to give him a toss—women never did when Devlin took an interest in them—but he liked her. He liked her.

And somehow Mr. Hopkins knew.

Someone here was watching him and reporting back to Mr. Hopkins.

He had to find that painting—before Devlin or Meadow or Four got killed.

"I like Josh and Reva the best." Meadow shoved another pillow behind her so she didn't have to crane her head to watch the fifty-inch television on the wall.

"They're *old*." Katie was sixteen, the youngest of the seven maids gathered in various poses around Meadow's bedroom to eat Jordan's hors d'oeuvres and to watch *Guiding Light*.

"Hush up. They're not old. They're classic." Rashida, forty, tall, black, opened her lunch bag, pulled out her sandwich, and used the bag as protection for her lap.

"Here, use the bed table." Meadow took it off the mattress where she'd shoved it and handed it over. "It's easier."

"Thank you, Mrs. Fitzwilliam." Rashida nudged Buzzy, next to her on the couch. "I told you she likes me best."

Buzzy shoved her and laughed. "You silly old woman. She doesn't know me yet."

The two women were different ages and different colors, but best friends of long standing.

Meadow watched their camaraderie with envy. Her best friend was miles away in Washington, the daughter of Russian immigrants, and Meadow had far too little time lately to spend with Firebird. When the doctors said Sharon was completely well . . .

When Sharon was completely well, Meadow would visit the Hunters' tiny home. She would be respectful of Konstantine, because he was a typical Russian patriarch—big, strong, and a little scary. She would tease Firebird's brothers. Zorana would pack a basket full of wonderful food, and she and Firebird would run off into the forest and have a picnic, and Meadow would tell her friend all about Devlin. . . .

"I like Gus and Harley, and they're classic, too." Katie sat on the Persian rug, a bowl of popcorn in her lap, an apple in her hand. "I love that she was wrongfully convicted of murder and suffered—"

"Is that Harley?" Meadow used a fistful of popcorn to point at the TV.

"That's Tammy," Buzzy said. "Mrs. Fitzwilliam, do you mind if I use your phone to call my mother? She's home alone, and I like to check on her during my lunch hour." She added hastily, "I already asked Mr. Fitzwilliam if I could use the hotel line, and he said it was okay."

"Of course I don't mind." Meadow handed over the receiver, then watched as Buzzy dialed.

As it rang, Buzzy told Meadow, "Mama watches *Guiding Light,* too, so we do the rundown during the commercials." Her attention switched to the phone. "Hi, Mama! Did you see what happened?"

"Her mama has MS," Rashida told Meadow in a low voice. "It's tough for Buzzy, but they're awfully close."

Meadow nodded. She understood.

Sharon's illness had been a trial for everyone in the family, but the anguish and the worry had changed them—the family that had lived to celebrate life seized each moment more intently, showed their emotions more freely, and treasured the time given them.

She liked watching Buzzy talk to her mother, seeing the affection, hearing the warmth.

"Oops. The show's back on, Mama. I'll call you at break, okay? Love you, too!" Buzzy hung up and handed the phone back. "Thank you, Mrs. Fitzwilliam."

"Is she okay?" Meadow asked.

"Some days are better than others." Buzzy used the kind of language that let Meadow know her mother was suffering.

Meadow swallowed. She hadn't been away from her mother since Sharon had been diagnosed. It was stupid to feel so anxious, as if a week away would make a difference to Sharon's health . . . but the anxiety was there, growing with each hour.

She wanted to call her, but she feared Devlin was watching the calls that went out of her room. Of course, Sharon always said, *Where there's a will, there's a way . . .*

If Meadow could just figure out the way . . .

The idea came in a lovely burst of genius. If all the maids made one phone call a day off her phone, that would be probably fifty phone calls, and that would surely confuse the issue. She sat up straight and announced, "You should all feel free to use my phone. Anytime! Long-distance!"

"You'd let us call long-distance?" Katie brightened. "Because my boyfriend's in Wisconsin and my folks get mad when I call him, and make me pay the bill."

"Mrs. Fitzwilliam doesn't mean long-distance," Rashida said.

"Really. Please." Meadow flashed a big, we're-all-one-happy-family smile. "It would make me happy to know you're in touch with your boyfriend. And everybody, don't forget your families!"

Katie stretched out her hand. "Please give me the phone."

"I'm next," Shelby said.

Meadow relaxed against the pillows and hoped her plan would work.

By the time the next round of commercials was over, Shelby had handed the phone to Rashida, who had called her brother in California.

When the show came back on, Teresa, their resident *Guiding Light* expert, pointed to the screen and told Meadow, "When Tammy was little she lived in foster homes; then her mama got married and she lived with her and her new daddy; then that daddy died; then her mama married a prince, but her real father kidnapped her—"

Meadow had already discovered that the wrap-up on these characters could take an hour, and ruthlessly interrupted. "So she's a good person."

Teresa's perky golden curls bobbed as she nodded. "But so put upon, poor lamb."

"I think she's stupid," Katie said. "Everybody could see that Jonathan was a creep, and she slept with him and set fires with him and—"

The outcry that followed caught Meadow by surprise.

"But he was cute—"

"He was just bad—"

"She's better off now—"

Passions were running high when Devlin stepped through the door.

His arrival cut conversation as if with a knife.

His cool gaze surveyed the scene. "What's happening here?"

Meadow lifted her chin at him. "The second cleanup crew is taking their lunch hour with me."

He'd been enforcing her prescribed bed rest: standing by while she showered, taking her clothes and leaving her pajamas and a robe, having her meals delivered on a tray, shutting the curtains when he decided she needed sleep. Worse, he was always right. Somehow he knew when a headache threatened. Somehow he knew when she was tired.

He had been *observing* her.

Now she was ready to shriek with the need to rise, to search the hotel, to escape this place before . . . before he . . . well, before he made good on the promise to spend the night with her. Because she knew one thing for sure—this time she wouldn't escape his bed unscathed. No woman ever had a *casual* affair with Devlin. It would be intense, desperate, passionate— and Meadow didn't have time. She needed to find that painting. She needed to get back home. Her mother needed her. Her father needed her.

So why did this whole episode feel less like a mission and more like escape?

"You're supposed to be resting." He glanced toward the television and frowned.

He had better not try to chase out the cleaning crew. He had better not. Belligerently, she said, "I am resting. I have been resting for the last forty hours. See? I'm in bed, I have pillows, I have pain reliever, which makes me feel *just* fine." She wiggled her eyebrows at him. "*Just* fine."

"How does your head feel?"

"*Just* fine."

"Vicodin," Rashida told Buzzy.

"I can tell." Buzzy's jowls trembled as she laughed.

"When the second cleaning crew finishes their lunch, you'll rest," Devlin said.

"Of course I'll rest. Just like I'm doing right now. Because the third cleaning crew is coming by for their lunch hour to watch Oprah. Oprah has Hugh Jackman talking about his new movie, and he's going to sing . . ." Meadow allowed her attention to stray from Devlin, and as she did an image on the screen caught her attention: a gorgeous guy crouched in the bushes and holding a crowbar. "Wait! Who's that spying on Tammy?"

"Oh, my God!" Teresa came to her feet and pointed. "Would you look at that? He's back!"

"I don't believe it!" Katie said.

"I told you so! Didn't I tell you so?" Buzzy exchanged high fives with Rashida.

Devlin stood in the midst of the screaming women, a lone male awash in a sea of estrogen.

"Who?" Meadow sat on her heels, bouncing on the bed. "Who? Who is he?"

Devlin swam toward her, caught her shoulders, picked her up, and laid her flat on her back. He held her there until she stopped struggling. He locked gazes with her. And he said, "This is not what the doctor ordered, and I won't allow you to hurt yourself out of pure obduracy. Now you can watch this soap, and you can Oprah, but only if you promise me you'll rest afterward."

He was so domineering. So macho. So . . . hot.

He made her want to lock her legs around his waist, bring him down on the bed with her, and show him exactly how rambunctious she felt.

How humiliating to discover that caveman behavior made her want to come right here, right now.

But she was very aware of the complete, riveted attention of the women of the second cleaning crew. Plus she had to face the fact that she couldn't handle the power of coitus with Devlin. Not because she was fragile. Oh, no. Because everything about him—the way he loomed over her, the grip of his hands on her shoulders, his scent of citrus and sandalwood, and that overwhelming air of sexual competency—convinced her she would expire from joy.

And she was too young to die.

"Okay," she said in a tiny voice, "I'll rest afterward."

He nodded once—the jerk never had a doubt she would do as she was told—and stood and faced the room.

Pink-cheeked, Meadow sat up.

"Ladies." He nodded pleasantly and walked out.

Each head followed his every step.

When he had disappeared, Katie whispered, "Whoa."

"I couldn't have said it better myself." Rashida's brown eyes were wide and awed.

Everyone looked at Meadow with a kind of ripe envy. Nobody paid a bit of attention as the credits rolled on *Guiding Light.*

Yep, Meadow needed to get away from the Secret Garden. Fast.

She had to take the chance she had sworn she wouldn't take.

She cleared her throat. "I was wondering . . . I would like to, ah, change that painting." She pointed at a print of *Water Lilies* by Monet.

Really, what a boring painting. It *did* need to be changed.

"During my wandering around the hotel, I saw a painting, but I can't remember where. . . . It looked like an oil of a Dutch domestic scene from the seventeenth century, a lady cooking while her husband taught the children their lessons. Have any of you seen it?"

Everyone shook their heads.

"Strong lighting effects, warm colors, a sense of tranquillity and contemplation . . ." She tried to express the elements that created a masterpiece.

Again the heads shook.

She had hoped that if she asked, someone would remember seeing the painting and she could be on her way. Instead, she now risked one of these ladies mentioning it to Devlin. Then he would be on his guard, and he had the resources to find the painting and the capacity to discover why she sought it. Disappointment tasted bitter in her mouth, and she lay back against the pillows. "If anyone sees that painting, would you let me know?"

"Of course, Mrs. Fitzwilliam." Rashida stood up. "Come on, girls. Time to go back to work."

Buzzy stood up, too. "Mrs. Fitzwilliam, would you like us to tell the third cleaning crew you're tired so you can rest up? For, you know . . . later?" She weighed the last word with significance, and glanced eloquently at the door where Devlin had left.

The others giggled.

"No! Really! I'm fine. Mr. Fitzwilliam simply overreacts; that's all." Meadow blushed again.

"Is *that* what you call it?" Teresa picked up her lunch. "How many more days are you supposed to rest, Mrs. Fitzwilliam?"

"I can get up tonight."

"If I were you, I'd angle to stay flat on my back," Buzzy said.

As the women left, laughing, Meadow heard someone say, "Amen, sister. Amen!"

Eighteen

When Meadow stepped into the office, Sam was already staring at the door with a resigned expression, as if he expected her. "Mrs. Fitzwilliam. How can I assist you?"

"I came to see my husband. I want to show him I've completely regained my health." Actually, she'd come to view the paintings Devlin hung on his walls, because she really needed to get out of Waldemar, hopefully before she spent another night sleeping with a very warm, very active, very horny Devlin.

"Your recovery is a relief to us all." Sam's flat tone belied his voiced concern.

But she knew that with the right incentive—and someday she would figure out what that was—he could be cajoled into a smile.

"Mr. Fitzwilliam is busy right now. Would you like to wait?" he asked.

"Sure." She wandered around, examining the office. "You've got a great place here." He did. The room was spacious and nicely furnished, with large windows looking out toward the ocean, oak file cabinets, a printer/fax/copier, and absolutely no interesting paintings on his walls.

Rats.

She wandered toward the file cabinet. "What did you do before you worked for Mr. Fitzwilliam?"

Sam looked up from his work and glowered.

Hastily she added, "Not that I have gender-biased thoughts about a guy being a secretary—"

"Executive assistant."

"Yes, executive assistant. That's what I meant to say. But you"—*with your constant scowl and impatient efficiency and your eyes, which are way too observant*—"seem to be more of a general." *Or a serial killer.* "Someone in command."

"I *am* in command. Of Mr. Fitzwilliam's time and a good deal of his organization." Sam went back to shuffling papers.

"I'm sure Mr. Fitzwilliam is glad to have you." And now she knew better than to ask Sam personal questions. Maybe he *was* a serial killer. "Is there a map for the hotel? I keep getting lost."

"There's a stack of maps on the corner of the credenza by the door."

She nabbed one, folded it up, and stuck it in her pocket.

"And if you remained in your room, you would not get lost."

It was obvious the guy didn't like her, and since he knew that she'd broken into the house, and suspected she wasn't really Devlin's wife, she supposed she could see why. But that didn't stop her from trying. "I get bored. You understand, Sam. You're very fit. You must play sports. Keep active. You must play football, like Devlin?"

"I lift weights and I run. Those are the two most efficient methods of staying fit."

"What do you do for fun?"

"Fun?" His brow knit in puzzlement.

Okay. That line of questioning wasn't going to pan out. She glanced at the open door to Devlin's office, and sidled toward it.

"Won't you have a seat while you wait?" Which was Sam's less-than-subtle way of telling her to sit down and shut up.

"Sure." She sat down in the chair opposite him, and smiled.

He didn't smile back.

"I guess Mr. Fitzwilliam keeps you really busy? Do you always work this late?" She glanced at the clock on the wall. "It's after five."

"Yes, he does. Yes, I do. So it is."

Not much of a conversationalist, our Sam. "How late do you usually work?"

"Very late. In fact, right now I need to finish typing up the requisition list for the groceries for the next week." He turned to his computer. His fingers hovered over the keys.

"That's a great telephone." She turned it toward her and examined it. "It's got four lines. Do you answer them all?"

"Yes."

"Is that all the lines for the hotel?"

"No. But I do monitor the use of all lines on that switchboard." He indicated the electronic panel hung on the wall. "For instance, I've noticed that your line has been almost constantly in use since about eleven." He bent a dark frown on her.

"How about that?" she asked cheerfully. "Is someone using it now?"

"Yes. One of the maids, I suppose."

"I suppose. Can we listen in?"

"It is against the law to listen to private calls in a hotel."

"Oh." She barely managed to keep from rubbing her palms together.

"Do you have any more questions?" Before she could speak, he added, "Because these last few days I've had very little sleep, and until this is done, and all the jobs after it, I won't be able to sleep tonight."

Testy. "I don't want to keep you from your work." She stared at him while he typed.

She didn't know if he was dedicated to his work, or immune to her charm, but he didn't pay her any attention.

Standing, she wandered over to the fax machine and frowned at it. "I'll bet this gets a lot of use."

"Yes."

If only she could get a glimpse into Devlin's office without having to actually confront

Devlin . . . She wandered closer to the open door.

She could hear voices. Devlin's deep, distinctive Southern accent, and a woman's thin, frightened tones.

"I'm sorry, Mr. Fitzwilliam. I won't let it happen again. At least . . . I'll try to make sure it doesn't happen again."

"Mia, I don't understand. Until three days ago you were a model employee. What's happened?"

"It's . . . it's my son." The cook sounded miserable and embarrassed. "He dropped out of school. He's getting in trouble. I try to keep control of him, but he's seventeen. Mr. Fitzwilliam, I told him we're going to starve if I don't keep this job, but he said he had a way to provide . . . provide for us . . ." Mia's voice was wobbling. "And I'm afraid . . . afraid . . ."

"Sit down. Take some Kleenex. For God's sake, stop sniveling." Devlin's voice was a slap in the face after Mia's miserable recital.

What a jerk. Didn't he see Mia needed special care right now?

"Yes . . . yes, sir," Mia said.

With a glance at Sam, typing furiously, Meadow moved close enough to peek into the office.

Mia sat in the chair opposite the desk, dabbing at her nose.

"Mia, are we romantically involved?" Devlin snapped.

She lifted her outraged face out of the tissue. "No, sir!"

"Then blow your damned nose. I don't care what it sounds like." Devlin scowled ferociously. "I just want you to stop sniveling."

She blew.

What a jerk! He really was as awful as everyone said. Meadow ought to go in there right now and tell him—

"All right. Look at me." Devlin leaned forward and stared right into Mia's eyes. "Your seventeen-year-old son has dropped out of school, your husband has abandoned you, you've got a thirteen-year-old daughter, and you're afraid your son's involved in drugs. Have I included everything?"

"My son cashed my last paycheck, and I don't know what he did with the money." Mia started to cry in earnest and stood. "I'm sorry, Mr. Fitzwilliam. I know it's not your job to worry about my family. Do you want me to leave now?"

"Not until we've figured this thing out. Sit *down*."

She sat.

"Now. Look at me."

She did.

"I have a project working on the island of Elmite."

"Where's Elmite?"

"In the Caribbean. I bought it."

"The whole island?"

"It was uninhabited. No water. I drilled. There's a huge reservoir under the island. I'm building a resort."

"Okay." Mia nodded.

"Since your son has already dropped out, what do you say I give him the incentive to get back in school?"

Mia stared, the beginning of hope flickering on her face. "Okay."

Perhaps Meadow had misjudged Devlin.

"If he were kidnapped"—Devlin paused to see if Mia would object—"and sent to work construction, hard construction labor, on an uninhabited island for the summer—"

"How soon can he go?" Mia's voice changed, became cool, poised, eager.

"Mrs. Fitzwilliam!" Behind her, Sam whispered, "Are you eavesdropping?" He tried to move her.

"Shh." Meadow shoved back at him. "I want to hear this."

Devlin glanced at the door, saw them, then returned his attention to Mia. "He'll go tonight."

She didn't waver. "Take him."

"On your way out, give my secretary the information he needs to find him. Then go back to work, and good luck. Jordan's in one hell of a mood today."

"I know, sir. Thank you, sir." Mia stood. As she marched past Meadow, she nodded—and for the first time since Meadow had met her, she looked happy.

Sam tried to move Meadow aside. "I'll announce you."

"Don't bother." She bounded into Devlin's office and shut the door in Sam's face.

Devlin did *not* look pleased to see her.

Yeah, because the big, bad, ruthless developer had been caught in a generous act.

She rounded the desk.

He stood up. "You should be in bed."

"Forty-eight hours are up." She shoved him back down on his chair, followed him down, and straddled his lap. "You are so nice."

"Mia's a good cook."

"The nicest man in the whole world." She put her lips to his and kissed him.

When she released his lips, he said, "If I fired her, Jordon would be furious."

"The nicest man in the whole world," she repeated, kissed him again, and pushed her hips further into his lap.

By the time she took her tongue out of his mouth, he would have agreed with anything she said. "I'm the nicest guy in the world." He looked into her eyes, a half smile on his damp lips, his hands holding her hips. "Did you lock that door?"

"No. Why would I have to? The nicest guy in the world doesn't screw women in his office chair."

"No, but he would screw his wife."

"You silver-tongued devil, you." She was as close in his lap as she could be, her arms wrapped around his shoulders, her breasts almost touching his chest, her scent warm and womanly. . . .

My God, she was smiling at him. Not at Four. Not at the old farts. Not at the maids or Sam or Mrs. Cognomi, but at him.

Yet he felt compelled to speak. "Really, I

didn't want to lose one of the few people from Amelia Shores willing to dare the displeasure of the old farts and work for me." What was wrong with him? Why was he talking her out of thinking well of him? He *wanted* her to smile at him.

But not to reward him for being a Boy Scout. Which he was not. He wanted her to smile at him because she felt at ease with him, because she wanted him.

Hell. She was smiling at him for the wrong reasons, and before this moment, he hadn't even known there were wrong reasons.

It took a discipline he didn't know he possessed to move her hips away from his crotch. "Look, I'll get my money's worth out of the kid, too. He's going to work like he's never worked before."

"Tough love. I get it. But without your help, Mia wouldn't stand a chance." Meadow kissed him again, then slid off his lap.

He wanted to stand up, but he couldn't move without groaning.

"Wow, look at all the monitors." She faced the wall where they all hung. "Man. What a bunch of monitors." She sounded uneasy, and she glanced around.

Her gaze lingered on the wall behind him—or rather, at the paintings on the wall behind him.

Damn it. She hadn't come here to smile at *him.* She'd come to check out his art.

As she walked down the corridor toward her room, Meadow took the map from her pocket, spread it out, and examined it. Every corridor was marked. Every room was clearly shown. This was exactly what she was looking for.

She glanced around her. But how spooky to know that every second someone—Devlin—was observing her. She'd known it before, but seeing those monitors had made the sensation of being watched so vivid that the hair stood up on the back of her neck. She was glad to get into the refuge of the sitting room, glad to be able to spread the map out on the table and with a pen, plot her explorations.

She didn't understand Devlin. One minute he was holding her on his lap and looking at her as if she were God's gift to South Carolina; the next minute he dumped her off, figuratively speaking. Then, as she was looking around, he grabbed her arm, hustled her out of his office, and, before he shut the door on her, he told her to order room service.

And Sam didn't let her open that door and charge back in, either. He must have been in football, because he blocked her attempts just by standing in front of the doorknob.

She had just wanted to tell Devlin he shouldn't be embarrassed because he'd been nice to Mia. Meadow wasn't going to tell anyone and ruin his image as a big, bad, ruthless developer.

She glanced at the phone. She wanted to tell her mother all about him, but Judith had said not to call.

Was Sharon okay?

Picking up the phone, Meadow ordered a room service dinner. When it arrived, it was succulent, glorious, and vegetarian. The hotel's reputation for fine food would be secure. She ate, she chatted with the room service server who picked up the tray, she took a shower, put on her nightgown, settled down to watch *Training Your Spouse*, a really lousy reality-TV show . . . and all the time she worried about Sharon.

She missed checking in with her mother. Missed hearing Sharon's assurances. Missed her earthy wisdom. And she worried,

worried so much, about Sharon's health. If she could at least give her mom a hint, not about what she was really doing, but about *him*, Sharon would be interested. Distracted from her illness.

And why not call her?

Meadow stared at the phone.

Why not?

She could tell Sharon some story about how she was sneaking a phone call during the seminar. A simple tale, because Mom had a way of hearing when Meadow lied.

And if Sam was still in the office, he might see that she was making a call, but he couldn't listen in.

Meadow looked out the window at the rapidly falling spring darkness, and made the decision she needed to make for her own peace of mind. Quickly she dialed her parents, and as it rang, she gripped the phone as hard as she could.

When she heard that beloved voice on the other end, she relaxed. "Mom. I have to go back to the seminar, so I can't talk long, but . . . how's it going with you and Dad?"

Sharon hung up the phone and lay back on the bed. Sweat beaded her upper lip and her forehead, and her face had that pallor that made River want to cry.

But her smile was genuine. "That was Meadow. She's having a wonderful time."

"How's the seminar?"

"She didn't want to talk about that. She wanted to talk about this guy she met."

"She met a guy?"

"She said he's different—grim and driven and intense. But he fascinates her."

"He doesn't sound like our kind of guy."

"He doesn't have to be. He has to be *her* kind of guy."

"I guess." River wasn't quite as altruistic as Sharon when it came to men dating his little girl, but they'd taught Meadow to trust her instincts, and now he had to trust them, too. He handed Sharon a glass of water and held out a handful of pills. "When is she coming home?"

"She asked if we minded if she stayed for a couple of weeks."

"A couple of weeks?" Dismay mixed with River's interest. "She really likes him?"

"I'm glad. She's only twenty-two, and it's been a rough couple of years for her. This is a break she needs."

"Yes, but . . ." He watched while Sharon

struggled to sit up, and fought the impulse to help her. She hated that; hated being treated like an invalid.

"Don't you want to spend some time alone with me?" One at a time, Sharon took the pills and, with great effort, swallowed them. Smiling, she stroked his cheek, then slid back on the pillow.

"Yes. Of course I do." He watched help-lessly as she closed her eyes and put her hand on her stomach, a clear sign that nau-sea, always so close, threatened again. "You told her you were fine." He didn't mean to, but the words came out as an accusation.

"I'll tell her the facts when we know them. When the final results come through. I prom-ise I will. Let's let her be happy for a few days."

He surrendered to Sharon. He always did. She had a strong will and a clear sense of wrong and right, but this time . . . he didn't know if she'd made the correct decision. He wasn't sure at all.

Nineteen

Seated in his office, Devlin watched the video screens.

It was close to midnight. The moon was full. And Four staggered up the stairs, drunk as a skunk. He didn't even drink that much; he just couldn't hold his liquor.

Was Devlin ever going to get rid of this guy? While Devlin was distracted by Meadow's injury, Four had taken up residence, and the trouble was, during his daily visits to the sickroom, he'd charmed Meadow. She liked him—far more than she liked Devlin.

To Devlin's surprise, that irked him.

How the hell did a guy like Four, who couldn't manage himself, much less a successful company, win over every woman he met? Did Four conceal hidden depths?

No. Devlin had known the guy for twenty-five years. If Four had hidden depths, they were buried too far beneath layers of vanity, cowardice, and alcohol to be accessed.

Now, as Devlin watched, Four reeled from wall to wall. He was lost, of course. The son of a bitch had lived here, on and off, since he was a kid—and he still couldn't find his damned bedroom. He claimed it was because of the changes Devlin had made; Devlin believed it was because Four was a dissolute idiot. Four was weak, without morals, and a lousy businessman. So much for Bradley Benjamin's proud breed.

Devlin wasn't wrong about Four. He wasn't wrong about Meadow. He sure as hell wasn't wrong about himself.

Devlin lifted the walkie-talkie from his belt and, without looking at the small screen, said, "Mr. Benjamin is on level two, corridor T-three. Send somebody to escort him to his bedroom."

A deep female voice came back. "Yes, Mr. Fitzwilliam."

Startled, he glanced down.

Gabriel had told him he'd hired a woman, but Devlin hadn't yet caught a glimpse of her. Even now he couldn't see her well—she stood somewhere outside. He caught a quick impression of middle age and competence, and an Eastern European stockiness. Gabriel had assured him she was experienced, so Devlin clicked off the walkie-talkie. "Sam!"

Sam appeared in the doorway. He looked tired—both of them had been working flat-out since five this morning trying to trace the sudden loss of water pressure to the hotel.

Of course, they both knew who was behind the sabotage, but that didn't make it easier to fix.

"No luck so far, sir. The manager of the water treatment plant still says he can't get anyone on the problem until next week." In frustration, Sam ran his hand through his hair.

"You know where he lives. Send someone over to knock on his door."

"Right now?" A measured smile grew on Sam's lips.

"Absolutely, right now. Then go to bed." With familiar bitterness, Devlin said, "Until we figure out a way to get a monkey wrench locked around Bradley Benjamin's nuts, there's going to be more trouble, and we'll never figure out a solution without sleep."

Devlin glanced toward the video screens. He rubbed his eyes. He should go to bed, because he was hallucinating. He had to be.

He thought that was Meadow running down the dim corridor outside their bedroom—in her bathrobe.

"What the hell?" He sat forward.

Sam joined him. "It's good to see that Mrs. Fitzwilliam is feeling so much better," he said in a neutral tone.

Meadow was flitting along without any care to a stairway or obstruction or a sudden veer, when one more smack on her head might actually give her what she claimed to already have—a memory loss.

At least she wasn't looking for paintings.

"By the way, the detective e-mailed. He's following up on all the phone calls from Mrs. Fitzwilliam's room, but so far he has eliminated only two numbers. Most people aren't home. One won't speak to him, and another threatened him with a lawsuit if he called again. Three go right to voice mail every time. He says caller ID is the bane of the detective. If a person doesn't know the number, they won't pick up. If they don't know the person who leaves a voice mail, they won't return the call. And the kind of questions he asks trip off all kinds of concern." Then Sam looked at Devlin, just looked at him, and the questions were clear in his eyes.

Sam hadn't been along on Devlin's trip to Majorca. He couldn't say for sure that Meadow wasn't his wife. But he knew better than anyone how Devlin had reacted when he'd first seen her, and of Devlin's search for her origins. Sam didn't believe they were married.

But Devlin's motivations were none of Sam's business, any more than Sam's lack of a personal life was Devlin's.

Sam had no relatives to plague him, no home that called him, no dog to pee on his rug. The guy showed a flair for business, but apparently had no desire to start his own, and occasionally Devlin wondered if he should keep an eye on Sam, because really—how could a guy so talented not have a single fault?

Yet based on Sam's impeccable references, Devlin had hired him, and until the day Sam announced he was seeking his fortune elsewhere, Devlin would utilize his skills, pay him really damned well, and trust him—or trust him as much as he trusted anyone.

"Where are the calls going?" Devlin asked.

"Most are local, but several calls went to Atlanta. California. Wisconsin. Texas. Washington. Florida. And New York."

Devlin never took his gaze off her. "She's a clever girl."

"Yes, sir," Sam said without an ounce of inflection.

Devlin took the ornate silver key out of the desk drawer and pocketed it.

Meadow headed toward the back door. She was going outside.

"I'm going for a walk to clear my head." He set off at a run.

He thought he would catch her before she left the house; instead, he arrived at the back door as it clicked shut behind her. He caught it and stepped out on the porch.

After his trek through the dim corridors, the moonlight almost blinded him. It turned the estate into stark etchings in black and white. The shadows beneath the trees sprinkled the lawn with dark coins, and when he looked up, he could see the full disk of the moon floating through a black sea decorated with stars.

Across the lawn, Meadow was running, her copper hair the single color in a black-and-white world. Only she wasn't really running. She was . . . skipping like a schoolgirl, her arms in the air as if to embrace the night.

Damn. The drugs had made her crazy.

But he knew that was bullshit. The drugs had nothing to do with it. She was just . . . crazy.

He spoke into his walkie-talkie. "Mrs. Fitzwilliam and I are going to be in the walled garden. We'd like our privacy. Tell the other security personnel to stay away."

"Yes, sir." It was the woman again, speaking to him from somewhere out in the yard. It didn't matter where she was—where any of them were—as long as he herded Meadow toward the walled garden. There they would have privacy.

He turned off the walkie-talkie.

Meadow disappeared over the rise toward the beach.

He sprinted after her. When he topped the rise, he saw her bathrobed figure on the winding path headed over the dunes toward the beach. "Meadow," he called. The breeze carried his voice away, so he bellowed, "Meadow!"

She turned. He thought she would frown at him, as she had when he broke up her soap opera party, or clutch her robe together in that maidenly skittishness she displayed whenever he showed the tiniest hint of his sexuality.

But no. She grinned and ran back to him. "Did you come out to play, too?"

"Come out to play?" He hadn't heard that term since third grade.

"Isn't it beautiful?" She waved an all-encompassing arm at the lawn, the dunes, the sky. "Don't you love living here? Don't you love the sound of the waves and the smell of the ocean and the scent of the pines?" She seemed giddy.

"Did you hit your head again?" he asked warily.

She laughed without a worry as to who might hear. "It's the full moon. Come on!" She grabbed his hand. "Let dance!"

She pulled him along, holding his arm in the air, stomping her feet in some weird version of Greek dancing.

"Isn't this fun?" she called.

He felt stupid, like an onlooker at a drunken party. Plus, security was watching for saboteurs coming up the beach, and he'd be damned if they were going to see him prancing around like a sailor on leave. He stopped and, like an anchor, hung on to her.

She stopped, too—she had no choice—and glared at him in exasperation.

"I have a surprise for you," he said.

"You do not." But she lavished that stunning smile on him. "What?"

"Come on." He led her along the winding path back into the depths of the estate.

"What's that?" She pointed at the ivied walls rising ahead.

"That's where we're going." He led her toward the tall, heavy, timbered gate. Pulling the key out of his pocket, he showed it to her.

He felt her flinch. He heard her draw a breath.

So she recognized it. It probably matched the one she'd used to get into the house.

Fitting the key in the lock, he turned it. He experienced an odd sensation, a sort of breathlessness, although he didn't know why. Then he realized—he actually anticipated the look on her face when he showed her. . . .

He pushed the door open and stepped aside.

Her expression of delight was everything he could have wished. "Look. It *is* the Secret Garden!" She bounded in, her robe fluttering behind her.

Her enthusiasm bubbled up like champagne, intoxicating him, and he hurried after her, calling, "Would you slow down?"

"Don't be silly!" She disappeared around the corner, and her voice called back, "How could I slow down when the moon is full and I'm in the Secret Garden?" She laughed, one of those full-bodied laughs that made his testosterone levels surge. Then, "Oh!"

He came around the corner and almost ran into her.

She stood stock-still before the wide expanse of lawn that was the heart of the garden. A tangle of pine and rhododendrons occupied one corner. An immense live oak spread its branches over a marble bench. An artificial waterfall sparkled over real boulders and into a pool, and frogs called their love songs.

And at the center of the broad sweep of the glade was a pergola where an ancient wisteria vine twisted up and over, thick with blooms.

It was just the way he'd planned it. He'd

seen in the garden a marvelous asset. He'd approved its cleanup, the plantings, and the installation of the waterfall. Transforming the garden from a tangled jungle into a romantic hideaway made financial sense—after all, the value of the Secret Garden increased once lovers started hiring the hotel to plan their weddings.

But he wasn't thinking of finance while he basked in the awe on her face.

"This is . . . so beautiful." Her voice choked with tears.

In the moonlight, the garden glowed with light and shadow, glory and mystery.

So did Meadow. The moon's glow lit her face, and at the same time she radiated pure joy. "Thank you for bringing me here. Thank you for showing me this. I don't care what everyone says about you. You're wonderful!"

Leaving him speechless, she danced away.

She twirled in a circle, around and around, laughing lightly. Then she did something that stopped his breath.

She shed her robe.

The moon shone through the thin white material of her nightgown. As she whirled, he could see her legs, her hips, her waist, her breasts in silhouette.

She was glorious, a white candle topped by flame.

Then . . . she pulled her nightgown up and off over her head.

He'd seen his share of naked women. He'd visited Mediterranean beaches where toplessness was a way of life. But he had never seen anything as bold and innocently sexy as Meadow worshiping the moon. She paid him no heed, but swayed to an inner rhythm, her feet bare, her thighs strong and muscled, her small breasts high and pale.

If he believed in witches, he would believe in her. She made him want to dance in the moonlight. She made him want to shout, to sing, to fuck.

She made him want to live. And that was goddamn stupid, because he was already living.

Except . . . as he watched her, he knew he was lying to himself. He hadn't been alive for years. Maybe he'd never been alive.

Her expression was fiercely exultant, as if the night were her lover and she the only woman who could satisfy him.

But no. Devlin wanted to be her lover.

He discarded his shoes.

Stupid move, but not fatally stupid, because he kept his pants on. As long as those pants were on, the two of them were safe from something so impetuous, it would be madness.

He walked toward her, seeing nothing but her.

As she twirled toward him, her smile blossomed.

"Let me show you what moonlight is made for." Sliding his arm around her back, he placed his hand on her bare back.

And for the first time, he got real benefit out of his Southern-gentleman training. Unhurriedly he guided her through the basic steps of the waltz, teaching her; then, as she gained confidence, he took her in wider and wider circles, speeding up, carrying her along with him.

She felt small in his arms, and with each turn her body brushed against him, teasing him. Her scent rose in his nostrils and fired synapses in his brain until he knew that if he were blindfolded and shoved into a crowd of women, he would identify her. The breeze sang in his ears, the trees and flowers and pond and pergola whirled past, and she smiled up at him as if *he* had enchanted *her*.

And she was naked in his arms.

Later he didn't remember planning to do what he did. He was a man who plotted and schemed every moment of his life, his business, and his revenge, yet a silent melody and a merry face swept him away to someplace where only the two of them existed.

The circles got wider and slower.

Her smile dissolved. Her wide eyes focused on him—just him. The two of them loitered through the last steps, their bodies pressed together.

They stopped and stared at each other.

She broke away.

She took his hand.

And she led him toward the pergola.

Twenty

Inside the pergola the fragrance of wisteria hung heavy in the air, and the moonlight lay shattered in bright bits on the marble bench, the flagstones, and Meadow's face.

She struggled to get Devlin's jeans unbuttoned and unzipped.

He didn't help her. Hell, why would he, and miss the accidental touches to his groin and occasionally—okay, more than occasionally—the touches to his dick?

For how could she not touch it? It was *gigantic.*

He wanted to chuckle at himself for his testosterone-fed flight of imagination. Trou-

ble was—his dick felt gigantic. It felt powerful. *He* felt powerful.

She pushed his jeans off. His boxers. She
ran her fingertips from his balls to his tip.

No other touch had ever felt so good, and
he groaned like a callow boy.

"Do you want to dance now?" she whispered, and her husky voice trembled with
suppressed laughter.

"You little tease." Picking the robe off the
bench, he spread it over the marble. In one
efficient motion he twirled her around and
flat onto her back.

For the first time she saw him with a face
stripped of guile. The moonlight showed her
his soul before the circumstances of his life
had stripped away his pleasure in life. Tonight he wasn't a control freak or a tycoon or
a mystery. Tonight he was just a man.

No, he was a *guy*, controlled by his testi-
cles and happy to obey their dictates.

And who was she? A woman who had
disregarded her mother's warnings about
the fatal combination of moonlight and men.

Now she was as helpless as he was.

She held up her arms to embrace him.

His dark eyes gleamed in the shards of
moonlight, and his teeth flashed as he

smiled. With his hands on her shoulders, he pressed her back.

Then those hands wandered . . . down across her breasts, brushing them, learning their shape, their sensitivity.

Her eyes closed as he caressed the curve of the underside, the small circle of her nipples. He knew exactly what he was doing, touching her in such a way that she thought only of the slow, warm slide into arousal.

She didn't know what to do with her legs. Put her feet on the ground? The bench would be between them. She would be revealed, and it seemed too early for that. Yet when she bent her knee and put one heel against the seat, he murmured, "Darling," and kissed her inner thigh.

They were going to make love, in this secret garden on this perfect night . . . and maybe this was what she'd planned all along. Her untried emotions felt new and raw, different from any she'd experienced. She felt like an adventurer visiting a place she'd only imagined.

When he slid his hand up her thigh and buried it in the carefully trimmed thatch of copper curls, she arched off the bench in a tumultuous excess of anticipation. "Devlin," she whispered.

"What? Do you like that?" His finger slid inside her, a deep, leisurely violation. "And this?"

Her eyes opened wide, and when she looked up at him, she saw a handsome face made wondrous by the desire he could fire in her. He was all strong muscle over heavy bones, a man made tough by the fight for success, for honor, for his identity.

He thrust his finger inside her again, and she was swollen, damp—her body betrayed her need with excruciating detail.

She wanted that shirt off him. She wanted it off now. "Take it off." It was *not* a request.

He smiled. He withdrew his finger from within her and straightened. His hands went to his buttons. One by one he unfastened them, and as unhurriedly as he moved, she might have thought him indifferent to passion.

But as his shirt fell open, she saw his sculpted chest and belly . . . and the proud erection that reached up from his groin.

He stood between her legs, one knee on the seat, masculine, dominant—yet he needed her desperately. She didn't even know if he realized how much he needed to be civilized . . . no, not even civilized.

Humanized.

The shirt still hung from his shoulders as he leaned down to kiss her breast, taste her nipple. Goose bumps rose in a wave, rushing away from the sensation like a wave, cresting in the sensation that lifted her hips toward him.

He laughed again, very much the man in command, the conquering hero.

She couldn't allow that.

She sat up on one elbow. She licked one finger and, with its damp tip, she swirled it around the head of his penis.

He groaned—a spontaneous, vibrant sound that made her laugh for joy.

She licked her finger again, but before she could touch him, he caught her wrist and squeezed. Not painfully, but somehow she knew . . . the moonlight, the scents, the passion had broken his fierce will.

They stared at each other, eyes locked.

Then he picked up her knees and spread them wide. He sat on the seat and dragged her toward him until they were groin-to-groin.

The pressure of his erection against her

wrenched a moan from her. She wanted . . . needed . . . She tried to position herself to thrust herself on him.

He didn't allow her that. Didn't allow her any control. He rubbed himself against her, a long stroke that massaged her clit and made her whole body clench in anticipation. He found the entrance to her body and gradually thrust inside.

He lifted her hips toward him, and each inch filled her past the point of comfort, but she didn't care. It wasn't comfort she sought; it was satisfaction, and the craving made her supersensitive.

The scent of him mixed with the fragrance of the night-blooming flowers, the grass, the air. Above him she could see the wisteria hanging off the arbor like ripe clumps of grapes, and beyond that the night sky and moonlight . . . so much moonlight. She could hear the rough rasp of his breath as he thrust all the way in, then reluctantly drew out, and she wanted to clutch at him, make him stay tightly inside her.

But like some Greek god, he sat above her, looking down at her, his gaze never leaving her. He held her hips and directed their movements until she wanted to scream with frustration.

Yet she did nothing but writhe and moan . . . because everything he did to her felt so good. Too good.

She clutched the robe-draped sides of the bench, bunching the material in her fists in building frustration. Each time he lifted her, he leaned in so his groin connected with her clit, and the pressure . . . the pressure built.

Her skin grew so sensitive that even the cool breeze felt like a caress. It hurt to breathe, hurt to have Devlin thrust inside, hurt to have him slide out. "Please. Please, please, please, please . . ."

She didn't care what he thought, whether her begging constituted some triumphant mark on his supremacy scoreboard. She knew only that he had better do something about this intense compulsion that drove her to madness or . . . or she really would lose her mind and her memories, and be lost in some glorious place with Devlin.

"Please." She kissed her fingertips and placed them on his lips.

His lips returned the kiss. Then his stark features tightened; his lips parted as he pulled air into his lungs. He lifted himself— and her—and rode her in a driving rhythm.

Her back went taut as a bow. She wrapped her legs around his hips, accepting him, welcoming him, taking him as he took her—and finally, finally climax seized her.

Thank God.

Devlin had held her off too long, and her orgasm was almost painful in its intensity. She screamed. Her hands went over her head and gripped the bench behind her. She heard him say one word: "Meadow!"

To hear his deep, warm, Southern voice call her name sharpened her response, and the climax, already so powerful, blotted out the rest of the world . . . except for Devlin. Always she was aware of Devlin.

And he was aware of her. Even as his balls drew up tight against his body and that shudder ran up his spine, he couldn't stop observing her—the way her small breasts lifted as she clutched the bench over her head, her taut belly, her expression of min- gled agony and exaltation. She was the most beautiful thing he'd ever seen. He wanted to spend every moment of his life inside her, kiss her mouth, her breasts, her belly. He wanted to pleasure her until she believed the

tale he wove of their love, until she remembered no life except with him.

He wanted this moment to go on
forever . . . and he couldn't stop the rush of
semen that spurted from him. He laid claim
to her in the ancient, primal way dictated by
the moon for generations past . . .

And it wasn't until he finished, until he
rested on her, panting, and felt the rise and
fall of her chest as she gasped beneath him,
that he realized—he hadn't used protection.

For the first time in his life, he hadn't used
a condom.

Twenty-one

Clad in the innocuous black-and-white uniform of a security guard, Judith stood under
the huge live oak and watched as Meadow
and Devlin pranced toward the house.

They'd had sex. Great sex.

So freaking lovely for them. The only time
Judith had had great sex was when she was
alone and had an unending supply of D bat-
teries. Men didn't seem to be interested in a
woman with a broad chin, thin lips, legs like
tree stumps, and a waist as broad as her
beam. It wasn't fair, but she was used to "not
fair."

What *was* fair was acquiring a sponsor

like Mr. Hopkins, who helped her get a job in the right place at the right time doing the right thing—being a security guard at the house where Isabelle's painting was hidden. Here she could keep tabs on Four and Meadow as they searched Waldemar, and when they found it . . . she would be the first to know.

But never for a second did she imagine she would end up with custody of the painting. She had made a deal with the devil, and better than anyone in the world, she understood the nature of evil—her father had taught her that—and respected its strength.

Besides, in the end, she would get what she wanted. Mr. Hopkins had promised she would have the credit for discovering that painting.

"Why are we sneaking back into the house?" Meadow stage-whispered.

"Because every security person in the place is watching and—" Devlin broke off. Why *were* they sneaking into the house?

He couldn't herd Meadow across the lawn and through the corridors to their bedroom without every security person on duty—and probably a few who weren't—seeing them.

And he knew damned good and well the conclusion they would draw from their disappearance—the right conclusion. Especially since he claimed Meadow was his wife. And because she was still dancing, although now she wore her nightgown and robe—but only because he made her.

And she was smiling. She was so happy.

Damn it. Damn it. Damn it.

He couldn't believe he'd been so criminally careless.

He couldn't believe he let her take his hand and swing it as they walked. He should have explained the danger they'd courted. Instead, he let her blissfully babble on.

"My mother always told me that mankind isn't as far removed from the primitive as we would like to believe," Meadow said. "That when we take the time, we respond just as our ancestors did to moonlight and springtime and nature. I think tonight we proved she was right."

He thought about cornering Meadow, asking her how, when she had amnesia, she remembered what her mother said, but Meadow grinned at him so mischievously he couldn't.

He'd made her sparkle. He'd given her

satisfaction. For some ridiculous reason, to-night she trusted him. With her joy and easy acceptance of their relationship, she made him feel like Scrooge—armored against the good things in life, suspicious . . . old.

And horny. She made him horny.

It was damned embarrassing, walking around like some bull moose following a fe-male in heat.

She'd been so small and tight. For a horri-fied, exultant moment he'd been afraid she was a virgin.

But no, only seldom touched, and not for a long time. And he, who had intended to take his pleasure of her—but on his terms and in his own time—had put his heart and soul into claiming her.

Without protection.

She could be pregnant right now.

"Watch your step." He led her up onto Waldemar's wide porch and opened the door.

Inside, moonlight streamed through the windows and lurked in square patches on the carpet, and, suddenly superstitious, he avoided walking through the white light. What if her mother was right? What if it was the moonlight that had caused his mad-ness? He certainly had no other explanation.

Meadow showed no such care. She skipped along, apparently energized by sex with him.

Great, fabulous, wonderful, earthshaking, marvelous, dick-building sex.

"Be careful," he called. "Don't run into anything."

"I won't!"

If she was going to race around in the moonlight every night, he would have to order the lights turned on. Or perhaps he should keep her in bed at night through whatever means he had at hand.

He shook his head. He had to stop thinking of sex or he'd knock that vase off that table and lift her up there and—

Did he have no sense of propriety? Was he like his father after all? He'd worked so hard to develop the moral character that his parent had so obviously lacked. Now he'd broken every rule he'd set himself about women and about life. He could have created a baby with her, and he remembered all too well how miserable his childhood had been as the one bastard offspring of the Fitzwilliams.

Which brought him to Bradley Benjamin— what had happened to his plan to use her for revenge against Bradley?

He had, of course, and thoroughly enjoyed Bradley's attack of angina.

But now Devlin had spent an hour ar-
dently enjoying her body to the point of mad-
ness. He slept with a liar, and one of the
hated Benjamin clan.

Worse, he wanted to do it again.

Meadow got ahead of him. He heard her
feet patter up the stairs, and like some
creaky old man chasing a two-year-old, he
pursued her, calling, "Don't trip."

She turned the corner at the top of the
stairs. "I won't!" Her voice floated back, full of
devilry.

Shit. What was she up to now? By the
time he reached the top of the stairs, she'd
disappeared.

"This way," she called.

Shit. He ran down the corridor toward their
room. The door was closed. The light shone
beneath it. He flung it open, fully expecting the
sitting room to be empty. And it was. Except
for her bathrobe pooled on the Oriental rug.

In the bedroom, he could see her nightgown tossed on the floor.

Did the woman ever keep her clothes on?

But it wasn't annoyance that made his
blood surge and his subsiding erection stir.

She was naked again.

He shut the door behind him. He locked it. He walked into the bedroom—and through the open bathroom door he heard the shower running.

For a long moment he shut his eyes. Water . . . sluicing down her body. Her copper red hair . . . getting wet and turning auburn. Her hands . . . caressing her breasts, her arms, her stomach, between her legs, leaving a soapy trail of bubbles.

He found himself standing in the doorway, staring at the glass shower enclosure.

The view was even better than he imagined. She stood with her head tilted back, her arms up, rinsing the shampoo from her hair. Dense white bubbles slid off her shoulders and down her chest, and one small batch broke away to perch on her nipple. She was pale and starkly bare against the claret tile, and so beautiful his eyes blurred, probably because all his blood had left his head and rushed to his dick.

As if she sensed his heated stare, her eyes popped open. In a laughing voice, she asked, "What took you so long?"

Twenty-two

"And I was afraid I would be too quick," Devlin said ironically.

Meadow's grin disappeared. Just like that, with a few words, he turned her from a merry water nymph into a woman who hungered . . . for him.

She popped the door open and gestured invitingly. "Let's test you out."

He glanced at the drawer by the sink. He kept condoms in there. There were condoms by the bed. Just in case, he needed to put some in the desk drawer in the sitting room. . . . Then somehow he found he had his clothes off. He stepped into the shower.

The multiheaded Hydra of a shower shot water onto their heads, into their backs, and vibrated their buttocks.

He told himself he was in here to do the responsible thing. He squirted shower gel on his hands and rubbed them together. "We have to talk. What we did in the garden was reckless." He rubbed her shoulders, and the combination of water and bubbles made her slickly erotic. "We can't allow passion to sweep us off our feet and onto whatever horizontal surface is available."

"Why not?"

"We're going to get caught." His hands trailed down her arms. His fingers entwined with hers, and he slid up and down each finger, then stroked the palm of her hand.

She leaned against the wall. "By who?"

"By security personnel. By one of the maids." He watched Meadow draw short, shallow breaths, then used another splash of shower gel on her chest. "By your ob-gyn, who will announce you're pregnant." He rubbed the soap into a lather, then used it to wash her breasts.

"W-wrong time of the month." Each word sounded like a moan.

"If I had a nickel for every kid conceived at the wrong time of the month, I'd be rolling nickels for the rest of my life." Was he trying to convince her or himself?

She slid her feet apart, put her hands against the wall, braced herself as if he were trying to knock her down, when all he was doing was washing her. "Nickels or nipples?"

"What?" He loved the texture of her boobs—the dense, warm, heavy flesh, the soft skin, the responsive tips.

"I'm trying to ask if you're planning to wash anything but my boobs."

"They can never be too clean." And he supposed he was acting like an obsessive tit man, when actually he was more of a butt man. It was just that *Meadow's* tits were so fine.

He slid his hands around her and rubbed her back with the lather, then moved closer and rubbed her body with his. She clutched his shoulders while they slipped across each other in a slow, warm, slithering ballet.

Gradually the soap washed down the drain.

With his lips, he followed the bubbles on their descent. He kissed her shoulder, her breast, her stomach, her hip. . . . She moaned as he pressed his mouth to the small froth of hair over her pubis. He was on his knees now, and the scent of her— lavender soap and clean woman—made him hungry for more.

With his fingers, he parted her nether lips and tasted her with a long, slow stroke of the tongue.

She whimpered, and when he glanced up, she had her fist pressed against her mouth and her head back.

Because she screamed when she came. He knew that now. And she wanted to muffle the sound.

Good luck to her. He intended to make her scream again.

He wrapped his hands around her bottom to hold her still, and licked her again. The flavor of Meadow imprinted on his senses, and he knew no matter how hard he tried, he would never forget this night. With his lips he found her clit and carefully drew it into his mouth.

"Devlin!" She jerked as if he'd given her an electric shock.

He sucked on her, used his tongue to drive her over the edge, and in only a few moments she arched—and screamed. He fed her sensations, reveling in her pleasure, until her knees collapsed and her cries died down to whimpers.

He drew away, intent on standing, sweeping her into his arms, and taking her to bed.

Instead she shoved him down to the floor of the shower. She followed him down. She straddled his chest.

The showerheads splashed down on them. The tile was hard as hell. But one glance at her face revealed a woman intent on getting exactly what she wanted from him.

"Wait—" He wanted that condom.

She took his very, very erect dick in her hands and rubbed it up and down.

"My God!" All the synapses in his brain exploded like popcorn.

She took him in her mouth.

His muscles gave way. He fell back against the floor.

She sucked hard.

He shuddered, so close to climax he was willing to promise anything, reveal any secret, for one more stroke.

She had different ideas. "No, you don't." She sat up on his groin and adjusted his dick and her vagina until they met, and then performed the kind of wiggling, panting, forceful ravishment he'd always imagined being forced to endure.

But he'd never met a woman who shared his dreams—until now.

He'd never met a woman whom he trusted to take charge—until now.

Until Meadow.

She took him inside her inch by inch, rising and falling as she pulled him in, and the sweet, hot friction broke his will. "Please. Meadow. Please." He didn't care that he sounded like a boy, that he'd lost his control as well as his mind, as long as she gave him the kind of pleasure that made him die and resurrected him, all at the same time.

She braced her hands against his shoulders and rode him with an expression of furious need, her lips open, water trickling into her mouth and eyes.

The shower rained down on them, drowning him, pushing her sopping hair into her eyes. Her desire burned his skin, his heart. Need, desperation, put him in pain . . . or was it pleasure? He was lost in the labyrinth of time. He braced his feet against the floor and thrust as hard as he could, meeting her, trying to reach the center of her being, as if that would somehow make her his.

And he did it.

Or rather, she did it. She drove herself onto him, a wild girl obsessed with her needs, and at some white point of fusion, their passions melded and became one. He came so violently he lifted her with his body, while inside her he felt the spasms of her orgasm sucking him dry.

Finally he *was* dry. Empty. At last he came to rest.

She withered down on top of him, and he experienced a savage gratification that she was as replete, as exhausted as he was.

He wrapped his arms around her and held her. Just held her. Opening his mouth, he let the water flow in, trying to replenish himself for the next bout—which his every instinct told him would be soon.

Very soon—or at least, as soon as he could guarantee that, out of pure repletion, he wouldn't flow down the drain. As soon as he could lift himself off the floor and somehow resume the character of the man he had been . . . only a few hours ago.

He felt her chest rise and fall in a sigh. Bit

by bit she inched into the sitting position. She looked down at him and smiled, a wobbly smile quite unlike her usual impish grin. She lifted herself off him and sat on the floor, her knees raised, her hands resting limply on them. "That was wonderful," she whispered.

"Yes." He knew he should say something meaningful. Something that expressed how earthshaking the night had been. But he didn't know what to say.

From the moment they'd met they'd been lying to each other, playing games as each sought some unknown goal. He didn't know how to tell her the truth—or even what the truth was. Somehow, tonight, the truth as he knew it had changed.

He didn't know what he wanted anymore.

But he did know they'd once again had sex—without protection.

"Son of a bitch!" Devlin surged to his feet.

Meadow looked up curiously. "What?"

"We did it again!"

"I noticed." Her voice was mellow, exhausted, pleased. "Do you want to lodge a complaint?"

"We did it without protection."

"I don't have any diseases. I swear to you I don't."

His mind, once so sharp, veered away from the subject at hand and onto the obvious track. "You're not active."

"You could make that sound a little more like a question."

Then the charade they were playing caught up with him, and he snapped, "How can you swear that when you don't remember your past?"

"Do *you* have a disease?"

A smooth counterattack. He appreciated her cleverness even as he answered, "No. But I am fertile, and I can hardly claim it was the moonlight again. What excuse can I use in the shower? It's the *soap*?"

She lowered her head and bit her lip to subdue a smile.

And with that smile, so beautifully provocative, he remembered the feel of her beneath his palms, her skin slick with bubbles. . . . Temptation struck him like a blow between the eyes. Not the temptation to take her again, although the urge hovered close. He actually wanted to admit that he knew she was lying about her amnesia, ask her

her real name, beg her . . . beg her for *what*?

Kicking open the door, he stepped out.

He had come *this* close to saying, Y*ou're not my wife.*

But damn it. No!

He wasn't the one who should step forward. Let her tell the truth. Let Meadow reveal herself, and then he would see if she was worth taking a chance on.

Meadow woke slowly and, without opening her eyes, inhaled deeply.

Devlin smelled so good. Like that peculiar man scent composed of strength and stubbornness, and with a hint of girlie lavender soap—or maybe Meadow was smelling herself with his scent on her.

Because she'd slept deeply last night, exhausted from her midnight adventures, but always she had been aware that Devlin held her as he held her now—tucked tightly against his body, her back against his chest, her butt in the cradle of his hips.

Devlin.

She hadn't believed a man could be what he was. A challenge. A lover. An enemy.

It was the stupidest thing she'd ever done

in her life, wanting him, taking him. Yet she wanted to roll onto her back and wiggle like a puppy when she remembered the raw, wild passion between them.

Groping behind her, she slid her hand along his flank. He was tall, and each part of him was long and muscled. Last night he'd ridden her hard, and she'd returned the favor.

This morning she ached between her legs. In her life she'd been with one man, and maybe he'd been a peewee. She didn't know. She knew only that the length and breadth of Devlin was echoed in the size of his penis. Last night had taken its toll. Her body couldn't easily accept him again.

But knowing he would cause her discomfort didn't stop the wanting.

If she had the choice between forgetting last night and saving herself the inevitable pain, and reliving it, she would relive it.

His breathing was slow and easy, and with great care she turned in his arms.

His eyes were closed, his face lax. He looked like a man worn to exhaustion by too little sleep . . . and unexpected pleasure.

She believed that all things happened for

good, and surely he had come into her life now for a reason. And how could that reason be anything but good? He was, after all, Devlin.

Never mind that he made her feel restless. Panicky. Unlike the Meadow she had always been. Something in him called to her, and she responded with such lust. . . .

She stroked his chest, then pressed against one shoulder and pushed him onto his back. Sliding her hand down across the taut skin on his belly, she reached his groin and closed her hand on his erection.

His temperature went up five degrees.

She smiled. Maybe he was asleep. Maybe he wasn't. But either way she made him wild with greed.

He was so afraid of raw, brazen sex— unprotected sex, he called it. He wanted that rubber as a barrier between them during their most intimate moments. Grudgingly she admitted the good sense of his precautions, for all the reasons, but at the same time she liked to feel his flesh in her flesh, his come in her womb.

Probably she'd be a lot more perturbed if she thought there were a danger of repercussions, but they were safe. Last night was time out of mind.

More important, the time of the month would keep her safe.

Leaning over him, she lightly kissed his mouth. Then his shoulder. His nipple. His stomach.

He was definitely awake now.

His hip . . . she slid beneath the blanket. Under here the sunlight was muted and the air was warm and dense with their mingled scents. She teased him with tiny kisses down one thigh. She circled to his other leg, his other hip. Deliberately she allowed the ends of her hair to trail across his groin, and chuckled when his whole body went rigid.

He clamped a hand on her head, holding her in place.

From the end of the bed, a woman's soft Southern voice asked, "Darling boy, what's this I hear about your marriage?"

A woman was in their bedroom? A woman had violated the sanctity of their privacy? A woman asked about their marriage as if she had the right?

And he dared to indicate he wanted Meadow to remain hidden?

She sank her teeth into his thigh.

He flinched. His fingers tightened on Meadow's neck. In a loud, emphatic voice he said, "How good to see you, *Mother.*"

Twenty-three

The ringing phone made Four jackknife up in bed. He stared at that instrument of torture, then at the clock.

Nine in the morning—again.

Was it *him*?

Of course it was him. Mr. Hopkins. Who else could it be?

Four didn't want to answer. He felt ill with whiskey . . . and fear. But the ringing kept on and on, as if the man knew for sure that Four was in his room. And that was just what Four feared.

Cautiously, Four hit talk. "Hello?"

"Four. I'm very disappointed in you." That

familiar, gentle, demonic voice made Four want to retch. "You've been drinking when you should be searching."

"No, I haven't."

"Four, lying won't get you out of trouble. Not this time."

"I'm not lying!" *Down, boy. Don't snap at Mr. Hopkins; you might piss him off.* "I drink a little, then pretend I'm drunk. But can you think of a better ploy to search this place than to stagger around every night like I'm lost?"

The short silence that followed made Four break a sweat. Then Mr. Hopkins said, "Why, Four, I'm impressed with your ingenuity. My kudos on taking one of your many failings and putting it to good use."

Even his compliments were carefully designed to make Four grovel. And Four could grovel with the best of them.

"Yet still, you've completely failed me, and after I did you the favor of buying stock in your company," Mr. Hopkins said. "Remember that company? The company you embezzled from?"

Four sat on the edge of the bed, his throbbing head in his hands. "I remember."

"Do you remember also that I didn't prosecute you when the theft was discovered?"

Neither had Devlin.

This was all Four's fault. He knew that. He was a screwup, always had been. But when he'd falsified those books in his father's corporation, he hadn't realized Devlin would get so pissed off. Sure, Four had personally convinced him to buy stock, but what was a couple of million bucks to a guy like Devlin?

But when he'd said that to Devlin, Devlin had looked at him, and Four had taken about five steps back. Even now he shuddered at the memory of Devlin's bitter dark eyes. Devlin had taken Four's little embezzlement as a betrayal, and no one betrayed Devlin without suffering repercussions.

So Bradley Benjamin the third had had to choose—sell Waldemar to the bastard son of the upstart Fitzwilliams, or let his son go to prison. It had been close, but now Devlin owned a new hotel, and Four's father's enmity toward his only son had deepened.

"Four, when I speak to you, I like to know that you heard me." Like a bulldog, Mr. Hopkins had his teeth sunk into Four's flesh, and he wouldn't give up.

"I remember everything," Four said.

After Waldemar's sale, Four had thought the worst was over.

But no. Because some guy he'd never heard of had bought a bunch of stock, too, and Mr. Hopkins didn't possess Devlin's kind, gentle soul.

Four's mouth dried as he remembered the warehouse where Mr. Hopkins and his men had taken him. He hadn't believed their threats at first. Stuff like breaking fingers and slicing off ears happened in the movies, not to the son of a distinguished Southern family. But those guys had done both, and all the time he'd screamed Mr. Hopkins had been talking, talking, talking.

All too soon, it was clear to Four he'd been played for a fool. Mr. Hopkins had known the stock was no good. He'd bought it to put Four into his debt, so he could send Four into the house where he'd once lived to retrieve a painting unlike any Four had ever seen there.

"How much more of the house do you have to search?" Mr. Hopkins asked.

"I've worked my way through all the rooms on the first two floors and the basement. I've been in all the closets. I've searched the pantry. No luck so far." Four hesitated, but what had he to lose by telling the truth? "You know, that painting you described—it's not even Isabelle's style."

"Please. Four. Don't tell me my *business*." Mr. Hopkins's voice sharpened.

For an instant Four thought he heard something—some tone, some accent—that sounded familiar.

But Mr. Hopkins's next words drove the thought from his mind. "Do you remember in that warehouse when one of my men held a knife to your . . . what's the anatomical name? Ah, yes. Scrotum."

Four swallowed.

"With one word from me, you could find another knife pointing at your scrotum. And with one word from me, you could find it cut off."

Four breathed heavily, trying to subdue his nausea.

"It's an unpleasant operation. There's a lot of blood. The victim screams a lot. And if he recovers, which is not guaranteed, he wishes he had died. Please keep that in mind as you search for the painting I described." The click as Mr. Hopkins hung up was almost inaudible.

Four headed for the bathroom. Holding himself over the toilet, he retched until tears came to his eyes.

The goddamned picture wasn't here. How could he find something that wasn't here?

And how much more time did he have before Mr. Hopkins took matters in his own hands, and sent his goons to kill them all?

How much time?

"Do you think she knew I was under the covers?" Meadow shimmied into her jeans.

"I'd wear a sundress." Devlin zipped up his beige linen slacks.

"A sundress? To meet your mother?" *Wait a minute.* He was distracting her. "So you *do* think she knew I was under the covers?"

"My mother will never acknowledge it if she did." The short sleeves of his polo shirt cut across his biceps in a most spectacular manner, and the dark blue made his eyes gleam when he looked at her undressed from the waist up. "And yes, when it comes to clothes, my mother's quite the fashion maven."

"But she should meet me as I really am." Meadow grabbed a cap-sleeved pink T-shirt and pulled it over her head.

He walked over to her and pulled the shirt back off.

"This is no time for that." The man was insatiable. She liked that.

He handed her a bra. "I've found, in dealing with my mother, that the less she knows, the better. She's like a steamroller, and once she starts rolling there's no escaping her. She'll flatten you unless you get out of the way."

Meadow looked at the bra, shrugged, and clipped it on. "You make her sound awful."

"She's not awful. She's a woman of power. She gets things done. *You'll* see." He tugged the shirt over her head and handed her a pair of sandals.

"That sounds ominous." She shoved her feet into the shoes.

"Ominous. Good choice of words." He took her arm and led her down the stairs to the elegant room where she'd hidden her key among the couch cushions. Eyeing the couch, she wondered if it was still there.

The room where the painting was supposed to hang on the wall over the fireplace, but didn't.

She flicked a resentful glance at the

pompous old gentleman who hung there instead.

The room where she'd first seen Devlin Fitzwilliam.

Well. So the place wasn't all bad.

She straightened when a dainty, elegant woman rose from behind the dainty, elegant desk in the corner.

Devlin's mother was absolutely the right weight for her height; her blond hair was carefully colored and highlighted; she wore a lightweight pink wool suit with a skirt; and her skin had the sheen and texture of porcelain. Yet for all that she appeared to be every inch a Southern lady, she projected the kind of authority Meadow saw in her son.

When she stepped forward to hug him, she projected a stiff affection.

He pecked her cheek. "Mother, what a pleasant surprise. What brings you to the Secret Garden?"

"You can imagine my surprise when I met Scrubby Gallagher in Atlanta and he told me he'd met my new daughter-in-law." Her blue eyes were cool as she observed Meadow, from her unpedicured toes to her unaccessorized top. Her glance at Meadow's hair was a critique, and Meadow realized Devlin's mother had most definitely known she was under the covers—and she did not approve.

She did not approve of any such ill-advised and passionate behavior. She did not approve of Meadow's attire or grooming. She most certainly did not approve of her son's marriage to a hooligan, and she was plain ol' pissed about being left out of the loop.

And obviously everything was Meadow's fault.

So Meadow responded in the best way she knew how. She opened her arms wide, said, "Grace, dearest!" and headed for Devlin's mother.

Meadow caught Grace on the first pass and gave her a hug that rumpled her jacket and disarrayed her careful coiffure. She caught a glimpse of Devlin's amused, appalled expression.

"Mother, this is Meadow. Meadow, please meet my mother, Grace Fitzwilliam."

"I'm so glad to meet you, Grace, so I can thank you for raising my wonderful husband." Meadow beamed at her. "I just knew we would get along!"

Grace winced and rather forcefully disengaged herself. "Yes. Well. Yes. Lovely. So glad . . . But to not tell me!"

"It's a long story, Mother." Before Meadow could hug her again, Devlin pulled her close to his side—and no matter how hard she squirmed, he wouldn't loosen his grip.

"I suppose *your* parents know, er, Meadow." Grace tidied her suit.

"Not . . . exactly." Meadow shifted her feet and hoped Grace wouldn't pursue that line of questioning. Based on nothing more than a pair of jeans and a T-shirt, the woman clearly considered her a misfit. If—when— she heard the story of Meadow's amnesia, she could consider her a head case.

"If you're trying to keep this union a se- cret," Grace said, "there are better ways to do it than to parade around Amelia Shores causing Bradley Benjamin a heart attack."

"She didn't cause him a heart attack," Devlin said frostily. "He suffered angina, and I hear he's perfectly healthy again."

"Although if he did have a heart, it would certainly attack him," Meadow said.

"Bradley Benjamin is one of our leading citizens," Grace answered.

Meadow couldn't believe Grace was de- fending him. "He was mean to Devlin."

"But he's older and in ill health, so we allow him his foibles." Grace sounded calm, smooth, and so civilized.

Sort of like Devlin sounded when he was angry.

Fascinating.

Seating herself at the desk once more, Grace sorted through the papers stacked there, found one she wanted, and extended it to Devlin. "There's the guest list. I'll need Meadow's list before I order the invitations."

Devlin glanced at the sheet and shrugged. "Invite whomever you like, Mother."

Meadow felt as if she'd missed part of the conversation. "What list? For what?"

Devlin continued as if Meadow had never spoken. "Perhaps we could combine that party with the grand opening of the Secret Garden."

"What party?" Meadow asked.

Grace handed her the list. "That's rather impersonal."

"Not at all. Having two parties in a row would dilute them both," he said.

"Hmm. Yes, that's a point." Grace brightened. "Plus, I'd have a bigger budget for both."

"What party?" Meadow was considerably louder this time.

"My goodness, Meadow." Grace blinked as if shocked at Meadow's tone. "The party where we officially announce and celebrate your marriage to Devlin, of course!"

Not a good idea. It was one thing to flirt with him. To tease him into enjoying life. To have a small fling with him.

But a party? Where Meadow met not just Four, but all Devlin's friends and business associates? How dumb would that be? It seemed every time she took a step on the way to finding the painting, the shit got piled higher and deeper.

"I think we're ready to meet people, darling." Devlin looked into her eyes.

She saw the mockery there, brought her foot down on his, and ground it into his instep. "I think I need time to get used to my new home before we make an official announcement."

He bore the pain stoically. "Let me do the thinking. You don't need to worry your pretty little head about a thing."

Using all her teeth, she smiled into his face. "I can't help but worry, *darling*, knowing how much this grand opening means to you."

"To us. To our future." How he enjoyed testing her! Would she break and tell the truth rather than suffer the ordeal of a party feting their union?

His mother, of course, was impervious to the undercurrents. "Since you two aren't agreeing about this, we'll do it my way." Going to the table, she opened the boxes and pulled out a froth of packing paper. "I brought some things to use as decoration. Just some small things, Devlin; I know how much you hate my taste."

"I don't hate your taste, Mother. But I have my own decorators."

"And they've done such a quaint job." Grace waved a hand around at the exquisitely old-fashioned room.

"Quaint or not, I can't afford your idea of decorating. It's expensive, and I need things done when I need them done, not when you get the time in your schedule." They'd had this discussion before, and he was tired of it.

"I know that. I'm not reproaching you." At the point of losing, Grace abandoned the argument and pulled out a piece of china. "I found this for your display case."

"Oh." Meadow went to the box as if she couldn't resist. "This is wonderful. It's nineteenth-century Chinese cloisonné, isn't it?"

Grace looked at her as if she'd suddenly sprouted horns. "Yes, a footed bowl."

"Gorgeous! What else do you have?" Meadow carefully removed some of the cardboard packing and found a covered casserole. "English, of course. Portmeirion, Botanic Gardens?"

"That's right," Grace said.

"A good pattern for a party. Expensive but not precious." Meadow put it aside.

At his mother's indigent sputter, Devlin subdued a grin.

"Well, of course, it's very nice." Meadow didn't seem to realize how deeply she was wounding his mother, who so despised *nice*. "You don't want to spend a whole party terrified that someone's going to break your precious antiques, do you?"

Devlin leaned a hip against the couch and settled down to enjoy himself. "Mother likes to spend her time torn between terror and triumph."

Grace glared at her son. "I simply don't believe Portmeirion is *ordinary*."

"I didn't say ordinary," Meadow protested. "I said it was nice."

She'd just condemned the Portmeirion to perdition.

Delving farther into the box, she brought up another, smaller box.

"Be careful!" Grace said sharply.

But Meadow unwrapped the tall vase inside with reverent hands. "A Steuben. I love their work. Look at the iridescence!" She held it in the sunshine and it flashed with purple, blue, and gold. Running her fingers around the rim, she said, "It's in good condition, too—no chips, only a few minor scratches."

The interaction between his mother and his lover fascinated him, but more than that, Meadow's knowledge and the way she handled the bowl made Devlin remember the night she'd arrived, and how indignantly she'd refused to throw up in the precious Honesdale vase.

His mother hated one-upmanship—if she was the one being one-upped. With a flourish she unwrapped a wide-lipped glass bowl with swirls of red and pink and orange and jagged hints of purple. "I'll bet you don't know this one." Before Meadow could identify the artist, Grace hastily added, "It's a River Szarvas."

"River Szarvas. Really?" Meadow pinned Grace with a look.

Grace actually squirmed. "It's reputed to be a Natalie Szarvas. But the dealer who sold it to me didn't believe it, and neither do I. Natalie is River's daughter, so he has reason to build her reputation, but the girl's only twenty. She couldn't make such a mature piece at that age."

"Of course not." Meadow cradled the bowl.

"It's like holding a drop of sunset," Grace said.

"Exactly." Meadow smiled.

Every day since Meadow had landed on the floor of his library, Devlin had carefully observed her. He couldn't quite read her thoughts yet, but he was getting there . . . and she had some interesting thoughts. "So this River fellow is setting up an art dynasty."

"He runs an artists' colony in the mountains in Washington," Grace said. "Very large, very well respected, and apparently quite . . . bohemian."

A grin broke across Meadow's face.

"Bohemian?" His suspicions were rapidly becoming certainties.

"I believe your mother is trying to say they're a bunch of old hippies," Meadow informed him.

"Well, yes. So I've heard." Grace grimaced. "Their home in the mountains of Washington was a lodestone for artists, glassblowers, and, for God's sake, environmentalists."

"Heaven forbid!" To his ear, Meadow sounded phonily incredulous.

"According to my art dealer, everyone is welcome, and there's scarcely a night when they don't have guests 'sacked out' "—Grace made quotation marks with her fingers—"on the floor in the studio."

"That *is* bohemian," Meadow said.

Devlin could almost see her hidden amusement.

"But they're artists." Grace lifted an elegant shoulder. "What can you expect?"

"Exactly." Meadow handed her the bowl. "That's quite a find."

"If you ladies will excuse me, I'll leave you to your decorating. I have some work to catch up on." As he left Meadow alone with his mother, he heard Grace grilling Meadow about her family, where she'd gone to school, and what she did for a living. Glancing back, he saw Meadow's deer-in-the-headlights expression, and he enjoyed himself far more than he should.

When he reached his office, he was surprised to see that Sam wasn't anywhere to be found. Poor guy, he'd been working full-tilt for days. Maybe he'd finally crashed.

Devlin went to his desk. He didn't even sit down, but typed in *Natalie Szarvas,* and after Google had chided him for spelling it wrong, it took him to her home page—and he found himself looking at a picture of Meadow, hair up, sweat sheening her face as she worked the glass.

Natalie Meadow Szarvas.

He'd discovered who she was. Now only two questions remained. Exactly why was she here—and how long could he keep her?

Twenty-four

Meadow walked out of the library at a sedate, reasonable pace, and as soon as she was out of sight she broke and ran up the stairs.

She could kill Devlin for leaving her alone with that woman.

Shallow, self-important, domineering—every one of those words fit Grace Fitzwilliam to a T. Not to mention that she'd interrogated Meadow about her family, her background, her talents, her disposition, and her fertility. Grace was absolutely ferocious in her defense of her son. In fact, that was the only thing Meadow liked about Grace, or would have liked if that scariness hadn't been turned on *her.*

Rounding a corner toward their bedroom, Meadow ran into smack into Sam.

He rocked back on his heels, but he was sturdy and muscular and took the hit well. "Mrs. Fitzwilliam, is there a problem?" As always, he didn't look as if he really cared; it was a polite question only.

"Yes. I mean, no." She flapped a feeble hand back down the stairs. "I just left Grace Fitzwilliam in the library."

"Ah, yes." Sam nodded as if he understood.

"Is she always like that? Because she's the only person I've seen who could make Devlin back off." Meadow smiled to show she meant no harm.

As usual, Sam didn't smile back. "It's easy to see where Mr. Fitzwilliam gets his strength of character."

"What a good way of looking at it! I'll remember that." She glanced behind her. "Is Devlin in his office?"

"I believe so. After he left the library, he went right there."

"How do you know that?"

"I watch the monitors."

"I thought the monitors were in his office."

"There are monitors on every level—if one knows where to look for them. Every inch of the hotel is kept under constant surveillance." He sounded as if he were issuing a warning.

"Except for the rooms."

"Except for the rooms," he agreed. "Did you wish to go to Mr. Fitzwilliam's office?" Sam asked.

"No, I think I'll wander around the hotel a little more." With an irony she enjoyed, she said, "It's really a work of art, don't you think?"

"It is quite lovely." Sam watched her walk away, then called, "Mrs. Fitzwilliam, be careful where you go. The hotel isn't as secure as one might like to think."

She turned back and stared at him.

He stared back, his eyes flat, black, soulless.

Apprehension chilled her. "Are you . . . threatening me?"

"Warning you." He walked away.

She looked around. What was he doing in this corridor? Devlin's suite was here. Her suite. The suite they shared.

And their door was open. Had he been in there looking for . . . for what?

She walked into the sitting room. It looked fine. Nothing out of place.

Sam was an odd man. He didn't seem to have friends. He wouldn't talk about his background. He said threatening things to her. Maybe he really was a serial killer. Maybe she should say something to Devlin.

But what would she say? *You know your secretary? The one you trust? He says sort of hostile things, and the way he looks at me makes me think he doesn't like me.*

She walked to the bedroom. Nothing out of place here, either. Devlin's slacks, shirts, and jeans hung in the closet with her sundresses. His underwear was in a drawer next to her panties. He'd ordered enough clothes—clothes befitting every occasion— to keep her here through the month.

Maybe she should stop worrying about Sam and concentrate on Devlin. A month's worth of clothes? Why would he want to keep her here so long? And . . . married? Sure, men lied all the time, but they didn't claim happily-ever-after. If he suspected she was lying about the amnesia and he was try- ing to smoke her out, that was one thing, but he was telling *everybody.* Didn't he worry about what was going to happen when this was all over and he had to explain what they'd been doing?

Even she didn't know what they were doing.

Again the question skittered across her mind.

What game was Devlin playing? Perhaps she should be a little more cautious. . . .

She irritably shrugged her shoulders, trying to release some tension. She wasn't afraid of Devlin. They'd made love so wantonly, so sweetly, and never once had she felt a niggling of anything but joy.

She needed to find that painting so she could tell him the truth . . . yet what did she think he would do? *Give* it to her? He wasn't crazy. The painting was worth a fortune, and it was legally his. When she started the search, she'd believed it was rightfully, if not legally, her grandmother's, and her grandmother had said it was her inheritance. Taking it from Bradley Benjamin had been one thing. Taking from Devlin Fitzwilliam was another.

Meadow put her hand to her head. What had started out as an easily justified action had become confusing, and no matter how much she loved being in Devlin's arms, no matter how fondly she recalled his kindness to Mia and Mia's son, she had also heard him talk about Waldemar, and possessiveness rang in every tone. She'd listened to his fury.

A footstep. In the bathroom.

Who was hiding in there?

With her gaze fixed on the door, she started backing up.

Then a maid walked out, carrying a wilted bouquet.

Meadow collapsed against the wall. All this subterfuge was getting to her. She was imagining threats where none existed.

"Mrs. Fitzwilliam!" The maid bustled toward her. She was probably sixty years old, short, plump, with curly gray hair and a sweet, rounded face. She looked like somebody's grandmother.

But Meadow couldn't remember her name. Or anything about her. She was usually pretty good at this stuff, but with this woman she drew a blank.

Should she confess her ignorance, or try to fake it?

While she hung on the horns of dilemma, the maid said in a lowered voice, "I think I found your painting."

Meadow caught her breath. "Really? Where?"

"In one of the rooms. C'mon; I'll show you." She set off at a great rate, her short legs moving so quickly Meadow huffed to keep up with her. For an older lady, she was in good shape.

Meadow caught up just as the maid took a sharp left turn. She used her key card to unlock the door, turned the handle, and flipped on the light. "The painting's in here."

Meadow peered into the depths of a narrow storage closet. She could see a linen cart, a bucket, a broom, and a long shelf piled with pristine white linens. "I thought you said it was in a room."

"I took it out and hid it. It's leaning against the back wall."

"Really?" Meadow stepped inside and shoved at the cart. "I don't see anything back there that could be a—"

She turned in time to see the door closing.

"Hey!" As the latch clicked, Meadow flung her weight at the door.

It was solid.

She groped for the handle.

There wasn't one.

She stood staring at the plate with the slot for a key card. "Hey!" She slammed her hand on the door. "Hey, let me out!"

The insulated metal door remained closed, and it muffled the sound.

She didn't understand. Why would one of the maids shut her in a closet?

She dug through her pocket. Her key card, of course, wasn't there. She'd slapped on her clothes so quickly she hadn't even brushed her teeth.

Ew.

She yelled and pounded on the door for another few minutes, then backed away and took a deep breath.

She wasn't claustrophobic, so she didn't mind the closet. Really, it wasn't the closet that bothered her.

It was the malice behind the act of locking her in. What had she ever done to that woman?

She looked around. The closet was really pretty big. Sort of overcrowded with the laundry cart and the shelf sticking into the room, and when she went to the back and dug around, she found no painting.

Wow, big surprise.

She sat back on her heels and stared at the door.

Why had that maid done it? Was she even a maid?

She had to be. She knew about the painting, and Meadow had told only the maids . . . but maybe one of them had talked. Or maybe someone else knew about the painting. Or maybe the maid had heard Meadow was searching for it and thought it must be valuable and wanted it for herself.

But she had such a sweet face!

Meadow wrapped her arms around herself.

Her mother would tell her she had reaped what she sowed, that stealing the painting for even the best of reasons was immoral, and that art as valuable as that painting would of course lead to crime, even violence.

But Meadow had come so far. She couldn't quit now. And Grandmother Isabelle said she had saved the painting for an emergency.

This was an emergency.

For all the cheer Meadow had heard in her mother's voice, she knew only too well the ups and downs of cancer treatment. She'd known far too many patients, only to see them leave the cancer ward in body bags.

The trouble was, she was enjoying herself here at the Secret Garden. With no regard for the truth, to creating good karma, to what might be happening in a little town in Washington, she was falling in love with Devlin Fitzwilliam.

Twenty-five

Oh, no. Natalie Meadow Szarvas, artist and wannabe thief, was falling in love with Devlin Fitzwilliam.

How could she be so stupid? He didn't even know who she really was. And she knew *he* was lying through his teeth.

But he was so good at it. Every time he told her a story about their affair in Majorca, she slipped a little deeper into enchantment.

She didn't think he kept her here for any good reason. She wasn't that far gone.

Still, her heart thrilled when she saw him. She wanted to stand at his side and be what he said she was—his wife. And how stupid was that?

But it didn't matter.

Did it?

She was doing the right thing.

Wasn't she?

As if in answer, the lights clicked off.

It took a minute of shock and fear before Meadow realized it was nothing dire. The lights were on a timer; that was all. Having them go off right now was not an omen.

But it was dark in here. Really, really dark.

She blundered toward the exit, guided by the thin line of light under the door. She banged her shins on the laundry cart. She kicked the mop. She got to the door and groped for the light switch.

And someone yanked the door open.

"What are you doing in here?" Devlin's dark eyes blazed with fury, and his feet were firmly planted at shoulder width.

"Devlin! Thank God. This maid shut me in." Meadow fell into his arms, embarrassed by her panic, guilty about the painting, and grappling with the discovery that she loved him.

He didn't hug her back; he only repeated, "A maid shut you in." He sounded unconvinced.

She didn't care. Closing her eyes, she inhaled his scent.

Yep. She was in love. His scent was ambrosia. Touching him made her melt all over him. And at the bedrock of her soul, she believed he would always be there to save her.

"Devlin," she whispered. "I knew you'd find me."

"You are so . . ." For one moment he shook violently, as if he fought his instincts. Then his arms came around her almost ferociously. He backed her into the closet. The door slammed behind him, and when she lifted her head to ask what he was doing, he kissed her—kissed her as if this kiss were as necessary as breathing.

The darkness wrapped them in intimacy. The odor of clean, bleached sheets mixed with the potent scent of Devlin's sexuality.

She loved him. She needed him—now.

And he needed her.

He held her head in his hands and held her still, and each stroke of his tongue called to a primal part of her no one had ever touched. She let him take her breath, then took his in return. Frantic desire swept them along, melding them together in the darkness. She grew damp with longing, and she felt him against her, erect, hard as one of the marble pillars that surrounded the Secret Garden.

She pushed him away, tugged at his shirt, heard a ripping sound.

Briefly the little noise brought her back to sanity, but only enough to make her realize she was in too much of a hurry to care whether he was completely naked. She wanted him—now.

She reached for his belt.

He unzipped her jeans.

Together they struggled against the fastenings, stripping each other with speed and urgency.

She kicked off her sandals, her jeans, and her panties, and reached for his penis. He was so hard, so hot.

He handed her a foil pack.

She ripped it open and rolled it down the length of his penis.

He groped behind her, shoved stuff aside, lifted her, and placed her on the shelf.

The painted board was rough under her bare skin. He tilted her backward, pressed her shoulders back until they rested on the wall. Sliding his hands up her thighs, he spread her legs wide, exposing her. The cool air shocked her; the fire of his body promised her pleasure. He stepped between her legs and pressed the heel of his hand over her clit.

She pressed back, started to shudder with climax.

"No." He pulled back. "Not yet."

She whimpered, in such need she ached.

But he waited, although she could feel the tremors of passion that shook him. Then he explored her, and when he discovered the dampness that awaited him, he muttered, "Perfect." He positioned himself. The head of his penis felt impossibly large, searing her flesh. With tiny rocking motions, he pressed inside.

She moaned, taking him into her body, growing so full she couldn't imagine a moment when he wasn't with her. She sank her nails into his shoulders, and the small pain sent him surging forward.

For a brief moment he pressed close. Outside, his groin ground against her clit. Inside, the tip of him incited the deepest part of her. She couldn't see him, couldn't see a thing, but she felt surrounded, inside and out, by him—by his scent, his passion, his caress, his breath on her hair.

When he withdrew, a slow and torturous process, she wanted only one thing—to have him return deep inside her. With her feet behind his back, she pulled him close.

They grappled with each other, both reckless with the need for satisfaction.

The darkness intensified each sensation. Nothing he did could stop her. Her breath grew constricted. The dark flashed with colored lights. She sobbed softly, needing everything he had to give, reaching but not quite able to release. She needed . . . something . . .

"Come now." His voice told her clearly that he wasn't asking—he was commanding. "Come now." He thrust hard.

She screamed. In an agony of rapture she curled toward him.

He drove into her, taking her, his hips coiling and striking over and over, and the motion carried her into another climax, and another, until she couldn't tell where one ended and another began.

Between her legs and beneath her hands, she felt him tense. Every muscle went rigid, and he climaxed so hard her fingers slipped as sweat sheened his skin.

As suddenly as they'd started, they

stopped. She breathed so harshly her lungs hurt. She trembled from the effort she'd put out, and she couldn't understand what had happened.

One minute he'd been opening the door. The next, they'd fallen on each other with a violence of lust. She'd never imagined such a mating—no tenderness, only heat and desperation.

Then his hand found her face, and he pushed her hair off her forehead. "Are you all right?"

"Yes." She was wicked and wanton, desperate for him, in love with him, wanting what she couldn't have . . . but she was all right.

"Are you sure? I didn't hurt you?"

"No. You didn't hurt me." She would walk like a rodeo barrel racer for the rest of the day, but he hadn't done anything to her she hadn't demanded.

Slowly he withdrew.

She bit her lip against a protest. Their relationship was so easy here in the dark. So basic. No lies, no deception, only two bodies straining together, searching for, achieving one goal.

If only love were so easy.

He lifted her off the shelf and steadied her while she found her feet. He pulled up his pants, zipped up, buckled his belt.

"Ready?" He didn't wait for an answer; he turned on the lights.

She flinched, shielded her eyes. When she looked up at him, her expression could not have been more embarrassed, more guilty.

What the hell was he doing? When had he lost all pretense at civilization and started fucking without restraint, without control, behaving like a sailor on shore leave?

But that wasn't fair; he didn't slam every woman into a closet, rip off her jeans, and thrust himself inside her.

Only Meadow.

"I, um, can't find my panties." She stood bare from the waist down, her jeans in her hand, looking helplessly around at the jumble of linens he'd shoved off the shelf and onto the floor.

He knelt, looking for her underwear, distracted by the length of her legs, which ended in the small, trimmed froth of copper curls over her slit. He wanted to spread her legs again, to taste himself on her, in her, until she once again cried out.

She filled his mind. She filled his senses.

It didn't matter how many times he screwed her; he always wanted to do it again, and as soon as possible. He'd managed to wait long enough to get a condom on—yay, him—but only because he'd had to clear a space on the shelf to fornicate. If she had not been so efficient at rolling it onto him, he would have dispensed with safety and taken the chance of making her pregnant—again.

He was not like his father. He was not.

At least, he never had been before.

"Here." He handed her the tiny lacy thong and tried not to watch her pull it on.

Damn it. What the hell was he going to do about her? About the little liar who lived under his roof?

Because that was what had triggered his aggression.

She had lied to him. She had lied to him *again.*

Somewhere along the line he'd lost sight of his original goal—to use Isabelle's granddaughter to stick it to Bradley Benjamin.

Instead he'd been doing everything he could to make Meadow trust him. He'd given her every opportunity to tell him the truth about who she was and what she was doing here.

Instead she'd fed him some garbage about some maid shutting her in the closet, when in fact, she'd been looking for the painting and shut herself in.

He knew it because Sam had watched her every move on the security monitor. Sam had reported her movements to Devlin. And Sam never lied, and Sam never made a mistake.

Twenty-six

Devlin walked Meadow to their bedroom, then paused at the door. "Are you sure you're all right?"

He sounded so courteous, Meadow wanted to fling herself off the cupola. She was in love, and he was . . . remote. "I'm fine. Are you?"

"How could I not be?" He brushed his knuckles across her cheek. "But I'm very busy."

"Do you want a description of the maid who shut me in the closet?"

The motion of his hand stopped. "Of course. Tell me what she looked like."

She told him about the sweet-faced grandmother in the uniform.

"She doesn't sound like anyone who works here." His voice was very even, very calm.

"I didn't recognize her."

"I'll look into it." He didn't sound worried.

But he wasn't really the kind of guy who showed his worries. "Why do you suppose she did it?" That bothered Meadow more than anything.

"I don't know. Why do *you* suppose she did it?"

"Maybe I offended this woman somehow? Or she's some kind of psychopath who sneaks into hotels and locks people in linen closets?" Even Meadow thought that sounded stupid, but, *Maybe it's someone after the painting,* seemed an answer fraught with peril.

If only he were less aloof . . . If only she trusted him a little more . . .

"I'll look into it," he said again. "Will you forgive me for leaving you here, now?"

"Sure, but . . ." *Are you embarrassed by what happened in the closet? What can I do to make you stay?*

Do you love me?

"What is it? Are you scared?"

"No. No, I'm not scared." *Confused, uncertain, worried, yes. Scared, no.* "I need to shower. I'll see you later?" *Needy, Meadow. And clingy.*

"Of course." One corner of his mouth crooked up in what might pass for amusement. "When Mother's with me, we dine in manorial splendor."

"Oh, nooo." Meadow leaned against the door frame and looked up at him in despair. "Will she interrogate me some more?"

"I believe she'll call it conversation." He sounded almost normal now.

Her anxiety eased. She felt a little more like Meadow and less like a woman facing a disaster of mammoth proportions. "You should have heard her in the library after you left. That was *not* conversation."

Abruptly his half smile disappeared. "She doesn't understand what got into me, marrying so swiftly and without warning."

The tension returned, thicker and more oppressive than ever.

She straightened. "But we aren't really married."

Stepping close, he crowded her against the wall and leaned close enough that his breath brushed her ear, that his heat seared her flesh. "We married in Majorca. Unless you remember differently?"

She loved him. She ought to be able to tell him the truth. He seemed to want her to tell him the truth. So she would. "I . . . I should. I . . . It seems wrong, like we're not married." *The truth, Meadow. Tell him the truth.*

But when he looked so cool, like a quarterback planning a new play, like the big, ruthless developer his reputation claimed, she choked up. Would he throw her out? Maybe she was betraying him by lying, but what other choice did she have? Betray her grandmother? Leave her mother to die?

He flashed her one of those sharklike smiles that expressed no amusement. "Until you say different, we were married in Majorca, and I intend to remind you every chance I get."

He was bullying her, and any sensible woman would shrink away.

Not Meadow. Her stupid body yearned for his, her blood surging in her veins. She leaned her head away from him, giving him access to her throat, wanting his kisses on her skin. . . .

He stepped away. Briefly, gently, he caressed her cheek with his knuckles. "Try not to get into trouble."

She watched him leave, his long legs eating up the distance, his hips rolling with that assurance that told a woman he knew how to give her pleasure.

He must have transferred his heat to her, for her cheeks grew warm. Flinging herself into their suite, she locked the door and fell back on the small sofa in the sitting room. She would have never considered Devlin Fitzwilliam someone she could love.

He was a developer, a guy who created hotels that attracted people to the wild places in the world, where they could ruin them with sewage and sunscreen.

Yet at the same time, he saved old buildings, bringing them back to life instead of tearing them down.

And clearly he didn't comprehend the advantages of viewing life as a positive experience. In college they'd called her a Pollyanna, and he was the exact polar opposite—whatever that was.

Yet when she thought of what they shared, she wanted to share it some more. Her eyes closed. Her hand crept to the seam of her jeans, and she rubbed herself between her legs, imagining he was here, watching, helping—

The shrill ring of the hotel phone brought her to her feet, wild-eyed and mortified.

All these damned security cameras had made her paranoid. She felt as if she'd been caught in the act.

But by who? Who was calling her here?

Devlin. Who else?

Snatching up the receiver, she put all her longing into her tone. "Hello?"

"Meadow? Is that you?" Judith's voice, sharp, nasal, anxious.

"Judith!" Immediately Meadow's mind leaped to the worst. "Is it Mom?"

"No, she's fine. Just fine."

"Then what are you doing calling me here?" Meadow lowered her voice as if someone could hear her. And that was impossible—obviously the doors were soundproof. But somehow the security in the hotel felt as if it were turned against her, and she wouldn't put it past Sam to have planted a microphone in their rooms.

"I had to take a chance. I've been so worried about you."

"How did you get through to me?" Meadow had visions of Judith asking for her at the switchboard, and whoever worked the desk running right to Devlin with the information.

"I called and got a maid. She told me your room number, and after that I could direct-dial." Judith's voice lowered, too. "Have you had any luck finding it?"

The painting, she meant. "None."

"Are you looking hard? All the time?"

"No. I search when I can, but I have to act normal." Meadow paced toward the window and gazed out on the estate. It was all so peaceful out there, and such turmoil inside.

"Is Fitzwilliam giving you trouble?" Judith sounded fretful.

"Not trouble exactly. He sort of wants me to stay here, and I don't know why."

"You know why," Judith said.

Meadow didn't like Judith's tone. "No. Why?"

"He wants to sleep with you."

Meadow didn't know what to say.

Her hesitation must have been telling, for Judith asked, "*Have* you slept with him?"

"Judith!" Meadow hoped her horror sounded genuine enough.

"I went on the Web and read about him. I saw the pictures. He gets around." Judith made it sound like the ultimate sin, and for her perhaps it was. Certainly never in all the years Meadow had known her had she seemed interested in a man. Or a woman, for that matter—art was Judith's obsession.

"Really?" Nothing could have surprised Meadow more. Going to the desk, she brought up the computer and typed his name into a search engine. "I thought he seemed too calculating to be indiscriminate."

"Some women worship football players, and he's handsome."

His photo popped up right away, a youthful one of him in his football uniform, a later, unposed picture of him in a hard hat. "Not handsome. Not really. But a mesmerizing juxtaposition of gorgeous and rugged." Meadow wished she could paint him, but that gift had been given to Isabelle and Sharon, and not to her. She touched the cool, smooth screen, outlining his jaw with her fingertips. "I can see why women would chase him, but it's not just for his looks."

"What do you mean? What else is there?" Judith asked sharply.

"When he talks to me . . . he concentrates on *me*." Meadow's eyes half closed as she remembered. "No one else exists. It's . . . intoxicating."

Judith took a ragged breath. "While you're flirting with this man, the painting goes undiscovered and your poor mother is *dying*—"

Abruptly furious, Meadow came to her feet. "She is *not* dying. Don't you dare put that out into the universe. My mother is recovering!"

"You're right. I know. I know." At least Judith had the good sense to back right off. "I'm sorry, I just . . . I'm so worried."

"All right." With an effort, Meadow controlled her temper. "Just . . . please don't say that. Don't even think it. And give Mom my love. Tell her I'll be home soon."

"With good news," Judith said heartily.

"Yes. With good news."

"Don't stop looking. Figure out a plan and stick with it. Everything's depending on you, Meadow! Everything's depending on *you*."

Meadow hung up and sat down, limp with the flash flood of rage Judith's blunder had caused.

Meadow thought that Judith had always wanted to be Sharon's dearest friend, but because of these kinds of slips, she'd never managed to get close.

Judith said she believed what Sharon believed. She acted happy, said the right stuff, ate the right things. But she would barely discuss her background, and as Sharon told her daughter, "I'm afraid she's hiding some trying times and struggles to maintain a good public attitude. She needs to believe from the heart, poor thing, and I wish I could help her do that."

But Judith was right about one thing: Meadow had to figure out her next move. She was here in the hotel, and she was solid—solid because Devlin claimed she was his wife and because—Meadow didn't think she flattered herself—because he was infatuated with her body. Possibly as infatuated as she was with his body, and that fascinating, intelligent, guileful mind. He saw life as a chess game, black-and-white, and a series of premeditated moves that ended in one of two ways—winning or losing.

But she wasn't playing a game.

Last night and today had been genuine for both of them.

So how would this end?

The man Judith described as nobody's fool accepted Meadow's story of amnesia, then claimed she was his wife.

What piece did that make Meadow on his chessboard?

Black . . . or white?

Pawn . . . or queen?

Winner . . . or loser?

Twenty-seven

That evening, before they walked into the dining room, Meadow stopped Devlin by digging her fingers into his arm. "Promise you won't leave me alone with that woman again."

"Four's in there. He'll protect you." Devlin was in no mood to make promises to Meadow. Not after this afternoon. Not after she had lied about the maid, and lied again about her silly amnesia.

"Four is a very nice man, but he's no match for your mother."

"I thought all women worshiped at his feet." Today Sam had pressed to send

Meadow away. Devlin had refused, but if there were very many more incidents like this one, he'd be forced to act.

"I only worship at *your* feet."

She was so good with the flattery. But in a few weeks he was opening a hotel. He knew from experience that a grand opening took all his concentration. He didn't have time to get Meadow out of a closet every time she screwed up and locked herself in. He really didn't have time to step inside and take her clothes off, or chase her through the garden in the moonlight, or fall in love . . .

She tugged him around to face her. "Promise me you won't leave me alone with her," she said.

Fall in love? With *Meadow*? That was impossible. She wasn't at all the kind of woman he admired. She was a liar, potentially a thief, a wild child without any sense of how to dress or how to keep her distance from the servants. If he got involved with her, really involved with her, he'd find himself rescuing stray dogs and eating tofu.

He didn't want that. That wouldn't work for him. He was a bastard, and his wife had to be like Caesar's—above reproach.

All of that was true. He knew it. So why, at

this moment, was he thinking of their night together and how he'd been so enraptured by Meadow's passion and joy that he'd taken her without a single precaution?

"Devlin!" She tugged him around to face her. "*Promise* me you won't leave me alone with her."

Damn. He hated that, with one simple phrase, she slipped under his guard. "I'll stick like glue."

"All right, then." She straightened her shoulders. "I'm ready."

She wore a simple, off-the-shoulder shirt in a flattering chocolate brown and a soft, swirling flowered skirt. Her shining copper hair hung loose around her neck, a beaded bracelet one of the maids had worked for her wrapped her wrist, and she wore sandals again—sandals with a heel, but sandals nevertheless.

She was in no way ready to face his mother, but he wasn't going to tell her that.

The shock of Meadow would be good for Grace Fitzwilliam.

He offered Meadow his arm, and together they walked into the grand dining room.

Actually, it had been converted into a conference room for their corporate guests. The

ong table seated twenty, and Devlin had
brought in a smaller round table and placed
t in the alcove. Two broad side tables held
computer setups, making the room multipur-
pose, yet elegant.

Grace leaned against the marble-faced
fireplace, adjusting the swirling glass bowl
created by Natalie Meadow Szarvas.

Four, of course, stood by the liquor de-
canter holding two cocktails.

"That's one way to get a head start," Devlin said.

Four grimaced, walked to Grace, and
handed her a drink.

Four didn't look well. He was pale, his
beige linen pants were rumpled, and his
loafers were scuffed. Devlin shouldn't give a
damn—Four had cheated him, then made
the mistake of thinking it was okay because
they were friends.

Yeah. Like it was okay for Devlin's father
to screw Grace, get her pregnant, show up a
couple of times a year and lavish attention
on Devlin, then abandon Devlin to the troubles his occasional appearance created.
Like it was okay for Nathan to ruin his own
business, take the money, walk away from
his legitimate family and his illegitimate son,

and never look back. Devlin had had enough of getting screwed by people who were supposed to care.

Yet long ago, when they were kids, Devlin had developed the habit of worrying about weak-willed, likable Four. No matter how hard Devlin tried, he couldn't seem to break that tradition.

Taking Meadow over to Four, he handed her over, and spoke in his ear. "Please, Four. Keep your wits about you tonight, or my mother will have Meadow flayed for dinner."

Four brightened, always pleased to be handed a job he knew he could manage. "Sure. I'll keep an eye on her." He asked Meadow, "Can I fix you a drink?"

Devlin went to Grace and kissed her cool cheek. "You look marvelous, Mother."

"Thank you, dear. So do you." She wore a knee-length black sheath with a red silk paisley scarf draped over her shoulders and diamond studs in her ears. Her blond hair was dressed in some swirly thing at the back of her head, and he could almost feel her exerting her will on the room. "Shall we sit down to dinner?"

"Let's. I'm starving!" Meadow viewed the

long table with dismay. "But we're not sitting there, are we?"

"We'll use the round table," Grace announced.

That surprised Devlin; he would have guessed Grace wanted the length of the polished wood to properly intimidate Meadow. As it was, sitting at the round table meant no one took the head. He wondered what Grace intended by such a democratic maneuver.

As soon as the servers had changed the settings and presented the little group with the first course, he found out.

"I've decided you two should remarry in a little more . . . proper . . . circumstances." Grace's tone made it clear a runaway wedding in Majorca was the height of immaturity. "With a little concentration and planning, we could pull it off by September."

To Devlin's surprise, Meadow shook out her napkin and shrugged. "Sure."

His eyes narrowed on her. She didn't care if his mother planned a wedding.

Why?

Because she didn't intend to be here for it.

Because she would be in the Cascade Mountains, blowing glass—or if she stole a valuable painting from him, in jail. "Excellent idea, Mother, but surely the maven of Southern planning and propriety could accomplish a wedding in less time than that. I hear June is an excellent month to get married."

"Pushing. Pushing," Meadow muttered into her water glass.

"I never thought I'd see the day that you'd get married not once, but twice, in a scandalous hurry." Four buttered a slice of his bread.

"What do you mean, in a *scandalous* hurry?" Meadow asked.

"Devlin's *so* concerned with appearances," Four said, "and this will look like he *had* to marry you—not once, but twice."

"I'm not amused," Devlin said. Not amused because perhaps, if the gods of fertility were against them, Four was right.

"Because I got pregnant, do you mean?" Meadow laughed. "Does anyone get married for that reason anymore?"

Devlin looked directly at her. "I do."

"But that's a recipe for failure. People marry because they have interests in common and because they're in love, not because they accidentally"—Meadow made quotation marks with her fingers—"made a baby."

"It's not easy for a child to be illegitimate," Grace said.

The intensity of her voice surprised Devlin. He hadn't realized his mother had even noticed.

Meadow looked at the three of them as if they were speaking a different language. "Is it easy for a child to have parents who don't care for each other? Or who divorce? I don't think so."

"Knowing my son, I'm sure it's a moot point." Grace utilized her society smile. "And it's not as if you two are hippies running around the woods like free-range chickens, having sex willy-nilly and without protection."

Meadow snorted into her napkin. "No, heaven forbid we should behave like free-range chickens."

In his lap, Devlin twisted his napkin into a knot. And heaven forbid that he should have knocked Meadow up.

Before Meadow regaled them with the assurance that moonlight really did act as an aphrodisiac, Devlin said, "Perhaps, Mother, we should ask Meadow how *she* wants to celebrate her wedding."

Twenty-eight

"I am sure, given Meadow's indifference to the niceties of society"—Grace coolly viewed Meadow's skirt and blouse—"she's happy to leave the details to me."

Until that moment, Meadow hadn't realized she'd fallen into a BBC costume drama. Yet here she was, the upstart who married the prince—that part was played by Devlin—and now had to prove herself worthy of her new role.

She only wished she could take it half as seriously as did Grace Fitzwilliam.

Free-range chickens, indeed.

She considered how best to express her

sentiments in a way Grace would understand. "As long as my friends and family are around me, the details are immaterial."

"See?" Grace gloated at Devlin.

Meadow gave in to her spirit of mischief. "But we can't have the ceremony until Eddy returns from Europe."

"Is Eddy your uncle?" Grace asked.

"No, Eddy's one of my dear friends—and my maid of honor." Meadow beamed at Grace.

"Tell me Eddy is a variation of Edie?" Grace's fixed smile expressed pain and hopelessness at the same time.

"I think it stands for Edmund." Meadow frowned in overdramatic fretfulness. "But he hates that, so everybody calls him Eddy."

Four looked between Meadow and Grace, then lifted his glass and drained it.

Devlin rose from his chair and walked to the window. He stared out into the garden.

But his shoulders were shaking. Meadow had wanted to see him laugh for a long time, so she piled it higher and deeper. "I've known Eddy since grade school, and we promised we would be each other's maid of honor."

"You promised." Grace sounded faint.

"We used to imagine what our weddings

would be like." Meadow relished Grace's horror. "We always knew he would be a lovelier bride than me—he's awfully pretty—and I made him promise he wouldn't overshadow me when I got married."

Grace fanned herself with her hand.

"Hot flash?" Meadow asked cheerfully.

A chortle escaped Devlin.

Four covered his ears.

"I don't have anything as vulgar as a hot flash, and if I did, it wouldn't be proper to mention it." Irritation tinged Grace's cultivated tone. Leaning back, she closed her eyes. "I feel faint."

"Only one thing to do for that." Meadow pushed back from the table, pulled Grace's chair out, grabbed her by the back of the neck, and pressed her head down between her knees.

Grace shrieked.

Devlin turned and stared.

"Sorry, old man." Four threw his napkin on the table. "I'm out of here." He left in such a hurry he almost burned a trail in the carpet.

"Best treatment for faintness." Meadow grinned when Devlin covered his eyes with his hand. "Nothing to worry about. She'll be fine in a minute."

"I'm fine now." Grace's voice was muffled.

"You shouldn't come up too soon. You don't want to faint again," Meadow said.

Grace struggled, but Meadow held her in an untenable position. She could have wrestled her way free, but dignified Grace wouldn't lower herself to physically fight.

At least . . . not until she was desperate. Then she shoved Meadow back and sat up, brushing at her hair with her hands. "That is quite enough of that. We'll return to the wedding plans when you two are feeling more reasonable." She stood.

"Don't forget we need to discuss the party, too!" Meadow said.

Grace started to close her eyes and put her hand to her forehead in another pretended faint. Then she remembered, shot Meadow a wary look, and made quite a dignified exit, considering the fact that the back of her dress had hitched up to show an incongruously silky pink undergarment.

Devlin waited until her footsteps had faded before he burst into laughter. He laughed so hard he collapsed into a chair and held his sides.

Meadow watched him in satisfaction.

Laughter.

She'd bet he couldn't remember the last time he'd laughed like that, with all his heart and soul and body.

And amusement had a way of making him look . . . not softer, but more dashing, like a man who understood what it was to live life to the fullest without the suspicion and wariness that dogged his footsteps. When he stopped, he still grinned at her. "Do you really have a transvestite friend named Eddy that you've known since grade school?"

"Of course. Eddy's a great guy. I remember . . ." But she was supposed to have amnesia.

"What else do you remember?" Like a cat viewing a mouse that was struggling beneath its paw, Devlin watched her.

He'd caught her in her lie again. He looked remote again. He'd made her feel . . . uncomfortable again. "It's odd the things I remember and the things I don't. I guess I never mentioned Eddy to you before?" She held her breath and waited to see if he'd let her go . . . again.

"No. You never mentioned Eddy before."

She released her breath. For some reason he still wanted her here. She was safe for another day. "I seem to be distressing your mother."

"As if you care." He grinned again.

"I care enough to wonder why she's so . . . so . . ."

"Judgmental? Overweening? Concerned with appearances?" With his hands on his hips, he looked Meadow over from head to toe, and she realized that Grace might find her lacking, but Devlin appreciated every last inch. "She's not used to girls who aren't in awe of her."

"In awe?" Meadow strolled over, taking her time, letting her hips roll and her legs flex. "Why?"

"Because she's so good at everything. Don't you watch television?" He gathered her close.

"Not much." She didn't really remember what they were talking about—or care. All she knew was that he held her in his arms, and the warmth they created between the two of them could illuminate Seattle in December. She unbuttoned his shirt and slid her hand inside, loving the texture of hair over his soft skin. Standing on tiptoe, she kissed his jaw on one side, then the other.

He stood still, eyes half closed, allowing her the freedom of his body.

She zoomed in on his lips and—

"Dears, I have an idea for the party. . . . Oh, my God, are you at it again?" Grace stood in the doorway, her hands over her eyes.

Meadow exhaled in frustration.

Devlin buttoned his shirt. "You should knock before you enter."

"It's only evening. This is the dining room. The door is open. The waiters could walk in at any minute!" Grace peeked between her fingers, and when she saw they had separated, she marched right in. "Listen for one second, and then you can go back to doing"—she waved a slender, expressive hand—"whatever it was you were doing."

"So it's been a while for her?" Meadow said out of the corner of her mouth.

Devlin jerked with suppressed amusement.

Grace glared at Meadow, then at Devlin.

Then her gaze lingered on Devlin, her blue eyes thoughtful, and Meadow wondered what was going through her mind.

Devlin seemed puzzled, too. "Mother?"

"All right, here's my idea. See if you don't like *this*, Meadow." Grace panned the room with her hands. "I see the whole party taking place outside. We'll turn the estate into a carnival. We'll have games—not electronic games, but games like, oh, knock down the pins with a ball and, er . . ."

She waved her hand at Meadow.

"Break the balloons with the dart," Meadow supplied.

"Exactly." Grace nodded with satisfaction. "I knew you would know what kind of games they played at *those* places."

"She's good with an insult." Again Meadow spoke out of the side of her mouth.

"The best," he answered.

"I can hear you!" Grace tapped her toe.

"I know, Mother, and it would be best if you didn't listen," he said. "If we hold the party outdoors, it might rain."

"It won't," Grace said. "The elements don't have the nerve to mess with my plans."

"Wow." Meadow was impressed. "You could teach a class in positive thinking."

"Mother, who will we get for the freaks?"

Grace waved him away. "Those will be the guests, dear."

Meadow blinked. Who knew? Grace never cracked a smile, but she had a keen sense of humor.

"We'll have cotton candy and those red apples, and the waiters will be dressed like carnival barkers."

Devlin viewed her cautiously. "Mother, this doesn't sound at all like your kind of party."

"Dear, the party has to fit the people it honors, and in this case . . ." Grace gestured eloquently at Meadow.

Meadow contemplated blacking her front tooth and painting big red freckles on her nose.

Grace continued. "The waiters will circulate with trays. They'll have tokens to play the games, and champagne and hors d'oeurves."

"Champagne and hors d'oeuvres. That's more like it," Devlin said.

"In honor of Meadow, the decorations should be natural—flowers, flowers, flowers! And, as the centerpiece"—Grace flung her arms dramatically upward—"a Ferris wheel!"

In that instant, Meadow forgave her the insults and for barging in at the wrong moment—twice. "A Ferris wheel would be fabu!"

"Exactly!" Grace's lips puckered as if she had bitten into a lemon. "*Fabu* was the precise word I was looking for."

Devlin began, "It's not the word I—"

"A real full-sized Ferris wheel?" Meadow asked.

"But of course! It wouldn't do to skimp," Grace said.

Devlin tried again. "A Ferris wheel is not—"

"With lights and music! How about a roller coaster?" Meadow bounced on the couch.

"No. That would be overdoing it." When Meadow tried to protest, Grace pointed a finger at her. "We're going to invite all the best people in the South, and newspeople, too. It will be an event, and we don't want to be perceived as vulgar."

"Or free-range chickens." Then Meadow perked back up again. "I bet we could get Dead Bob. He performs at the Renaissance festivals. Oh, and the Fantastic Juggling Oxenberries."

"Very clever! A few shows would add to the ambience."

Devlin could hardly contain his exasperation. "Mother, I appreciate the thought you put into this, but—"

"Listen, Meadow." Grace's eyes gleamed. "The Ferris wheel will be the visual centerpiece of the party, and you and Devlin will announce your marriage from the top of the wheel."

"That's sick!" Meadow said.

"Sick?" Grace was taken aback.

"You know—awesome!" Meadow explained.

"Ah. *Awesome.*" That pucker was back. "Another word I was looking for."

"Ladies!" Devlin's single snapped word finally got their attention. "There will be no cotton candy. There will be no carnival barkers. And make no mistake, there will be no Ferris wheel." He stopped their outcry with a firm gesture. "That is my final word."

Twenty-nine

Devlin couldn't believe he had a Ferris wheel spinning in his yard, or that it released a shower of flower petals every time it reached the top, filling the air with a whirling, scented snowstorm. He couldn't believe he had carnival barkers and games, and, providing the music for the afternoon, an antique steam calliope painted blue, red, and yellow, and decorated with liberal amounts of gilding. He couldn't believe that Dead Bob was doing his act on the stage in the walled garden.

What Devlin really couldn't believe was that people, adult people, his distinguished guests, were eating and playing and riding the riding the Ferris wheel while shrieking like children.

This grand opening may have been his mother's concept—but it was Meadow's fault. Without Meadow's influence, Grace would have never thought up such an outrageous extravaganza.

Of course . . . the two women were right. He'd already seen three camera crews covering the event, and recognized at least five travel writers taking notes—and grinning. It was a huge success, but damned if he would admit it to Grace and Meadow.

Hands on hips, he stood on Waldemar's wraparound porch and surveyed the scene.

The waiters circulated through the crowd. Gregory Madison, federal judge, sat at one of the red-stripe-covered tables, eating from a pewter bowl full of cotton candy. Mr. Volchock, owner of last year's winning Derby horse, threw baseballs at stuffed clowns, while Mrs. Volchock clutched a teddy bear he'd won her. Jessica Stillman-Williams, Grace's boss, owner of two hundred cable stations across the United States and a ballbuster if ever there was one, wore a balloon animal hat while she stood in line for the Ferris wheel.

Four slouched against the trunk of the great live oak, drink and cigarette in hand, conversing with that girl, what-was-her-name. The cute one from the hospital.

She wore a shirt cut so low she was in imminent danger of fallout, and she was blatantly using her chest as an enticement.

It was working. Four hadn't once glanced at her face.

When he finished the cigarette, he ground it under his heel, then glared down at it. With great and obvious irritation, he picked it up and threw it in the garbage. Meadow had cured Four of his habit of tossing out his cigarette and leaving it. When she was finished with him, he'd be cured of his cigarette habit altogether.

If she stayed.

Like the call of a siren, the sound of her laughter drew his gaze toward her. He saw her at once, of course. She wore a wide, floppy straw hat decorated with a huge blue flower—his mother said it was so vulgar she might as well leave the price tag attached—a long-sleeved blue T-shirt, shorts that displayed smooth legs, and a liberal application of sunscreen. *Complete coverage is the price of fair skin*, she'd said, laughing up at him.

Hell, he'd be aroused if she wore a nun's habit.

There were better-looking women here— two rock stars who'd made it on their bodies, not their voices, three gorgeous models, and at least seven trophy wives—but the guys all stared at Meadow. She had a way about her; when she was around, it seemed the world was brighter, kinder, more joyous, and men, all men, wanted her to light their fire.

The lecherous sons of bitches. She was *his* fire.

The last two weeks had been marvelous and horrible. Marvelous because they'd been together every day and every night, because she looked at him as if he were the moon and the stars.

Horrible because he'd been working at a madman's pace, and while he did, she made a methodical search of the mansion and each of its rooms. She tried to disguise it as casual wandering, as visiting with the maids, as approving the decorations, but Sam kept track on the blueprints. She never returned to the same room, and once Devlin had caught her scowling at her map.

He felt almost sorry enough for her to tell her what she needed to know—but she kept her silence. She pretended to be an amnesiac.

And he refused to make himself a fool over a woman. He refused to find himself abandoned, scorned, and betrayed like Bradley Benjamin.

Devlin would not be the one to give his trust—and it really pissed him off that she made him want to.

Off to his left, the Amelia Shores Society of Old Farts sat on the porch, observing the proceedings with varying reactions.

Scrubby Gallagher sat with his feet propped on the rail, nursing an iced tea and watching the women. He couldn't have looked more content.

Penn Sample rocked a little too fast to be anything but annoyed by the hubbub.

Begum, one of the world's top models, sauntered by, and Wilfred Kistard adjusted his toupee, unbuttoned the top button of his tropical-print shirt, and went after her. Good luck to the old fool.

H. Edwin Osgood wore his trademark bow tie and thick glasses, and as he watched the frivolity it seemed the stoop in his shoulders became more pronounced. Probably the carnival made him feel old.

Bradley Benjamin sat stiffly on a straight-backed chair beside Osgood. He wore a summer-weight wool suit, a white shirt, a tie, and a straw hat. All he needed was a slave boy fanning him with a frond to be the picture of a wealthy nineteenth-century Southern planter. His posture, his scowl, everything about him was a criticism of the Secret Garden and the party.

His glower, and the opportunity to needle him, almost resigned Devlin to the cost of that antique calliope.

Devlin strolled over. "Enjoying yourselves, gentlemen?"

"This display of tastelessness"—Bradley Benjamin gestured at the party—"is a disgrace to a fine old estate."

"But really, you didn't expect any different from a common bastard like me." Devlin enjoyed delivering the line before Benjamin could.

"You don't show Mr. Benjamin the respect due him for his advanced age and noble position." Osgood's mouth puckered, and his skinny lips wrinkled.

"Oh, be quiet," Bradley snapped. He did not like having his age called into play.

Penn Sample's blue eyes twinkled with

that artificial kindness he played so well, and which Devlin had learned meant trouble. "It would be a shame if something happened here before you could open your hotel."

"Such as?"

"We saw a cell tower had been erected." Benjamin never bothered to hide his hostility, but today he visibly bristled.

"Yes, it's hard to miss, isn't it?" Devlin leaned down to Benjamin's eye level. "See the people mingling with the crowd? The ones in black and white with headsets and mouthpieces? Those are my security force. They're on top alert."

"You had security before." Benjamin's papery lids drooped over eyes heavy with malice.

"Gabriel Prescott, the national head of the firm, is here and mingling with the guests. There won't be any incidents—or rather, any more accidents." Devlin straightened. "I declare that from this moment, the hotel is officially open."

Benjamin glared in helpless fury.

Devlin looked around at all of them. "Trust me, gentlemen, before the decade is out, you'll see three more hotels along this strip. But then, that's what you're afraid of, isn't it?"

It was. He could almost see them shivering in their fine leather shoes.

"Hey, Mr. Fitzwilliam!" Christian, the pastry chef, held up a football. "Look what I won!"

"Cool!" Devlin clapped his hands.

Christian launched the football at him. His aim was off, and Devlin had to dive to keep it from hitting Bradley Benjamin right in his pompous, offended old schnoz.

"Sorry, Mr. Benjamin!" Christian waved apologetically, and grimaced at Devlin.

Devlin shrugged in response and shouted, "Go long."

Christian backed up and up and up, and Devlin shot the football right into his arms.

The crowd around the porch applauded—Southerners loved football, and they really loved having their own winning quarterback right in their backyard. He was pretty sure it was the only reason they still had electricity—the head of the local power company was a fan.

Devlin waved, and dusted his fingertips.

Grace stalked up the stairs and toward the house, her arms straight at her sides, the picture of offended dignity.

Devlin hurried toward her. "Everything all right, Mother?"

She showed him the lapel of her white jacket. "Frank Peterson was waving a pimento-cheese sandwich and hit me with it. Ill-bred lout. He's the handyman. I don't know why you invited him."

"I didn't invite him."

"Then what is he doing here? Did he crash the party?"

Meadow walked up licking a three-scoop cone. "Who?"

"Frank Peterson," Grace snapped.

"*I* invited him." Meadow's tongue massaged the ice cream. Her hat brim bobbed. "You couldn't expect him to stay home while his wife was here."

Grace waited for Devlin to speak, but he was busy watching Meadow catch a creamy drop before it trickled onto her hand. So, with a resigned sigh, Grace asked, "His wife? Who is . . . ?"

"His wife is Jazmin, who works at the hospital." Meadow sounded patient, as if she were reciting information they all should know.

"And you invited her because . . . ?" Grace lifted a perfectly tweezed eyebrow.

"She was nice to me after the wreck." Meadow's cheeks were flushed with pleasure as she looked out at the carnival.

"I'll bet you invited Miss I-Have-Perky-Breasts-and-I-Know-How-to-Use-Them." Devlin indicated Four and the young girl.

"Weezy!" Meadow said.

"God bless you." Grace brimmed over with irritation.

"Her name is Weezy," Meadow said patiently, "and I invited her because I couldn't invite Jazmin without hurting Weezy's feelings. Besides, Weezy's keeping Four entertained."

Devlin noticed that Meadow's tongue had turned bright pink from the red sprinkles. He broke a sweat.

Weezy tucked her hand into Four's arm. As they strolled past, the silence on the porch varied from freezing disapproval from Grace to wide-eyed lecherousness from Penn Sample.

"He's taking me on a personalized tour of the house," Weezy called to them.

"I'll bet," Devlin said.

Meadow grinned and tugged at his arm. "Down, boy. You're married now. All you get to do is run to the end of your leash and bark."

From the direction of the old men, Devlin heard a series of horrified gasps and choking laughs.

She glanced at them. "Hi, Mr. Gallagher,

Mr. Sample, Mr. Osgood, Mr. Benjamin. Got your hearing aids turned up?"

Scrubby Gallagher laughed. "And loving to hear you jerk that leash. Keep it up! You'll get him trained!"

Meadow gave him a thumbs-up, then went back to work on her cone.

As he viewed Isabelle's granddaughter, Bradley Benjamin's faded gray eyes blazed with irritation—and something Devlin had never seen there before.

Maybe the emptiness of a life badly lived?

God, Devlin hoped so. That would make this whole farce well worthwhile.

That, and the pleasure of getting into Meadow's pants every night.

"I suppose you invited the whole hospital staff so no one got their feelings hurt," Grace said.

Meadow looked down at her feet as she scuffled them. Her hat brim hid her face, but everyone knew the answer.

"Oh, for God's sake!" In a dramatic, exasperated gesture, Grace put her hand on her forehead.

"You told me I could invite my friends!" Meadow used her tongue to push the ice cream down into the cone.

Devlin wondered how long he could keep his erection below half-mast.

"Your *friends*, not the people who are in service to you," Grace said.

Devlin slid his arm around Meadow's waist. "Meadow makes everyone a friend."

Meadow shoved her hat brim back and looked up at him, and he saw the mischief in her face. "I suppose I shouldn't tell her I invited the rest of the household staff, huh?"

The expression on Grace's face was worth the price of the Ferris wheel. She stammered, "You . . . you invited the staff. The staff of the Secret Garden?"

"Well, sure. I told them to drop in when they weren't working. Look! They're having a marvelous time." Meadow gestured widely. The cone went flying and landed splat on the handrail.

Grace flinched and tried to protect her still-pristine white slacks.

In a voice that insulted and sneered, Bradley Benjamin said, "Mrs. Fitzwilliam, it might help if you maintained enough sobriety to hold on to your food."

"I haven't had a drink. I'm always this way!" She smiled at him with that special edge she maintained for Bradley Benjamin. "But it's okay. I'm an artist. We get to be eccentric."

Benjamin's gray eyes would have frozen bourbon in the glass. His lips moved soundlessly, but he wasn't swearing. Devlin saw it. The old guy said, "Isabelle."

Meadow saw it, too, because she removed her hat and inclined her head at him.

All Devlin's suspicions shifted, changed, became certainties. Meadow knew—had always known—about Bradley Benjamin and his position in her grandmother's life. And Meadow, who liked everybody, didn't like Bradley Benjamin.

"An artist?" Grace said. "I didn't know you were an artist."

"Oops," Meadow said softly. Wheeling on her, she said, "Grace, you've got something on your lapel."

Grace gave an exasperated huff. "If Meadow noticed, then I've *got* to go change. But I'll be back. Don't make your announcement until I am!"

"We wouldn't dream of it." Meadow watched her leave; then, the picture of guilt, she waited.

Waited for Devlin to question her about

her art, he supposed. But he wasn't disposed to be an asshole today.

They had Bradley Benjamin for that.

Instead Devlin lifted her chin and kissed the corner of her mouth. "Ice cream," he said.

"Right." Scrubby put all his disbelief, all his envy, into that one word.

Devlin didn't care. All he cared about was having Meadow gaze at him as if she adored him.

The raucous music from the calliope, the clamor of the crowd, the smell of food and sunscreen—they all faded away. He was aware of nothing but Meadow's delightful smile, her warmth as she leaned into him, the scent of the lemon rinse she used in her hair.

"Mr. Fitzwilliam, if I could speak to you in your office?"

Sam startled Devlin out of his reverie.

When Devlin glared at him, Sam added, "It's important."

"Of course." Reluctantly, Devlin allowed Meadow to slip out of his grasp.

She stepped away from Sam. Looked at him *very* oddly. It was as if she knew Sam had been watching her when she'd shut herself into that closet, and blamed him for telling Devlin the truth.

"Don't be too long." She replaced her hat and skipped down the steps.

Devlin glanced over at the old guys. All of them watched her go, and all of them had that wistful, walking-down-memory-lane gleam in their eyes.

All of them except Bradley Benjamin. He looked furious—and old.

The fool. Did his pride keep him company when he sat alone every night?

Or had it occurred to him that if he'd kept Isabelle, he could have had Meadow for his granddaughter?

Thirty

Sam indicated the bank of monitors in Devlin's office. "Usually while Mr. Four wanders the halls, he's reeling drunk. But today . . ."

Four walked along the corridor on the third floor, Weezy on his arm.

"He's probably looking for somewhere new to get laid," Devlin said. *Like the linen closet.*

"I wouldn't have come to get you if that was the case," Sam said. "Watch him."

Four was wild-eyed, his motions jerky, as he stared at each painting. Once he stopped before a landscape, leaned in, and looked at the signature in the corner. Weezy looked bored to death, and when she tugged on his arm, Four turned on her. It was obvious that he snapped, for she flounced off.

"He's looking for a painting, too?" Devlin couldn't believe it. It was too odd. Too similar to Meadow's behavior to be a coincidence. "What the hell do they think they're going to get out of the damned thing?"

"Sir?" Sam frowned at Devlin.

"Nothing." Devlin waved the question aside.

"Sir, do you think perhaps it might be a wise idea to send Mrs. Fitzwilliam and Mr. Four away until it's ascertained that this painting isn't on the premises?"

"But it *is* on the premises."

Sam stepped forward, and he projected a surprising menace. "Would you explain yourself, sir?"

Devlin considered what to say, how much to say. "The painting is not what everyone hopes. It's not an important lost masterpiece. It's an early work, and a hurried work. I like it, but I have my reasons. Why?" Why, of all the people in the world, did Sam care so much?

"When Mrs. Fitzwilliam started searching, I took the liberty of looking over the appraisals of all the art in the house." Sam went to the file cabinet and pulled out the file. "There's nothing here that would indicate the kind of interest Mrs. Fitzwilliam and Mr. Four are displaying."

"Exactly." Devlin noted that Sam hadn't answered the question, but before he could ask, his walkie-talkie beeped. He glanced down and saw his mother framed in the small screen.

"I'm ready, and if you don't hurry, Meadow will go off and jump in the large"— Grace waved her arms—"blow-up clown thing."

Meadow thrust her head in front of the camera and rolled her eyes.

"I'll be there in a minute." Devlin clicked the off button and said to Sam, "Is there anything else before I go back?"

"I have the report on Mrs. Fitzwilliam from the detective."

"About damned time." Nothing else could have held Devlin in place. Nothing else.

"It took him a while to sift through and find the right information." Sam handed him a manila folder filled with papers and photos. His cool, dark eyes met Devlin's. "Mrs. Fitzwilliam has never visited Majorca."

"Let's keep that our secret."

But Sam still stood there, balanced between what he wanted to say and what he should say. He must have decided they were one and the same, because at last he used a low, slow voice to ask, "Have you thought that perhaps she's sleeping with you just so she can stay here and search for this . . . painting?"

When had Sam become so interested in all this? When had he started looking and sounding like the man in authority? "Of course I've thought it. How could I not? But if that's the case, it's worth it—and I'll bear up and suffer through."

"Yes, sir. Do you want me to do anything about Mr. Four?"

"No. Let him search. It won't hurt, and maybe it'll keep him away from the booze."

"Yes, sir." Sam turned away to his office.

Devlin stared at the folder, at Sam's neat printing on the tab.

Natalie Meadow Szarvas.

He should go back to the party. He was the host. But Meadow hid too many secrets, and he'd not had time to search them out. He wanted to know everything about her, about her family, about her art, about her background. He held the answers in his hand, and he couldn't wait any longer.

Sitting down at his desk, he opened the folder and started reading.

When he was finished, he stood up.

Everything had changed. Everything.

He had to find Meadow. This time they would work this thing out.

Instead, when he stepped onto the porch, his mother saluted him with a glass of champagne and called, "It's the bridegroom! Come on, Devlin; we've cleared the Ferris wheel. It's time for you and Meadow to make your announcement!"

The day had been long and exhausting.

Devlin and Meadow had ridden the Ferris wheel to the top and made the announcement of their marriage to the cheering crowd. No one had left until after ten, and then only the local half had driven away. The rest of the party had retired to the bar. It was after two by the time the last of the guests had staggered off to their rooms at the Secret Garden, sending the staff into a frenzy of work as they delivered extra towels, antacids, and bottles of water.

By the time Devlin came to bed, Meadow was asleep.

As he climbed under the covers with her, he resolved that he would talk to her in the morning.

But the second Meadow stepped out of bed, Devlin woke up. He lay there for a moment, waiting to see if she turned on the bathroom light.

But no. She slipped into her robe—and left the room.

Perhaps he was a fool, but he knew she wasn't sneaking off to visit another man. And the moon wasn't full, so she wasn't off to dance naked in the garden.

This was about her mother. That single sentence in the detective's report had explained everything.

Meadow wanted that painting to pay for her mother's treatment.

And how deeply Devlin resented the fact that she hadn't told him her troubles. Told him the truth. He'd given her so many chances, yet it seemed that while she trusted him enough to sleep with him, she didn't trust him with her secrets.

He got up and pulled on his jeans and a

T-shirt. Going to the closet, he dug out his Reeboks.

All right, maybe some of the things he'd done, and some of the things he'd said, and some of the things he'd encouraged others to say about him, led her to believe he was a ruthless, unyielding jerk.

But didn't she know? Didn't she realize?

With her, he was different. He felt . . . young. He believed in possibilities. In wiggly puppies and in spring showers that brought May flowers. In miracles.

The idea of Devlin Fitzwilliam being silly in love seemed absurd—except that he was in love with Meadow.

He tied his shoes.

Well. Tonight he would teach her to trust him. He would do what he had sworn he would not—he'd confess the truth, all the truth. Kind, generous Meadow would realize the error of her ways, and she'd stay with him.

He headed out, figuring he could check the monitors across the dimly lit corridor, see where she'd headed off to search, and find her.

But when he accessed the room, the security panel was black.

He stared in horror.

Had Meadow turned off the whole system to look for her painting?

Because with the hotel full of guests, including the Godfather of Amelia Shores, Bradley Benjamin, the chances for undetected sabotage, for theft and disaster, had radically increased.

Devlin tore down the hall and toward his office on the main floor. He hit the landing at the top.

Someone was going into his office.

He shouted.

Gabriel shouted back, "I'm on it!" and disappeared inside.

Devlin took the steps two at a time.

As he neared the first floor, he realized someone had dropped a bundle of towels at the bottom of the stairs.

But as he got closer, he realized that it wasn't towels or rags or someone's clothes. It had a head of copper hair that shone dully, limbs arranged at an awkward angle, and it lay unmoving. Unconscious.

Meadow.

Dear God. Dear God. Please, no, God . . .

He knelt beside her. His hands trembled as he touched her face. Still warm. He pressed his fingers to the artery in her neck. Her heart beat. He called her name. "Meadow?"

But she didn't respond.

She'd fallen down the stairs.

A small trickle of blood stained the carpet beneath her head.

But he didn't dare move her, because this time . . . this time she might have broken her neck. This time . . . she was really hurt.

He leaned down close. "Meadow. For the love of God. Don't die. Please, don't die. I love you."

And he stayed there until the ambulance took her away.

But she never moved. She never answered him at all.

Thirty-one

Dawn was lightening the sky when Devlin quietly let himself in the front door of the Secret Garden.

"How is she?" Grace stood silhouetted in the entrance to the library, her hands tucked into the wide sleeves of her robe, her eyes worried.

"She has a hell of a gash on the back of her head and a lot of bruises on her arms and legs. They say she's fine, but they kept her overnight for observation. Dr. Apps says Meadow's been hit on the head too many times in the last month." He tried to grin. "So why do *I* feel punchy?"

"I knew it. That girl wouldn't let a fall down the stairs faze her. She could probably fall out of an airplane and bounce."

He only wished Meadow had looked a little less pale, and been a little less confused by where she was now and how she'd gotten there. "Yes. She is indomitable, isn't she?"

"Rather like me."

He was very tired, and it took him a minute to process her observation. Grace had paid Meadow the ultimate compliment. He almost staggered from the shock. "My God, Mother. You like her!"

"I don't like her. I think she's lying about half the things she says. She dresses horribly. She's impertinent. She doesn't comprehend the most basic of proprieties. Neither of you has given me the slightest clue about her background, by which I must assume both parents are serial killers. And she's a Yankee." Grace's voice got sharper with each complaint. Then her face softened. "But she makes you happy, so that impertinent, unsuitable child of Yankee convicts . . . is fine."

"Thank you, Mother. That's very . . ." He started to say *sweet.*

She shot him a glare.

". . . open-minded of you." He laughed a little and rubbed his head. When he'd gotten out of bed and gone after Meadow, he'd been irked as hell that she hadn't confided in him, yet prepared to make the grandiose gesture of paying for her mother's cancer treatment.

What a great guy he was.

Yet Meadow seemed to think he was wonderful, and, even more amazing, so did his mother.

"Meadow told you she's an artist," he said. "I believe you know her. She made that glass bowl you placed on the mantelpiece in the dining room."

"No, she didn't. That bowl was created by River Szar—" Grace stopped in midsentence. She looked at him. She walked to the dining room. She looked toward the fireplace. She turned back. "Meadow is Natalie Szarvas?"

"Natalie Meadow Szarvas."

"She told me she was an artist, but I thought . . . Well! That explains everything. No wonder she's so eccentric. This will be so much easier to explain to my friends." Grace's eyes gleamed with satisfaction.

"And we all know how important that is." His mockery hid his real pleasure in her approval.

"I am friends with important people!"

"They're only important because they're your friends."

"As Meadow is important because she's your wife." In her peculiarly inept way of comfort, Grace came to him and hugged him. "It's late. You're tired. You've had a shock. Go to bed."

"Yeah." He was well aware that his confession of love to Meadow had been unheard—and unanswered.

Worse, he was relieved. He was a stinking coward—he didn't want to be the one who took the chance and offered his love, only to have the new, fresh, never-before-experienced emotion rejected.

He wasn't the kind of man who imagined Meadow had never danced naked in the moonlight, or that her open affection for him might just be . . . Meadow's affection for all of mankind. He was certainly one of her only lovers, but when it came to love . . . he might be one of the crowd.

Grace walked with him toward the stairs. "What does Meadow say happened tonight?"

"She says she doesn't remember." He grimaced. *Yeah, right.* More amnesia. But this time . . . he believed her.

After he'd gotten Meadow settled in a room, Dr. Apps had called him aside. "I see this kind of injury far more than I like to. A blunt object inflicted the wound on Mrs. Fitzwilliam's head."

He had stared at the doctor, his worst fears confirmed. "You're saying someone hit Meadow and pushed her down the stairs?"

"Actually, Mr. Fitzwilliam, in cases like this, that someone is almost always the husband." Maybe Dr. Apps didn't flirt with other women's husbands. Maybe she didn't flirt with wife beaters. But at that moment, she sure as hell hadn't been flirting with him. She had stared at him, arms crossed, eyes hostile.

"In this case, it isn't. But I will find out who it was." He had walked away, knowing full well that Dr. Apps believed in his innocence about as much as she believed O. J. Simpson's.

But the fact remained that someone had struck Meadow and pushed her down the stairs, and he intended to discover who— and make that person suffer.

It was because of that person that Devlin had had to face a horrible fact: He loved Meadow, and that love had the power to make him suffer.

He didn't want to suffer.

He didn't want someone else to hold power over him.

He had, in the space of only a few hours, been proven a coward and a weakling.

How had he come to such a pass?

But his mother stared at him as she always had, as if she didn't know what to do with him, so he knew his vulnerabilities remained hidden. At the foot of the stairs, he patted her on the back. "It's late. You need to get some sleep."

"I'm fine. I'm putting off the first day of filming for the new season. I must see Meadow with my own eyes, and really know she's well." Grace stood there, waiting for . . . what?

Oh. "That's great, Mother. I appreciate it, especially since I know how important the show is to your fans."

"Anything for my son and his wife." She presented her cheek.

He kissed it and watched her make her way upstairs.

Then he headed for his office.

There he found Sam and Gabriel reviewing the security tapes.

He seated himself behind his desk. He

placed his hands flat on the cool surface, and coolly considered them both. "Well?"

Gabriel began. "The security system was off five minutes before my personal alarm sounded."

"Why so long?" Devlin asked.

"Because it was shut off by someone who knew what he was doing, and it was done remotely. The only reason he didn't circumvent my alarm was because I installed it right before the party. New technology. And I wouldn't have done that if you hadn't had the break-in three weeks ago. Stuff like that makes me twitchy." Actually, Gabriel didn't look twitchy. He looked furious.

Devlin switched his attention to Sam.

"I reviewed the tapes at the time the cameras went off, and again right after they came on. The only people in the corridors or on the perimeter were security personnel, Mia from the kitchen, who had finished cleaning up and was heading home, Miss Weezy Woodward, who was leaving Judge Gregory Madison's room, and near the top of the staircase . . . Mr. Bradley Benjamin the fourth."

Devlin found himself on his feet, and in a voice hoarse with rage he said, "Four? Four did this?"

"Sir, Four does not have the technical skill to shut off the security system," Sam said.

"Who else could it be? Do you have another suspect?" Devlin demanded.

"Perhaps one of my security people." Gabriel made his suggestion steadily. "They all have good references. Some have worked for me for years. I pay them well. But security guards are always a prime target for corruption."

Devlin paced out from behind his desk. "Have any of *them* been sneaking around my hotel after a painting?"

Sam shook his head. "But sir, Four isn't violent. I can't imagine he would strike Mrs. Fitzwilliam."

"Let's find out." At a deliberate pace, with Sam and Gabriel on his heels, Devlin walked up the stairs and down the corridor to Four's room. Just as deliberately, he slid his master key card into the lock. And even more deliberately, with all his force, he slammed the door open against the wall.

"Shit," Gabriel muttered.

Devlin flipped on the overhead light.

Four catapulted out of the bed.

"Four, you son of a bitch, is there something you want to tell me?" Devlin used to be a football player. He knew how to make himself look bulky and menacing.

He did it now.

His technique worked, because Four gave a sob and cringed back against the bed. "Please, Devlin, don't kill me."

Guilty. Devlin could scarcely stand it. That feeble little asshole was guilty.

He took a step inside. One step only. If he took any more, he'd go and wring Four's skinny little neck. "Give me one reason why not."

"It's not my fault! He's making me do it. It's Mr. Hopkins."

"Mr. . . . Hopkins?" Gabriel asked.

Four's attention switched to Gabriel. "He's this silver-haired devil with a smooth voice. So smooth. He calls me and he says . . . he says . . ." The pansy-ass wore a pair of silk pajama bottoms, and the knocking of his knees made the fine material shiver. "He says he's going to geld me! Or worse."

"Have you seen him?" Sam asked.

"Yes. I didn't see him well—he sat there in shadow—but he did this." Four pinched his ear.

Gabe turned to Devlin. "Remember, I told

you about Mr. Hopkins. If he's got his finger in this pie, we're in deep trouble."

"We are. We are!" Four said.

"I've hired a couple of his people. My security's been compromised." Gabriel looked at Sam. "Can you handle this?"

Sam nodded.

Gabriel walked back down the corridor.

Four watched the interplay with feverish eyes. "He knows everything that's going on here. He's watching me. He's watching the house. You do understand, Devlin?"

"I understand. You're working for him." Devlin waited for Four to deny it.

But he didn't. All he did was confirm his own cowardice. "I had to! He's going to hurt me if I don't get that painting. He's going to kill me!"

So Four had pushed Meadow down the stairs. He'd tried to break her neck to save his own. The lying little weasel. "You should stop worrying about *Mr. Hopkins* killing you."

"Man. Please. You're going to help me, aren't you?" Four had the guts to look hopeful.

"You hurt my wife." Remembering how Meadow had appeared, crumpled at the bottom of the stairs, made Devlin want to sob, too. Instead, he promised, "Now I'm going to kill you myself." He started after Four.

Four tried to back up. Fell on the bed. Scrambled backward.

Sam grabbed Devlin and planted his feet.

"Kill your wife? Kill Meadow? When? What are you talking about? I never hurt her. I never hurt anybody!" Four's blond, gelled hair stood up like an exclamation point.

Devlin strained against the restraint. "What a pile of crap. You charmed her. You made her like you. Then when you figured out she was looking for the same painting as you, you cut that steering fluid line."

"I didn't do that. He did. He did!"

"And when you saw her on the stairs, you smacked her on the head."

"I never touched her. Devlin, I swear to God"—like a goddamn Boy Scout, Four held up one trembling hand—"I would rather go up against Mr. Hopkins by myself than hurt Meadow."

"Get out." Devlin could scarcely speak for rage. "Get . . . out . . . now."

Four listened. He listened well, because he raced to the closet, pulled out his clothes, and flung them on the bed.

But he kept talking. He babbled as fast as he could. "Listen to me. I didn't hurt Meadow. If someone smacked her on the head, you'd better take good care of her, because if Mr. Hopkins knows she's after that painting, he'll take her out. No kidding, Devlin. Mr. Hopkins is going to kill me for failing." Four paused in the process of unzipping his suitcase.

He looked right at Devlin, and if Devlin didn't know better, he would have sworn Four was telling the truth.

"Devlin, honest. Mr. Hopkins will kill Meadow . . . just for trying."

Thirty-two

The next morning, as Devlin stepped inside his office, the clouds had closed in and the gray day echoed his mood. He hated that Gabriel had spent the night firing some of his security staff and trying to track down one who'd gone missing. He hated that Four had betrayed him. He hated more that his tolerance for an old friend had led to Meadow's injury.

Worse, now he saw traitors everywhere. When Sam looked up from his desk, all Devlin could remember was his unusual interest in that painting. There was something damned odd about his attention to *that* detail.

"I hope Mrs. Fitzwilliam is doing well today, sir." Sam looked the same as he always did—a mix of Asian and Hispanic, calm, unflappable, efficient.

But when Devlin got back from the hospital and settled Meadow into her bed, he was going to do some research on good old Sam. "I spoke with the hospital this morning. They tell me she's resting comfortably and, other than bruises, has no residual trauma. I pick her up at eleven."

"Good news, sir." Sam rose to his feet. He squared his shoulders. "Mr. Fitzwilliam, I refused to wake you, but you have a visitor. He didn't want to be seen by your departing guests, so I put him in the dining room."

Devlin was in no mood to play games. "Who is he?"

"His name is Carrick Manly."

"Carrick Manly. Well. Daddy's *legitimate* son." No wonder Sam had made such a big deal of this announcement. He didn't know how Devlin would react.

Hell, Devlin didn't know how Devlin should react.

Nathan Manly had had one wife, and among his other breeding activities, he'd managed to father one son with her, making

Carrick the anointed heir to his father's industrial kingdom. Only Nathan had ruined his business, taken the money, and run out on everyone, including Melinda and Carrick Manly.

In all the years since his father had disappeared, Devlin had never heard from any paternal relative.

Well . . . he hadn't gone looking for them, either. With a parent like Nathan, who knew what his offspring would be? Devlin had enough problems with friends like Four.

Four. Devlin had thrown him out, then almost sent someone after him. Because . . . what if Four was telling the truth?

But Sam had talked him out of it. "Sir, if this Mr. Hopkins really is searching for the painting, then Four is better off away from the action." Then he'd tried to pry more information about the painting out of Devlin.

Sam was definitely due for an investigation.

"Did Carrick say what he wanted?"

"He refused to speak to me," Sam said, "but I thought you'd wish to see him regardless."

"You thought right."

"I also thought you'd like information before you spoke with him, so I took the liberty of researching him and making up a file."

Sam handed Devlin a manila folder full of information he'd gathered off the Internet: press clippings describing Carrick's privileged childhood in Maine among American aristocrats, many more news stories from the time of Nathan's disappearance, and a mention of Carrick's graduation from college with a brief recap of the disgrace. The newest pictures were not clear; Carrick had clearly developed a talent for avoiding the photographers.

And finally, from January, the news that the U.S. government had filed charges against Melinda Manly, accusing her of collusion in the defrauding of the Manly Corporation's stockholders.

Devlin had heard about that, of course. He simply hadn't given a rat's ass. "Why did the government wait so many years?" he asked rhetorically.

Sam answered just as vaguely. "It's the government."

Devlin handed the file back. "You put him in the dining room, you say? Good choice. He can entertain himself in there." With the computers. With the books. With stealing the antiques, if he took after their father.

Devlin strode toward the dining room.

He opened the double doors, half hoping to catch Carrick pilfering the silver.

Instead he was sitting by the window, reading a well-worn paperback—one of his own, by the looks of it. He put down the book, rose, and extended his hand. "My name's Carrick Manly. I'm your half brother—and that's a phrase I've been using a little more often than I am used to."

Those recent, blurred photos didn't do him justice. He was approximately twenty-four, tall and broad-shouldered. His hair was dark, like Devlin's, and his brown eyes were intelligent.

Devlin thought they probably looked alike, and as he shook Carrick's hand, he said, "The apple doesn't fall far from the tree."

"So I see." Carrick checked him out as carefully as Devlin had him. "You look completely different from the last half brother I met." Clearly Carrick had been raised among the finest old families on the East Coast; his voice had a patrician accent, and although the clothes he wore weren't expensive, he wore them well.

"Who would that be?"

"His name is Roberto Bartolini. He's Italian."

"No more than half Italian, surely." Devlin gestured Carrick back into his seat.

Carrick corrected himself. "Italian-American."

"I believe I've heard of him. Saw his photo in the paper. " Devlin remembered the *USA Today* story he'd read at the airport last month. "Didn't he marry that famous crime-fighting lawyer in Chicago?"

"I was at the wedding." While Devlin seated himself, Carrick sank back and waited.

He showed an unusual amount of self-possession for a young man, and Devlin had to admire his handling of the situation. The other man didn't know if he would face overt hostility, amusement, or evasion, so he lingered in silence.

"Did you find him?" Devlin could think of no other reason Carrick would have appeared out of the blue.

"Our father? No. He's gone; the money's gone. Nobody knows anything. But perhaps you've heard—the government has accused my mother of collusion in Nathan's destruction of his industry and the disappearance of the money. I'm looking for any information he might have told you or your mother."

Devlin's ire rose. "After all this time, you come and ask a question like that?"

"Mr. . . . Fitzwilliam. After my father left, times were difficult for my mother and me. Nathan absconded not only with the money from the company, but also with most of my mother's family fortune. The part of her fortune she managed to preserve she's used to maintain the estate, but other than that, we lost everything." Carrick held up his hand. "We had a lot, more than most people, certainly more than the rest of my half brothers. Nevertheless, my mother is ill suited for economizing, and times were difficult. Tracking down my brothers—a difficult business because, like so many things, my father took care to obscure his indiscretions—took a backseat to simply dealing with our circumstances."

"Yes. I see." Devlin did—reluctantly.

"After so many years, this indictment has caught us by surprise. My mother is not well, and she . . . considers this another disgrace visited on us by my father. She refuses to defend herself, and it's up to me to clear her. The only legacy my father left me was my brothers. Through them I hope to discover what a family truly is."

He was very good, this brother of Devlin's. Carrick sketched his circumstances, he stated his case clearly, and his appeal was both unsentimental and brief. In the past, Devlin had heard enough to know that Melinda and Carrick Manly had been abandoned as surely as Devlin had been; his only thought, if he had one, had been a brief, *Good*. But that had been years ago, immediately after his father walked out; he'd been very young then, and hurt by the knowledge that he'd been nothing more than another notch on a very scarred bedpost.

Now Devlin had other interests, and none of them concerned Nathan Manly.

Instead, they concerned Meadow. Meadow and her quest for a painting that would pay enough for her mother to have all the treatments she needed to be cured of her cancer. Meadow, who would do anything for family.

Devlin had worked so hard to avoid having anything to do with his half brothers; maybe he should take a lesson from Meadow. Maybe it was time to forgive.

So he would give Carrick what information he sought, move on with his life, and perhaps someday he would host a reunion of the Manly sons at one of his hotels. "On his last visit," Devlin said, "a few weeks before he pulled his disappearing act, Nathan gave me a ledger and asked me to keep it until he returned."

Carrick sat forward. "A ledger? That's more than I would have ever hoped."

"I looked at it then—believe me, I wanted to think it was a treasure map or a secret message telling me where to find him."

Carrick laughed, a brief, harsh laugh. "Oh, yeah. I did that, too. I kept thinking that he would . . . walk back through the door. . . ."

The two brothers looked at each other, united by the bitter memories left by a father's cruel abandonment.

They had more in common than Devlin realized, and perhaps Carrick's life as a disgraced son had been as difficult as Devlin's as a bastard—certainly Carrick had suffered a shock when his social standing and income suddenly dropped, and Devlin had not. Maybe being tough right from the start was an advantage he hadn't imagined.

"Have you thought that he may have left no trail that would lead to the fortune?" A likely state of affairs, in Devlin's view.

"My father—our father—did everything in

his power to make himself and his fortune disappear, and he's been a rousing success. But I have to try," Carrick said simply.

With that, Carrick convinced Devlin. "The ledger is yours."

Thirty-three

Dr. Apps finished the exam and put her stethoscope in her jacket. "You're going to be stiff for a few days, and you can't wash your hair until the sutures come out, but all in all you came through a tumble down the stairs very well."

Meadow sat up in her hospital bed and grinned at Devlin standing guard by the door. "Plus I managed to get out of the party cleanup today."

"We'll put you on the riding vacuum cleaner," he said dryly.

"Really?" Her eyes sparkled.

"No." He crossed his arms over his chest,

stood with his feet apart, and exerted his authority. He was good at exerting his authority.

"But that would be fun!"

Either he'd lost his touch, or his authority didn't exert in her direction. "We do *not* have a riding vacuum cleaner."

"Oh." She looked crestfallen—and so much better than she had last night.

He hated that he wanted to kiss her, to hug her, to hold her until he was assured of her health, of her happiness, of her safety.

"Do you remember any more about what preceded the fall?" Dr. Apps didn't look at him as she asked. Obviously, in her eyes, he was still a wife beater.

"I got up to . . ." Meadow glanced at him, then said, ". . . to look for a painting I want to locate—"

He took a long, deep breath. She had at least begun to trust him.

"And when I got to the top of the stairs, someone was there. I started to turn and . . ." She shook her head. "That's all. I don't really remember much until this morning." She put her head down and shivered.

Coming to the bed, he sat on the side and put his arm around her.

She put her head on his shoulder and leaned into him.

Yes. Trust. At last. "If you hadn't turned off the security system, we would know who hit you," he said softly.

She lifted her head. "I didn't!"

"Are you sure?"

"I would surely remember that."

"Okay."

"Really. I didn't do it!"

"I believe you."

"Just like that?"

"Just like that." He didn't intend to tell her the truth about Four. Not yet. He knew her well enough to realize Four's treachery would break her heart.

Then she smiled at him so sweetly, he felt like the bastard he was. Because she thought he believed her because he had faith in her word.

And he did. But proof helped.

"We're going to have to talk about this painting," he said.

"I know. But you'll understand."

Dr. Apps cleared her throat. "I have some news about your condition, Mrs. Fitzwilliam, which I think might be a surprise."

What the hell . . . ? Devlin's arm tightened around Meadow.

"Last night, among the other tests we ran, we ran a pregnancy test."

He couldn't move.

Meadow didn't move.

"It was positive." Their stunned silence spoke volumes to Dr. Apps, and she added hastily, "But you don't need to be concerned about the effects of the fall. The baby is fine, you're in good health, and it should be a successful pregnancy. As soon as you're home, call my office and I'll give you a recommendation for a good ob-gyn. You should make your first appointment immediately, and the doctor will figure out your due date. Do you have any questions?"

Meadow shook her head no.

Devlin still couldn't move, couldn't speak, couldn't think.

"Then I'll give you a few minutes to get yourself together. Just let them know at the nurses' station when you're ready for a wheelchair to take you down to the entrance." Dr. Apps backed out of a room so thick with atmosphere she almost choked.

"A baby," Meadow whispered, and pressed her hand to her stomach.

They'd made a baby. They'd made a miracle.

"I'll bet it happened that night in the moonlight. Don't you think it had to be that night?" Devlin didn't answer, but Meadow was thinking out loud, thinking of herself and how this affected her. "I know you don't know this, but my mother has cancer."

"What happened to your amnesia? Did you *forget* about your mother?" His sarcasm cut right through her reverie.

"What?" She blinked at him.

His face was blank, his eyes impassive. He was in shock, poor guy.

Taking his hand, she smiled. "I sort of lied about having amnesia. Don't tell me you didn't know."

"I knew. That's why I *sort of* lied when I said we were married." His voice had an edge she couldn't define.

But remembering that moment when they met, when their falsehoods had topped each other, made her chuckle. "When you said we were married, I didn't know what to do. I thought the situation would be temporary, that I could find the painting, take it out of the house, and you'd never know. Then I found out about your security and all the people working at the hotel, and things got more and more difficult."

"You were going to steal from me."

"Not really *steal*. My grandmother left it in the house in case of an emergency, like my mom's illness. So it was my legacy, but I had the bad luck to arrive about a year too late. You already owned Waldemar. I walked into a secure place, fell and hit my head, saw stars . . . and haven't been the same since." She placed her hand on his. "Because I've gotten to know you. Being with you has been wonderful, an experience like no other in my life. So like so many things, what looked like bad luck actually became good luck."

"By what stretch of the imagination do you think this is good luck?"

"What do you mean? Haven't you *enjoyed* our time together?" He had. She knew it.

"Yes. But we're having a baby." Abruptly she remembered his panic when they'd failed to use protection. She remembered his illegitimacy and the taunting he'd had to face as a child, and from people—like Bradley Benjamin—who should know better.

"I know we didn't plan it, and you don't like it because you've got these archaic notions about what it means to be illegitimate—"

"Archaic notions? Lady, I have walked the walk and talked the talk."

"I know," she said hastily. *He's sensitive, Meadow. You be sensitive, too.* "That was patronizing. But what I mean is, a baby always brings such joy. And when you think about how many blessings we have in our lives—the grand opening was a huge success, my mom's in remission. . . ."

He stirred beside her, looked at her hard.

Meadow kept talking. "It makes me realize why our baby came along now. If Mom gets sick again, a baby will give her something to live for."

"What an *incredibly* stupid reason to have a baby."

His words, his tone, slapped her across the face. Still, she tried to be upbeat. "You're right. I didn't set out to do this on purpose—neither of us did—but since it's happened, shouldn't we find every reason to rejoice?"

He stood up and moved away from her touch. "Rejoice? About bringing a child into the world with a sometime father and a disgruntled mother?"

Obviously this was not a subject to be easily managed with compassionate words and a loving touch. "I am not disgruntled, and you have no reason to be a sometime father."

"Oh, really? Where are we going to live so that I can be a full-time father—*Natalie Meadow Szarvas*?" His eyes blazed with an eerie triumph as he produced her name and placed it between them like a hot coal.

He was really angry. At her? At him? At their baby? Whatever it was, she didn't like this side of him. He roiled with fury and old, dark, angry memories.

And she . . . she fought a feeling of betrayal. "How long have you known my name?"

"I learned it the day my mother came with those glass pieces. I realized you were an expert; then it didn't take much research to find out your name or where you lived—which is the issue here." He leaned toward her. "We live on different coasts. Unless you've got some brilliant solution, one of us is going to have to move. I've got a business that is centered here. You've got a mother who's critically ill. Which one of us do you think it'll be?"

"You know my name. You've known it for weeks." For some reason, that made her feel as if he'd been laughing at her. "You lied to me about . . . me."

"I wouldn't start flinging accusations around, Meadow, or Natalie, or whatever you like to be called." He mocked her with her own names. "There's plenty of reason for finger-pointing."

"You know what I do for a living. You know about my family." Her breath came in uneven gasps and burned in her chest. There was an issue here, a bigger issue. She knew it, but she was afraid to look at it. But she had to.

"I know your age, your weight, your IQ."

"You knew about my *mother*?" And that was the real issue. He had known about her mother's illness, and he'd let the farce go on.

He lifted his chin. He stared down his nose.

"You did know. You knew and you didn't offer to help? You knew I was looking for the painting that would pay her bills—and you just let me look?"

In her eyes, Devlin subtly shifted shape. He was no longer the man who frolicked with her in the moonlight, who teased her at dinner, who watched her eat an ice cream cone with a hunger that had nothing to do with the ice cream and everything to do with her. He had become cruel, indifferent, unyielding in his determination to win.

They stood on the chessboard, and she was a pawn.

She had feared that, but she had imagined she could change him, teach him that life was more than winning or losing. She'd fallen in love with him; he was the father of her child—and he was a monster.

Suddenly she found herself reclining on the bed. A red mist swam before her eyes, and her stomach roiled, but as the buzzing in her ears cleared, she could hear him saying, "I found out about your mother yesterday. I was going to offer to help, but I never had the chance. Then *this* happened."

She turned away. She didn't want to hear his excuses. She didn't want to hear him talk about their baby as a *this*.

Maybe he'd been wounded by his father's indifference and his mother's coolness. Maybe he'd been wounded so much he was an emotional cripple. Maybe . . . maybe Meadow had made the ultimate bad choice in men.

"Look, the solution is clear." He walked

away, but not far enough—she could still hear him talking.

"We'll sneak off and get married so no one knows we conceived this child out of wedlock."

"Out of wedlock?" She wanted to laugh. She wanted to cry. "I can't believe you care about such a minor matter."

"You wouldn't think it was a minor matter if you'd spent your childhood fighting little snots who called you a bastard." He ran water. "After we're married, I'll build you a studio. The child will have a home with two parents." His voice grew near. He placed a cold wet towel on Meadow's forehead, and directly above her he said, "We'll make the best of a bad situation."

She clenched her teeth against a wave of nausea. Her face flushed; sweat broke out on her forehead. She fought her way back from the brink. "I will not marry you."

"Don't be ridiculous."

"My marriage is not going to be 'making the best of a bad situation.'"

"Possibly I phrased that badly."

"Perhaps you did. And perhaps you meant it just the way you said it."

"Meadow . . ." He tried to take her hand.

She jerked it away. "It doesn't matter. I will never marry you. Not because you're illegitimate, but because what the gossips say about you is true. You really are a bastard."

Thirty-four

Meadow stalked into the house ahead of Devlin. "I am not going to discuss it anymore."

"You haven't discussed it at all." He followed her in and slammed the door. "You simply keep saying no."

"Which part of *no* do you not understand?"

"You're not being logical." And that heated his temper to a simmer. She had to be logical. How else was he going to keep her?

"Logic is overrated," Meadow said coolly. "And superfluous when it comes to love. My grandmother taught me that, and she was the bravest woman I know."

"But not the smartest," he said in frustration.

"No. That would be my mother."

"What's going on?" Grace stood in the doorway of the library, looking from one to the other in alarm.

"Nothing, Mother."

"I'm leaving your son," Meadow said.

"Damn it!" He didn't need the whole household in on this fight.

"Leaving him?" Grace held out her hand to Meadow. "Why?"

"Because like a free-range chicken, I managed to get pregnant." But for all her ire, Meadow couldn't resist Grace's outstretched hand.

"A baby? You're going to have a baby?" Grace held Meadow's arm out and gazed at her midsection, searching for proof. "I'm going to be a . . ."

"A grandmother." From inside the library, Bradley Benjamin cackled. "Did you hear that, Osgood? Grace Fitzwilliam is going to be a grandmother, and to the child of someone named *Meadow*."

"That is too rich," Osgood said.

Great. Just what Devlin needed. The old farts were still here.

Grace walked back into the library, dragging Meadow with her. "You leave her alone, Bradley Benjamin. If you want to take out your nastiness on someone, you take it out on me. I'm not in a delicate condition!"

Devlin followed and found only two old farts—Bradley sitting in the alcove in a brown leather recliner, smoke curling up from the cigar in the ashtray, and Osgood, on Bradley's right, sitting on a straight-backed dining chair, shoulders slumped, hands folded in his lap, his brown eyes wide behind his heavy glass lenses.

Osgood didn't matter. He blended into the scenery. Always had. Always would.

But Bradley sat like a petty god in his own fine heaven, breathing fire as his pretended indifference crumbled one feeble brick at a time.

"Don't worry about him, Grace," Meadow dismissed Bradley. "I have to go pack, anyway."

"No, you don't," Devlin said.

"Please, no," Grace said.

"You don't understand, Grace," Meadow began.

"Make her understand, and maybe I'll get it then, too." Devlin's voice rose with his frustration. "Because right now, I sure as hell do not know why you insist on leaving me."

Meadow interrupted at full volume. "Because I am not raising my child with a man who doesn't understand the difference between right and wrong. You only understand winning and losing."

"But you can't leave him." Grace took Meadow by the shoulders and shook her. "He's worth saving!"

"I don't need to be saved." Devlin couldn't believe his mother thought such a thing.

"I'm not in the salvation business," Meadow said flatly.

"Look, I know he has issues with . . . with intimacy and all that junk, but that's my fault. I'm his mother, and when he was a kid I was so busy trying to get my business going I didn't take the time to show him how to . . . love." Grace rubbed her forehead fretfully. "I don't think I'm very good at it anyway."

"Our relationship, Mother, has nothing to do with this," Devlin said.

The women looked at each other, then at him, and dismissed him with identical shrugs.

"He's an adult, and at some point everyone has to take responsibility for themselves. He's long past that point, so you can stop blaming yourself for your son's being a big, fat jerk." Meadow glared at him.

A cackle came from the chair in the alcove, and with a broad smile Bradley Benjamin rose to his feet. "I am so glad I stayed to look the old place over. I wouldn't miss this for the world!"

"Good! Yes!" Meadow flung an impatient hand out to indicate him. "Hang around and be exhibit A, the lonely, miserable old man Devlin is going to shrivel up and become."

Bradley's smile vanished, and his military posture became stiff and offended. "I am not lonely."

"Just miserable. You want to stay here and gloat over our troubles, because then you can go home to your lonely dinner with its place setting for one, and you can smoke your stinking cigars and no one will complain, and you can die alone and no one will discover you until the other tie-wearing old men notice that, for the third day in a row, you're not at lunch. And, of course, your funeral will be attended by all the right people, but who's going to cry, Bradley?" Meadow's voice shook with conviction. "Who is going to mourn?"

"Meadow." Devlin touched her arm. Later she would be ashamed of the things she'd said.

But not yet.

She jerked away. "Devlin is right. Someone will notice you're MIA before you've been dead for three days, because your little buddy H. Edwin Osgood sticks close, because somehow he gets his sense of importance from you."

"Well, really!" Osgood's lisp and his indignation were pronounced.

"Now I am going to call my mother"—Meadow flipped open her cell phone—"and tell her I'm coming home today. Because she loves me"—her voice thickened with tears—"just because I'm me."

She dialed the number and walked out of the room.

An uncomfortable silence fell.

Devlin looked at the other three.

They looked at him.

And he knew Meadow was right.

He was like his mother—stiff, uneasy with affection, and unschooled in love. He *did* see everything in terms of winning and losing, but that didn't work with Meadow. Because it didn't matter if he held the power in their relationship—if he didn't have Meadow, he had lost everything.

He started out of the room after her.

"Are you going to crawl after that girl?" Bradley Benjamin couldn't have sounded more masculine and more offended.

Devlin stopped and looked back at him. At exhibit A.

Meadow was right. If he didn't stop worrying he would turn into his father, and brooding about the abuses of his childhood, and worrying that someone somehow would take advantage of him right now, he would become Bradley Benjamin, a man without real friends, a man without a family . . . a man without his love.

By God, Devlin was not going to replay Bradley's mistakes. "Am I going to crawl after that girl? On my belly." He turned to walk after Meadow.

"True love triumths," Osgood lisped.

"Shut up, Hop," Bradley said.

Devlin stopped in midstride. He turned to face the two old men. "Hop?"

"Hop. It's his old nickname. Hopkins. H. Edwin Osgood." Bradley sounded impatient, as if that were a fact everyone knew.

And maybe at some point Devlin had

known it, but until last night when he heard Four's story about a behind-the-scenes murderer, Osgood's real name had meant nothing.

Of course, it could be a coincidence—but Devlin didn't believe in coincidence. He focused on Osgood. On his glasses, his dyed hair, his bow tie. Was it possible? Could it all be a disguise?

Osgood came to his feet. As Devlin watched, the foolish, womanizing, Bradley-butt-kissing sycophant faded from view, leaving an old guy with sharp brown eyes that observed him coolly.

Like gunfighters, Osgood and Devlin squared off.

"*You* never have trouble with money." Devlin spoke slowly as he thought the matter through. "*You're* in a good position to know everything that goes on here. *You* live alone in your mansion . . . do you collect art, Mr. Hopkins?"

Grace moved closer to Bradley. "Do you know what he's talking about?"

Bradley looked from one to the other. His gaze lingered on Osgood. "No. What is it you think he's guilty of, Devlin?"

Both Devlin and Osgood ignored him.

Osgood inclined his head. "I have interests in a lot of fields, Mr. Fitzwilliam." He didn't lisp at all. In fact, his voice sounded completely different than Devlin had ever heard it.

"I'll just bet you do." This old fart had been searching the hotel for Isabelle's painting. This crony of Bradley Benjamin's had threatened to kill Bradley's only son, Four. This man whom no one really knew had ordered someone to hit Meadow and push her down the stairs. Devlin took one big step toward Osgood, wrapped his hands around that prissy bow tie, and lifted him up on his toes. "I ought to kill you."

"Devlin! He's an old man!" Grace wavered between horror and confusion. "He's one of us."

"Not unless you're a murderer, Mother. And he's not as infirm as he puts on." Devlin plucked the glasses off Osgood's face and looked through them. A minor correction only. He chunked them aside. "What about the hair?" he asked. "Is it shoe polish?"

"Nothing so crude." Osgood looked into Devlin's eyes, unafraid, slightly contemptuous. "Are you going to snap my neck? Because it's getting damned uncomfortable up here on my tippy toes."

Devlin jerked his hand away. "No. I'm not going to kill you." He went to the security alarm and pushed it.

Osgood massaged his throat. He put his hand to his mouth, held it there a moment, then cleared his throat. "Coward."

Two security guards appeared in the doorway.

"Take Mr. Hopkins into custody." Devlin hesitated, remembering Gabriel's doubts about his people, remembering, too, the reports about Hopkins's long reach and shadowy background. "We'll need more people." He picked up the house phone and dialed Gabriel. With a few brief words he filled him in on the situation. When he hung up, he said, "Gabe's going to call the police and the FBI."

"Do you think that will be enough firepower to keep me?" Mr. Hopkins mocked him, but the old guy looked a little pale and sweaty.

Good. He was worried.

"Osgood. What the hell is wrong with you?" Bradley snapped. "You're acting very oddly."

Osgood looked at Bradley. "Am I?"

"You sound peculiar." Bradley searched

Osgood's face with his gaze. He took a step forward. "My God. Who are you?"

"'*What* are you?' would be a better question." Devlin glanced upstairs. He wanted to follow Meadow. He wanted to crawl, to explain that they would not be copies of Bradley and Isabelle. They would be themselves, Devlin and Meadow, in love forever.

But he wasn't going to leave Osgood until someone got here whom he completely trusted.

"Mr. Osgood, are you well?" Grace asked in alarm.

Osgood pulled at his bow tie. "Perhaps . . . not." The sweat was a slick sheen all over his face now, and when he shed his jacket, the armpits were stained.

Grace started toward him.

Devlin caught her arm. "No. Don't go near him. He's dangerous."

"Could I have a chair?" Osgood asked.

One of the security guards started forward, but before he could reach Osgood, Osgood groped behind him, then collapsed in a heap. He clawed at his arm, his chest.

"Heart attack." Bradley massaged his own chest.

"I don't believe it," Devlin said. The old guy was faking it.

"Honestly, Devlin. Look at him!" Grace said.

Osgood turned blue as he tried to get his breath.

So he wasn't faking it. But this was suspiciously convenient. "Are you okay, Mr. Benjamin?" Devlin asked. "Mother, help Mr. Benjamin to sit down."

Grace took Bradley's arm and took him back to his leather chair, then stood there and patted his hand until he snatched it back.

"I'll call an ambulance." One security guard headed for the phone.

The other guard shed his coat. "I'm CPR certified."

Gabriel walked in, took in the situation with one glance, and turned to Devlin. "What happened?"

"I think he took something. He put his hand up to his mouth, then cleared his throat." Devlin watched Osgood spasm.

Hands on hips, Gabriel nodded. "Good probability. That's pretty impressive, that he'd rather die than be arrested."

"Ambulance is on the way." The report from the guard was terse. "Everyone will hold their position until he's gone."

"You're seeing the hotel's emergency plan at work," Gabriel told Devlin. "In case there's a scheme to rescue him."

"Right." In the distance, Devlin heard the wail of sirens.

Emergency personnel poured into the hotel, took charge of Mr. Hopkins, stabilized him, and put him on a gurney.

Devlin and Gabriel followed them out of the library.

Sam stood by the open front door. "I'll ride with him."

Devlin lifted his eyebrows. *Interesting.* Apparently today was a day for all kinds of revelations. "Why should my secretary ride with such a dangerous man?"

"I'm federal agent Sam Mallery. Catching Mr. Hopkins is the reason I'm here." Sam walked out onto the porch, keeping the gurney in sight.

In key places around the yard, security personnel stood at the ready. Gabriel went to talk to the team leader.

Devlin wasn't letting Sam off with revealing so little information. "A federal agent? What is a federal agent doing working for me as my secretary?"

Sam pulled a small, efficient pistol from his holster inside his jacket and scanned the area. "We've known about Mr. Hopkins for years—he controls crime in Atlanta and most of the state of Georgia. We couldn't get a handle on who he was; talking to people in Atlanta got us a lot of information about his voice, about what they thought he might look like, but nothing concrete. He was a ghost. A very efficient, highly corrupt ghost. Then his influence started to edge north, toward South Carolina, and that gave me a lead." Sam never looked at Devlin; he kept his gaze on the emergency people, on the security guards, and most of all, on Mr. Hopkins. "I heard he collected art. He's one of those ubiquitous 'private collectors' you always hear about right after the museum loses a Picasso. That led me to a solid rumor that Waldemar hid an undiscovered masterpiece, and that led me to my career as your secretary."

"You're a damned good secretary for a federal agent." Devlin supposed this meant he didn't need to investigate Sam.

"Had to be. That's how I earned my way through school."

Fascinating. "Did you suspect Osgood?"

"I suspected everyone."

"Except me." Devlin enjoyed the irony of that.

The EMTs were loading Osgood into the ambulance.

"And then only because I knew what you were doing with your time." Sam walked down the stairs and waited for them to finish strapping Osgood and his gurney in place. "Also, Mrs. Fitzwilliam—or rather, Natalie Szarvas—was too young to be Mr. Hopkins. I did realize, though, that she was searching for the painting, and that put her in danger. That's why I had her locked in the closet by one of my agents."

"What?" *What?* What the hell kind of game had Sam been playing?

"I wanted her gone. I as good as told her to leave. I thought that if she told you what sounded like a crazy story about how *she* got locked in by a strange maid, and *I* told you she had locked herself in—and I had a tape to back up my accusations"—Sam grimaced like a man with resources—"you'd throw her out. But you never asked to see

the tape. It was too late for me to step between you. You were already in love."

It was almost a knee-jerk reaction. "Not in
love. Not then."

Sam climbed into the ambulance and
perched on the seat beside Osgood's prone
body. "From the first moment you looked into
her eyes."

Thirty-five

The ambulance hit potholes. Osgood felt like crap, but just as it was supposed to, the drug was wearing off. He jolted along. He stared at the ceiling, his eyes wide and unfocused. The federal agent sat beside the gurney, his pistol out, his expression still and tense.

Smart man.

Osgood waited . . . waited.

The wheels struck the pavement. The ride smoothed out.

And the ambulance slammed to a stop.

Before Sam had finished coming to his feet, the back doors whipped open. Two men stood pointing Uzis into the back.

Ah, it was good to have a contingency plan, as well as a contact with the local police who set that plan in motion.

Osgood freed himself from the restraints. He lifted himself up onto his elbows.

Sam looked to the front. The assistant driver had a pistol pointed at the driver.

The EMT on the other side of Osgood held a pistol on Sam, too, and handed Osgood a bottle of water—and the antidote.

Slowly Sam sat back, put his pistol down, and lifted his hands.

"Very wise, Mr. Mallery." Osgood swallowed the pill. He allowed the EMT to give him a hand onto the road. He dusted off his jacket, nodded to Sam, and walked to the waiting black car. Just before his men shut the door behind him, he heard the sound of the pistol as it fired.

He hoped it was one of his men killing the driver or Sam.

But he didn't really care.

When Devlin reentered the house, he saw Meadow.

Her tears had dried up. She held the phone as if it were a grenade. She was pale, but perfectly composed. She flicked a glance at Devlin, a glance that observed and dismissed him. She walked into the library.

Devlin followed.

Grace stood looking out the window.

Bradley Benjamin still sat in the chair, staring into space. He'd just been revealed as a fool, betrayed for years . . . by his old friend.

Meadow wobbled as she stood there, but her gaze steadied on Bradley Benjamin. "I talked to my father. My mother's back in the Hutchison Cancer Institute in Seattle."

Devlin put his arm around her, supporting her.

She didn't notice. All her attention was on Bradley. "She needs a bone-marrow transplant. I've already been tested. I don't match enough markers. But you might."

Bradley Benjamin stood. He looked around. "Me? Why would I match?"

"Because you're her father." Her tone was flat, no-nonsense.

"I am not her father." His faded eyes flashed. "In case you never heard the story—"

"*I* heard the real story." Meadow tapped

her chest. "I know the truth. When I was eight and my grandmother got sick, she told me."

"That sounds just like Isabelle. Regale an eight-year-old with the story of her affairs, like they were something to be proud of." Bradley's voice shook with scorn.

"She didn't tell me about her affairs. She told me about *you*." And obviously Isabelle had been none too kind. "She told me she loved you, but you made her miserable with your rules and your functions."

"She was inappropriate," Bradley said, as if that were a crime.

"She was real. When she had my mom, you and your dictates got worse—she was supposed to give up her art and become the right wife and the right kind of mother, as defined by *you*." Meadow's scorn was as lively as Bradley's. "When you came to her and accused her of infidelity, she couldn't believe you would think such a thing."

"Her affairs were legion." Bradley's teeth barely separated, and his lips were stiff.

"*After* you divorced her!" Meadow took a breath, and with all the conviction in her slight body, said, "She was faithful to you.

You're my grandfather. My biological grandfather. My mother is your daughter."

"Whoa," Devlin whispered. He had never
imagined this.

Meadow swiveled. She looked him in the
eye. "It's true."

"I don't doubt that for a minute, my love."
How could he? The evidence stood before
his eyes.

Meadow was a blend of grandmother and
grandfather, mother and father, and an
essence all her own.

Bradley trembled like a leaf in a gale.
"That's twaddle. Isabelle told me she'd slept
with that artist."

"No." Meadow walked to the couch. She
bent, dug among the cushions, and pulled
out a silver key, one to match the key that
opened the secret garden. She lifted it,
showed it to Bradley on her outstretched
palm. "You had the garden cleaned up for
her. You loved her. You'd had a child with
her. She thought you trusted her. Then you
accused her of sleeping with Bjorn Kelly.
She agreed because she didn't want to live
with a man who knew and valued her so little."

Bradley stood straight, his hands lax at his sides.

Devlin could see the thoughts racing across his mind, the incredulity, the possibility. . . . Devlin was willing to bet the old guy refused to believe Meadow, because if he did, his whole, bitter life was a waste.

Apparently Meadow thought the same thing, because she closed her hand over the key. She made a fist. "Look. It's a simple test. You provide a little DNA and you find out I'm telling the truth. Then you go to Seattle, donate the bone marrow, and save your daughter's life."

Bradley still didn't speak.

"You don't have to. But this is my mother we're talking about, so let me tell you what I'm willing to do to make you comply. I'll drag up the old scandal about Grandmother and you, and how you threw her and her child out without a dime. I'll sue you for what remains of your fortune, and I'll ruin what remains of your life." Meadow sounded cold. Meadow sounded ruthless. Meadow sounded like . . . Bradley.

"My God," Grace whispered. She looked between Bradley and Meadow. "My God."

"The alternative is a simple operation to harvest your bone marrow," Meadow said. "You'll be saving a life. Your daughter's life."

At last Bradley reacted. He staggered backward, fell into the chair.

"He's having a heart attack." *Two in one night!* Devlin leaped toward him.

Meadow followed. "He can't die now!"

But the old man put his head in his hands and gave a rasping sob.

Devlin stopped. He backed up.

The old son of a bitch was crying.

Meadow halted. She stuck the silver key in her jeans pocket. She shuffled her feet and, at last, knelt in front of Bradley. She touched his arm. "Are you okay?"

He took a few long breaths, then lifted his head. His papery cheeks were wet, and he looked at the tears in his hands as if he didn't know what they could be. Then he gazed at Meadow, and his eyes filled again. "My grand-daughter?" He touched her cheek. "You're my granddaughter?"

"Yeah."

"She didn't betray me, then. When she said she slept with him, I just . . . just wanted to kill them both."

Meadow caught his hand and squeezed. "I know."

"Because I loved her. I loved her so much."

"She knew that. She told me she knew that."

"Did she? Did she really? Because I don't want to imagine she died thinking I didn't love her."

Meadow nodded.

"I've got to go. I've got to get a plane ticket." Bradley slapped at his pockets. "All right. I've got my wallet. All right." He started to walk away, then made an abrupt turn and came back to Meadow. He bent and kissed her forehead. "Thank you. Thank you."

Devlin sent his mother a speaking glance.

"I'll show you to a phone." Grace tucked her hand into Bradley's arm, and together they exited the room.

As soon as they were out of earshot, Devlin said, "Meadow, we need to talk."

Whatever compassion Meadow felt for Bradley Benjamin, she clearly didn't feel for Devlin. She walked toward the door. "We've already said it all."

"No, we haven't. Please, Meadow. I don't want you to go."

She didn't slow.

He went after her. "I want you to stay, to marry me."

She headed for the stairway.

"You're like her, and I'm like him, but we are not your grandparents."

She climbed the first steps.

He held on to the newel post and looked up at her. "Meadow. I love you."

She turned on him, her cheeks flushed, her blue eyes narrowed and furious. "You would say anything to win, wouldn't you?"

Of all the reactions he'd imagined, he'd never envisioned this one. "You think I'm lying? I've never said that to another woman."

"*Anything* to win," she repeated.

"I'm not saying that to win. I'm saying that . . . because it's true. I love you." How could he articulate it so she believed him?

With Meadow, one way always worked.

He ran up the stairs. He pulled her into his arms. He tried to hug her, to kiss her.

She held herself stiffly. She dodged his lips. In a voice rife with irritation, she said, "Look. Yesterday I was feted as your wife. Last night I was knocked unconscious. Today I found out I was pregnant, that my mother has come out of remission, told my grandfather the truth—and got my heart broken. Let's just drop this for right now, shall we?"

"No." She was slipping away even while he held her. "I can't let you leave me."

She looked up at him and spoke slowly and clearly. "Listen to me. I won't marry you."

Thirty-six

Devlin let her go. "Before you leave, don't you want to see how I recognized you?"

Meadow so badly wanted to walk away. But she couldn't. The clever bastard had said exactly the right thing to keep her here. "You always knew who I was?"

"From the first moment you opened your eyes."

Her heart took a hard thump. Her eyes. He'd recognized her eyes. "So tell me."

"I have to show you." He walked toward her, toward the door.

She stepped back. She didn't want him touching her. She might say she didn't want him, but that was only her mind and her good sense talking. Her body thought otherwise.

He didn't look at her or acknowledge her caution, although she never doubted that he noticed. He noticed everything, so he could win—by any means. With Devlin, it was victory at any cost.

But he walked past her and down the corridor, not looking back to see if she followed him.

At first she didn't. Stupid, but she suspected a trick.

"I found the proof in the attic," he called back.

That made her start walking, although she kept a safe distance. "What attic?"

"Did you think a great house like this would not have an attic?" He pressed the up button on the elevator. The doors opened at once.

She stopped a few feet away.

"Would you rather take the stairs?" he asked, and to his credit he used no mockery.

She thought about it before she answered. She didn't want to step into the small, confined space with him. She didn't want the discomfort of standing shoulder-to-shoulder with him, not speaking, pretending they were strangers while he sucked up all the oxygen. Or worse, having him talk to her about *whatever,* while she remembered the times, so numerous over the last weeks, when he'd taken a private moment in the elevator to kiss her silly.

"This is fine." She stepped in.

Fine. A tepid word indicating indifference— a false indifference, but he got the message. He didn't like it—his hands clenched— but he kept his voice low and soothing. "When this house was new, the servants lived in tiny rooms under the eaves, and one huge attic room was used for storage. It still is."

She'd seen the dormers sticking out of the roof, but... "There isn't any access."

He stared at her. "You looked."

"Of course I looked. I even asked the maids. They said there wasn't; they should know."

"Not this time."

The elevator doors opened on the third floor, and he led her down the corridor toward the blank outer wall paneled with dark wood. Leaning down, he reached into what looked like an outlet and popped a latch. He pressed on one side—and a five-foot section of wall swung on a pivot, revealing a dim, airless passage and, off to the left, narrow, steep stairs. He flicked on the light switch and gestured with an open hand. "You first."

The stairs had a worn carpet covering the treads, and ended in an open space—a corridor above, or perhaps the attic he'd talked about. The passage smelled old, closed up. She didn't like this place. The atmosphere felt . . . unhappy.

"Do you want me to go first?"

She didn't care that he sounded sardonic, as if he believed her vacillation had less to do with an impression of sorrow and had more to do with him. "Please."

"Then be careful. There's no rail." He started up, ducking his head to clear the low ceiling.

She followed. The walls on either side of the stairway weren't more than two feet apart, and she put her hands on them to balance herself.

One tread creaked. "I'm having that one replaced," Devlin said. "Step lightly."

She was glad to do as he instructed. The landing came none too soon, and she breathed a sigh of relief to be on level ground.

But the sensation of unhappiness increased as she stared down a corridor lined with closed doors.

"The servants' quarters." Devlin strode toward the great room at the end.

"What's in them?"

"Rusty iron bed frames. Battered cupboards. Trunks full of junk. When I bought the house I had everything appraised. Some of the better pieces were cleaned, and we're using them in the main part of the hotel. But most of the stuff up here is worthless." Entering the main part of the attic, he moved from one window to another, flinging them open. "Once the hotel is running smoothly, I'll get rid of it."

She followed him. The ceiling slanted from the peak at the middle down to the three-foot-high walls, with windows jutting out in dormers every twenty feet. The sunlight streamed in, and dust motes danced on the beams. The pine floor was unpolished, but in good condition. Scattered throughout the room was a jumble of shabby trunks, cracked vases, and wardrobes tilting drunkenly on three legs.

He stood with his hands on his hips and shook his head. "It's worse than I remember it."

"What a waste." She picked up a pottery bowl, and it fell into jagged halves.

The South Carolina spring made it warm up here. The open windows flushed the heat away, but by no means did they make it cool. She wanted to go hang out the window and pant like a dog in the car. Instead she loosened the top button on her shirt. "Where is this reason why you knew who I was?"

"Watch your step." He wove in and out of the wrecked furniture, making his way to the far wall.

"I will," she said, glaring at a spot right between his shoulder blades. Since he'd discovered she was pregnant, he acted as if she needed to be enclosed in bubble wrap. "I'm simply going to have a baby."

He glanced back.

She banged her knee on the corner of a steamer trunk. She cursed—quietly. That was going to leave a bruise.

Red and blue and yellow oil paints splattered the wall with color. A dusty wooden easel and a large framed canvas was turned backward and leaned against the wall.

Meadow's skin chilled, then heated.

Fifty-five years of accumulated junk had been piled into the room, but she had located the source of the unhappiness.

This was her grandmother's studio. Here Isabelle had painted her last painting. Here she had decided to walk away from Bradley Benjamin. Here her heart had broken.

Was the painting leaning against the wall *the* lost painting? Had she found it at last?

Devlin knelt on the floor before it. "Come and see."

She almost couldn't bear it. She so badly wanted it to be *that* painting, yet even if it was, even if Devlin allowed her to take it to pay for her mother's treatment, it wouldn't make any difference now.

The only thing that would save her mother was a match to her bone-marrow donor. To Sharon's father.

And the chances of a match were never great. Never.

Everything Meadow had done had been for nothing. She'd achieved none of her goals, and she'd had her heart broken.

She pressed her hand to her belly. At least she had her child.

Besides, the painting couldn't be the

painting she sought, or Devlin wouldn't have recognized her eyes.

She shrugged off the hovering sense of defeat.

Perhaps the sorrow was not, after all, emanating from the attic, but from her.

Yet she had made the right decision for her and her baby. She didn't dare take the chance of having her child grow up with a father as sour and demanding as Bradley Benjamin. She only wished she were sure Sharon would be there to play the soothing chimes during Meadow's labor, and lift the newborn to the sky and offer it to the sun, and put its handprints in plaster and hang them beside Meadow's in her art studio.

Devlin watched Meadow without smiling, and in a soothing voice he said, "The bone marrow will be a match. Bradley Benjamin has to do one good thing in his life, and this is it."

Devlin's intuition about her thoughts gave her an uneasy feeling, as if she'd already allowed him too much familiarity with her mind to easily dislodge him.

"What is that?" She knelt beside him.

He turned the canvas—and she gazed into a face dominated by large blue eyes framed with sorrow. She saw the tanned skin, the jutting chin, the dark hair, so black there were blue highlights. The technique wasn't polished, and Meadow had never seen her look so young, but she recognized her anyway.

"Grandmother." She broke into a smile. "That's my grandmother."

Thirty-seven

Meadow examined the portrait from every angle. "It's a self-portrait. I'd recognize her style anywhere."

"I know. Look. She signed it, 'Isabelle Benjamin—*Herself*.'" Devlin pointed at the scrawl in the corner.

"She's so solemn!" Meadow touched the paint that formed her grandmother's cheek lightly with her fingertip. It felt dry and almost crumbly. "She must have painted it right before she left Bradley."

"I think so."

"But I don't look like her." She rubbed her

fingertips together and frowned. A hint of rose pigment stained her skin.

"Your eyes are exactly like hers."

"Do you think so?" she asked, pleased to think she resembled the woman she had loved so much. Pleased that he thought her eyes were as expressive and beautiful as her grandmother's.

"You can't argue with me. This is how I knew who you are."

She didn't want to argue with him. She was already alone with him in a secluded spot—and considering the short time they'd been acquainted, she comprehended the workings of his mind far too well. He would try to convince her she wanted to stay with him. And she knew the danger there, for her body was a traitor to her mind.

So she ignored the remark and asked the next logical question. "Where did you find the painting?"

"Right here." He gestured at the wall. "After she left, Benjamin must have hidden it so he didn't have to look at the face of the woman he loved."

"Yes. Serves him right," she said. "Poor, stupid old man."

"What will *I* look at? I have nothing of you." He managed to look rugged and gloomy at the same time—an impressive feat.

"You have photos from our engagement party. You have the clothes you bought me hanging in your closet. And what the heck—as a memento, I'll make you a glass vase." When she realized his shoulder pressed against hers, she ruined her derisive effect by scuttling to the side, away from him.

"Will a glass vase contain your smile? The way you burst into the morning full of enthusiasm for the day? The way you dance in the moonlight, naked and glorious? Will it contain the love you've lavished on me without a single thought to how unworthy I am?"

"Right now, I'm thinking about how unworthy you are." She kept her gaze on the large painting, bordered by a wide frame of black enamel and gold leaf. "Look, I'm not going to let you seduce me again."

"I've never seduced you. Not once. You took me every time, took me on joyous trips into forgetfulness, into celebration. So no. I'm not trying to seduce you." His voice grew deep and smooth, as irresistible as heated glass and just as dangerous. "I want *you* to seduce *me.*"

It was true. Always she'd allowed her joy in him to carry her into intimacies. Stupid, ill-advised intimacies. Exasperated, forlorn, she faced him.

A mistake.

His rugged, Liam Neeson face hadn't changed; it was as striking and as manly as ever. But his eyes, his wide, dark eyes, humbly pleaded with her.

But she had learned her lesson. She didn't believe them. She would not believe him. And it infuriated her that she wanted to. "What do you want? Is this about *winning*? Before I walk out of your life, do you have to *win* one last time?"

"Yes. You're walking out of here, taking all the sunshine with you, taking my soul, taking my heart. You're going to go across the country, and I'll see you once a month when we fly to some airport to hand our baby to each other, and the best I can hope for is that she looks like you. I want you to stay here with me. I want to make you happy, and have you make me happy. I consider that winning." He sat down on the floor, crossed his legs, and looked at her. "So yeah. This is all about winning."

Clever, clever man. He'd managed to take a humble, supplicant posture—as if she believed he could ever be humble or a supplicant. "I'd be more impressed if you'd mentioned your heart and soul before you found out I was pregnant."

"I didn't even realize I had a heart until you said you were leaving me. Haven't you wondered why, once I knew who you really were, I didn't go to your family and demand an explanation? Why, once I learned of your mother's cancer, I didn't corner you? Threaten you to discover what you thought you could find? I didn't want to expose you. If I did that, I would have had no reason to keep you by my side." He took her hand. "Meadow, I love you."

She pulled it away. "You wanted to use me to get to my grandfather."

"Honey, I did that the first time he saw you. That angina he suffered was perfect. Not fatal, just painful."

"Typical." And very like Devlin. *Don't kill your enemies; hurt them so you can watch them suffer.*

The trouble was . . . she wanted to believe him so badly. She wanted to live with him, have him there while she delivered the baby, watch him carry their kid around in a little hard hat while he dealt with his construction projects. She wanted to dance in the moonlight with him, wake up at his side, make love until they were both exhausted.

But he'd proved she didn't know him at all.

She didn't know his mother, either. She had thought Grace would jump at the chance to get rid of her unconventional daughter-in-law. Instead she'd been upset, and her pleading stuck in Meadow's mind. *Please give him a chance. He's not bad— yet. You make him happy. You can save him.*

She didn't want a man she had to save. She wanted a man to stand at her side, solid and dependable, a man to be the father to her children, a man who supported her art . . . a man who loved her.

Devlin could be that man.

Or he could be a fraud, lying in every way about everything.

There was no in-between.

And in her heart of hearts, she didn't think he was a fraud.

"The baby . . ." she began.

"I like children. I've never had much to do

with them, but no matter how this turns out between the two of us, I promise I'll be a good father to our child." He took her hand again.

Typical. Never give up.

He continued, "But the baby has nothing to do with this. I would still love you so much I'd make love to you without a thought to a condom, because whenever I'm with you, all the shields I've built over all the years disappear and I'm as open and as vulnerable as any fool in love." He tapped his chest. "You can refuse me now and know I'm bleeding."

She couldn't help it. She grinned at the way he phrased it. "So if I refuse you now, you'll bleed and never try to make me change my mind." She watched him struggle to find the best, most tactful way to explain he didn't give up.

She checked her watch.

He opened his mouth.

She interrupted him before he could get a single word out. "Never mind. I know you too well."

"I'll give up when I see you're sure."

He was pretty good at needling her with the truth, too. "We've got nothing in common," she burst out. "We come from different parts of the country. Our backgrounds couldn't be more dissimilar. You're in a cut-throat business with suits and wrecking balls. You read construction magazines, and I read—"

"The Secret Garden."

"Yes! I'm an artist to the very roots of my soul."

"And yet we love each other."

"A shark may love a bumblebee, but where do they build a house?" she asked tartly.

"I would build my house anywhere you want if you would live in it with me." In a voice that enticed and beckoned, he said, "We could even live in Majorca."

"Really? I've always wanted to go there." *Focus, Meadow.* "I don't know if we can find a middle ground."

"We don't have to find a middle ground. If you want to live in a commune, I'll live there with you. I can't promise I won't improve the place. . . ." He searched her face. "This concern is so practical. So un–Meadow-who-dances-in-the-moonlight."

"I remember my grandmother very well." She looked at the painting, touched it again. The paint felt dried-up, bloodless. "She made her life. She painted. She raised Sharon. She walked. She took lovers. She was happy. But underneath . . . something was missing. She never loved another man after Bradley. She wanted him, and they couldn't live together. They were too different."

"The circumstances are similar, but not the same, because I'm not Bradley Benjamin, and you're not your grandmother. Look, Meadow, all I can promise is that you're the best thing that ever happened to me, and I'll love you forever. But if it makes you feel any better"—he pulled a paperback out of his jacket pocket and placed it on the floor between them—"things in common is a bridge that can be built."

Thirty-eight

The Secret Garden.

Meadow picked up the book.

It had been read. The spine was bent and a corner of the cover frayed.

"While you were in the hospital, I went to the gift shop—and found this. They'd received one copy that day. Now, I'm not a man who believes in signs"—Devlin had a talent for understatement—"but I couldn't ignore this one. So I bought it."

"And?"

"Read it in the waiting room." Her incredulous stare made him add hastily, "Not *all* of it.

But I finished it before I went to sleep this morning."

"Weren't you afraid the other guys would think it was mushy?" She sounded snotty even to herself.

"When have I ever indicated I cared what the other guys thought?"

"All right." She couldn't stand to wait. She had to know. "What did you think?"

"Do you remember the miracle at the end, when Archie's dead wife called him back to the garden?" Devlin leaned toward her, and his eyes glowed. "It sent chills up my spine."

She told herself she was inured to his charms, but she couldn't help herself. She had to respond with enthusiasm. "Wasn't that cool?"

"And proof that love never dies, but sometimes goes astray."

She should have known every word he said was to make his point.

But apparently he was finished talking, because he reached out and took her in his lap.

She tucked her head down to avoid his kiss.

He nipped at her ear.

With a gasp, she lifted her head to admonish him.

And the kiss he gave her made her forget how to scold, how to speak, how to breathe. Or perhaps he made her forget any reason to do anything except kiss him back.

When he lifted his head, she lay sprawled across his lap, eyes closed, a smile on her face. But she wanted him to know, without a doubt, that she hadn't been swayed by his kiss. Or at least . . . not only by his kiss. "I'm marrying you because of Mia," she informed him.

"Who?"

Her eyes popped open. "In Jordan's kitchen. Mia. The saucier."

He still appeared bewildered.

Yet she would bet he remembered. He recalled every person in his employ. "If you had never done a single noble thing before in your life, I'd know you were a hopeless case, but you helped that woman."

"I did?"

"You hired her when she desperately needed a job."

He stopped pretending he didn't know what she was talking about and gave her a cool, pragmatic response. "I needed someone local in the kitchen. I gave her the position because she fit the bill."

"You gave her a position and a decent wage. That's more than anyone else in this town was willing to do."

"She's doing a good job or I'd toss her out the door, divorce or no divorce, family or no family." The glint in his chocolate brown eyes was frosty, as if she'd accused him of nepotism.

"You gave her a chance, and then you gave her another chance. When most employers would have fired her, you helped her with her son." Meadow tapped his nose. "She worships you."

"Good God." His mouth, his wonderful mouth, turned down in dismay. "I can deal with only one woman who worships me at a time."

"Who do you have now?" She innocently blinked at him.

He kissed her again.

"Oh, yeah. I remember." She sat up and pushed her hair out of her eyes.

"So we'll get married right away." He was never a man to rest on his laurels. "In Majorca. On the beach where we first took our vows, with the breeze blowing softly over our flushed faces and—"

She interrupted before he could tempt

her. "Nice try. We'll get married in Washington at my folks' place. Grandmother would like that." She glanced at Isabelle's portrait and saw a chunk of paint in the corner of the canvas that had crumbled. Leaning closer, she frowned. "Grandmother must not have known what she was doing. This is the wrong kind of paint. Look." She touched the chip—and a two-inch patch of pigment crumbled to dust.

She caught her breath in dismay. "Oh, no!" All around the hole the paint peeled back, begging to be removed. The canvas beneath glistened with golden light.

She stared it, snared by an absurd thought. Excitement caught her by the throat. Was it possible . . . ? Could her grandmother have been so devious? With her middle finger she thumped the bare spot. More paint crumbled.

"What are you doing?" He caught her wrist. "Be careful. This is the art you've been searching for!"

"I think you're right. I think it might just be." In that corner, the other corner, her grandmother's forehead, all over, the paint was flaking off. Meadow leaned close, so close her nose was almost touching the canvas. "There's an oil painting underneath."

"An oil painting. Why would she paint over oil with water-based paints? That doesn't make sense."

"It does if she was trying to hide something very valuable . . . in plain sight." Gently Meadow removed his fingers from her wrist. As she picked at the chips, she revealed bits and pieces of the domestic scene—a Dutch mother holding a child, a father reading to his sons, a fire in the hearth, and steam rising from a kettle.

"But . . . Isabelle's self-portrait." He sounded appalled.

"She painted other self-portraits, and I promise they're better. She didn't waste time on this one. This one was not for posterity." Meadow held out her hand. "Give me your handkerchief."

Pulling it out of his pocket, he handed it over.

She used it to scrub at the painting until all of the overlay crumbled onto the floor.

Now every part of the scene shone. The oils looked as fresh and glorious as the day they'd been painted by a master hand.

"The Rembrandt," she whispered in awe.

"Rembrandt? It can't be a—" He stopped.

Stared. Imitated her by leaning so close to the painting his nose almost touched.

She grinned as she watched amazement dawn on his face. He looked up at her. "It's a Rembrandt!"

"The lost Rembrandt. There have been rumors about it for years. My grandmother found it hanging in one of the guest bedrooms here at Waldemar. She tried to tell Bradley, but he laughed at her. She tried to tell Bjorn, but he laughed at her. She was on her way to fame in the art world, but this was the fifties. No one believed a mere woman could find the lost Rembrandt."

"Surely she could have convinced someone!"

"When she found it, she was in the last stages of pregnancy."

"Ladies don't put themselves forward while they're expecting." He understood.

She had thought he would, son of the South that he was.

"After my mother was born, Isabelle's unhappiness intensified. Her mother-in-law held sway in her house. Bradley didn't want her to paint anymore. They installed a horror of a nurse who barely let her near the baby."

Suddenly nervous, Meadow rubbed her palms on her jeans.

"My mother wouldn't dream of interfering with our baby. We'll be lucky if she deigns to speak to it until it's eighteen." He put his arm around Meadow. "And I'll let you hold the baby when I'm not."

Meadow laughed and relaxed. Leaning her head against him again, she examined the painting once more. It was beautiful. It was a miracle. For the first time since she'd received her mother's call, she believed her mother would be cured, that Bradley Benjamin's bone marrow would match, that once again Sharon Szarvas would be healthy and vibrant.

Returning to the story, she said, "Grandmother knew she was going to leave Bradley. She couldn't stand to take anything of his, but she didn't want the painting to be thrown away, either. She considered it her daughter's heritage. When I was old enough she told me all about it. I was thrilled. I wanted to go and get it right away. But when I told my mother, she said no. She wanted nothing to do with her father, and considered that taking a painting out of his house would be stealing."

"Ah. That's why you didn't tell your mother where you were going."

"That's why."

"I wonder how she's going to greet Bradley Benjamin."

The answer was easy. "The universe sent me here, now, to get him for her. Why else would all this have happened?"

"That's coincidence. Actually, the universe sent you here, now, so I could get you." He kissed the top of her head, and when she looked up at him, he kissed her mouth. "What do you think the painting is worth?"

"At least twenty-five million," a strange woman's voice said.

They looked up, startled.

Judith stood beside a tall wardrobe near the entrance.

"Judith!" Meadow half stood. "I've been worried about you. I haven't heard from you since . . ." A recent memory, truly forgotten and now recalled, stirred in her mind, and horror chilled her.

Devlin put his hand on her thigh. "Meadow. Who is that?"

She didn't look down at him. Didn't take her gaze off Judith. "That's the woman who's an old family friend. That's the woman who's supposed to be with my mother." She locked eyes with Judith. "That's the woman who pushed me down the stairs."

Thirty-nine

When Devlin looked at the woman by the door, he saw a threat to be eliminated. He also saw the broad expanse of floor between them, the clutter of antique trunks, warped cabinets, and a myriad of broken appliances, vases—the clutter of bygone days—as well as Judith's cold, steady, calculating eyes.

He wasn't at all surprised when she pulled a pistol from the holster under her black jacket.

His gaze flicked around the huge room, seeing the chest, close to him but not much protection.

In a tone that mocked Meadow's chagrin, Judith said, "And I'm the woman who wants you to bring me the painting." She leveled the black eye of a pistol at Meadow. "Now."

Devlin remembered Judith's face. He'd seen her before. But where?

"Has my mother been alone the whole time I've been gone?"

As always, Meadow surprised him. This woman with the cold, flat eyes of a snake held a pistol on them, and Meadow asked questions about her mother.

Judith shrugged irritably.

Devlin diagnosed her reaction with surprise. She felt guilty.

"Your father was with her." Her husky, New York–accented voice tipped him off.

"You're a security guard here," he said. He'd seen her shadowed face on the tiny screen of his walkie-talkie. Now he could assess her. She was short and stout, and she wore the uniform all female security guards wore—a straight dark skirt, a plain white shirt, dark jacket, and sensible heels. She resembled a fifties housewife, if fifties housewives carried a Glock 26 made of superlight plastic polymer with a steel slide and sixteen rounds.

She wanted that painting, and she would kill Meadow and him, walk away, and never glance back.

Her gaze flicked to him. "I had the best references—from Mr. Hopkins."

"He just went to the hospital with a heart attack." And Devlin *had* done Four an injustice.

"So I'll get the credit *and* the painting." Judith smiled like a warped Mona Lisa.

He glanced again at the furniture. At the windows in their dormers. The night table with the cracked marble top. The tall antique wardrobe that staggered under the influence of a broken leg. The wardrobe held potential as a weapon. . . .

"Be quiet, Devlin!" Meadow said fiercely. She turned back to Judith. "My father can throw clay and blow glass, but he can't balance a checkbook, and you know it!" In an exasperated gesture, she pushed her hair off her forehead. "How could you leave them alone?"

"When you came out with the painting, I needed to be here to take it off your hands." Judith's voice was soft, emotionless. Her pupils swallowed the color from her eyes, giving them all the compassion of a snake's.

"You were going to steal the painting from

me? The painting that would save my mother's life? Why? Why?" Meadow was almost stammering. "You have money. Why?"

"It's a *Rembrandt*," Judith said fiercely. "Do you know how much prestige goes to the person who discovers a lost Rembrandt? By God, I may not be able to throw clay or blow glass like you or your father, or paint like your mother or your grandmother. But I'll go down in history as the woman who discovered the Rembrandt." She glanced at the painting, and her eyes gleamed avariciously. "Mr. Fitzwilliam, bring me the Rembrandt"— the gun focused on Meadow—"or I'll shoot her."

She'd been watching him, or listening to rumors, or both, for she knew exactly how to force his hand.

And he would give her the Rembrandt. The painting didn't matter to him—except that it was his, and what was his remained his—but he knew very well that once she had the painting, she could escape only if she killed him, and Meadow, and his child. That he would not allow. "Get behind the wardrobe," he said to Meadow.

He wasn't at all surprised to see her lift

her chin at him. "What am I supposed to do, let her shoot you?"

"I can run and dodge." He used his eyes to reassure and command. "You . . . you are carrying my child." He waited until she nodded, reluctant but acknowledging. "Now . . . get behind the chest of drawers."

"It's not the chest of drawers that will protect me." She turned the large painting long side up and pulled it in front of her.

"What are you doing?" Judith's steady hand suddenly shook. "Meadow, what the hell are you doing?"

Genius. His little darling was a genius. Judith wouldn't shoot the painting, and Meadow had provided a distraction—for him.

He hit the floor and rolled behind a trunk.

A spray of bullets followed him. Splinters flew.

But he wasn't hit yet.

With the three-legged wardrobe as his goal, he dodged from the trunk to a cabinet.

The shooting stopped. Judith wasn't sure which way he'd gone.

"Judith, this isn't what we do." Meadow was moving.

Damn it. He could hear her shuffling to

the side. Why couldn't she do as she was told? Why couldn't she just stay put?

But she used her words like poison darts. "I can't believe you're willing to kill for a *thing*. Possessions aren't art. It's the soul that matters—"

If she said, *What goes around, comes around,* he was going to kill her.

"—And you know what goes around, comes around."

"Shut up." Judith had probably never meant anything as sincerely in her life.

He heard her footsteps moving into the center of the room, away from obstructions . . . looking for him.

She shot as he dashed toward the entrance. Toward the three-legged wardrobe.

Bullets followed him, spraying wood chips in a path . . . toward his ass.

Agony ripped his calf.

He was hit. He was hit.

Goddamn it. Judith had put a bullet in his leg.

He stumbled. Made it to the buffet. The mirror shattered as the ammo smacked it. Glass pierced him. Shards pierced him. He didn't care. His leg hurt so fucking bad . . . in football, some big, stupid defensive tackle had broken his tibia, but the pain was nothing compared to this. This was agony. This was hell.

He glanced down. Saw the splash of crimson on his jeans, the shredded denim, the broken flesh.

He measured the distance to the wardrobe.

He wasn't going to have the speed he needed to knock over the wardrobe. Not and walk away alive.

Well.

So be it. He had experienced the greatest love a man could know, all in the space of three weeks. He had created a child . . . with Meadow. If he didn't survive . . . She would. She must.

If he threw himself across the open space, even if Judith shot him, his body would smack the wardrobe as a projectile.

He planned that it would strike Judith. He trusted Meadow to get out alive.

And he had to run before his leg was worthless.

Dimly he heard Meadow talking, talking. "The value of the painting is nothing if it's stained with blood—"

"Shut up," Judith said fiercely. "Just shut up and give me that painting."

"If I give it to you, you'll kill me," Meadow said, "and I carry the future within me. Don't you see, Judith—"

Devlin gathered himself to dash into the open.

As he did, the floorboards in the corridor creaked. He caught a flash of movement out of his peripheral vision.

Four, that damned fool of a Four, staggered out of the corridor and into the room, bottle in hand.

He spotted Devlin. He pointed—damn him, pointed right at Devlin—and in a slurred voice he yelled, "See, Devlin? I told you it wasn't me. I didn't push Meadow down the stairs."

"Go back," Meadow yelled.

"Fuck," Judith said, and blasted Four with a shot.

Four screamed, spun, and dropped like a rock.

Devlin didn't wait to see him hit the ground. Using his arms, he lunged up and over the buffet.

Judith reacted a second too late. She shot. She missed.

And he was still alive.

He smacked the wardrobe with all the force of a linebacker.

With a groan and in slow motion, the wardrobe tilted toward Judith. For a split second it hung in the air. The doors flew open. Books, dried tubes of paint, the bare ceramic base of a lamp fell out and rolled across the floor toward him.

Judith backed up, hands up to protect herself, eyes bright with fury, pistol pointed at the ceiling.

With a crash that shook the floor, the wardrobe slammed down. One door flew into the air. The cloud of dust blinded Devlin.

"Bastard!" The epithet exploded from Judith with force and virulence.

He hadn't killed her.

He couldn't stop yet.

But when he tried to take a step, pain ripped through him. His leg collapsed.

Through the settling dust he saw Judith. She sat on a rickety trunk, blood trickling from a gash on her cheek and soaking her sleeve. She held the pistol with both hands, and she pointed it right at Devlin.

He had nowhere to go.

His leg couldn't go there even if he did.

He was going to die—and he hadn't saved Meadow. She was going to die, too.

His gaze met hers.

No time for apologies. He was losing consciousness. He put his hand on his heart to indicate his love.

Meadow inclined her head and, in the most detached voice he'd ever heard her use, she said, "Judith, if you shoot him, I'm going to stab the Rembrandt."

He couldn't believe it. No matter how long he lived, he would never forget the sight that met his eyes.

Meadow held the painting at an angle in front of her, the large silver key poised, point down, above the canvas.

"What?" Judith whirled and stared at Meadow.

"You can try to shoot me. You might succeed. You might hit the Rembrandt or damage it." Meadow's amazing blue eyes narrowed until she looked . . . menacing. Very unlike Meadow. "But if you shoot Devlin, I guarantee you're going to end up with a painting so mutilated, the only thing you'll get credit for is screwing up a masterpiece."

He'd never seen Meadow sound so calm.

He'd never seen anyone look so cold as Judith.

Carefully she aimed the pistol at Meadow's head.

Meadow's cool look of menace was reflected on his face. Picking up the base of the lamp, he used all of his rusty football skills, aimed, and threw it at Judith's head. It hit with a resounding smack, knocking her off the trunk and out of sight.

He subsided, breathing harshly, pain-racked, covered with sweat.

He was done.

He had to trust Meadow to handle the rest.

He drifted on a sea of pain.

And when the pain turned into agony, he opened his eyes with a start.

Meadow sat beside him, eyes intent, ripping off his leg.

He was all for it if that would make the misery stop.

Dr. Apps materialized out of nowhere with a large, white-coated goon carrying two huge bags. She didn't even say hello. She merely took over the job of ripping off his leg.

"Hang on, Devlin." Meadow kissed a hand. His hand. "Just hang on."

Two of the security people walked past, holding handcuffs.

The pain in his leg eased. A little.

The security people walked past again, Judith staggering between them, a round, bloody circle in the shape of the lamp on her forehead.

"Nice throw, Devlin." The volume of Meadow's voice wavered as if someone were changing the volume.

Devlin tried to speak, but could only shape the word with his lips. *Four?*

"The emergency people say he'll be fine."

Devlin looked up at Meadow. He'd lost a lot of blood. He couldn't feel his fingers. The bullet had shredded his leg. The world was narrowing to the tiny pinprick of light that was Meadow. He was dying, and he didn't want to go. He wanted to stay here with her. He whispered, "Remember Majorca. Remember, you were walking down the beach in a sundress and you saw me and kissed me. . . ."

"Because I loved you the first time I saw you." She smiled at him, but her smile trembled as though she were scared. "Then I took your hand and led you down the beach to a secluded cove, where we made love."

He couldn't see her anymore, but he could still hear her. And in his mind he could see Majorca, and feel her hands on him, and remember falling in love with her for the first time all over again.

The story he'd made up wasn't a lie.

It just hadn't happened yet. . . .

Forty

At the sound of the scream, Devlin's head whipped around.

His gaze followed his mother's pointing finger. Then he ran past Eddy and Firebird, down the beach through the small, muttering crowd, and toward the waves.

"She's making a break for it."

"I knew she wouldn't make it through this wedding without trying to escape."

"Poor thing. All this trauma has been too much for her."

In a panic he plunged into the Mediterranean, ruining his leather shoes and soaking his Armani suit to the knees. Reaching down, he caught his nine-month-old daughter as she plunged under the surface. Lifting her out of the water, he held her to his chest and headed back for shore.

She squalled and kicked at being pulled out of the waves, while from under the flower-strewn arbor he heard Meadow laughing—laughing because she had taught Willow how to swim and was proud of their fearless daughter.

Sharon headed for him, her arms outstretched. "Aren't you a smart girl?" she cooed.

Willow wailed louder and tried to climb over his shoulder toward the sea.

"Don't encourage her." Devlin pulled out his handkerchief to wipe the sweat of fear off his face, and realized it was soaked with seawater.

"But of course we should encourage her," Sharon said. "She's learning her path, and as her guides, we should help her find her feet."

"Maybe she could find them somewhere besides underwater," Grace snapped. Then, in a mournful tone, she said, "Oh, look. She ruined her outfit."

At the sound of Grace's voice, Willow's

crying cut off as if by a knife. Her bald head swiveled around, her big blue eyes fixed on Grace, and with a gurgle of delight, she held out her arms.

"No." Grace backed up, her hands fending Willow off.

Willow leaned forward, babbling her joy at seeing her grandmother.

"No, no." Grace wore a stylish hat, open sandals, and a beige linen suit, ironed within an inch of its life.

"Here. Let me take her." Sharon wore a yellow, off-the-shoulder cotton shirt and a gathered tie-dyed skirt and and she was barefoot.

Willow shook her head no at Sharon, and again reached for Grace.

"Come on, honey. Your *other* grandma loves you." Sharon also wore a scarf wrapped around her bare head, and a wide hat to protect skin made fragile by a massive dose of radiation and the subsequent bone-marrow transplant.

"Oh, for heaven's sake. Give her to me!" Grace took the dripping child and held her away from her pristine designer outfit.

Willow gave her a big, one-toothed grin.

"Oh, for heaven's sake," Grace said again,

and cuddled his baby. Revulsion at the sopping diaper battled with delight at Willow's adoration. She smirked at Sharon.

Devlin exchanged a look with Meadow.

Their mothers were fighting again—what a surprise. Two more different women there could not be, and their rivalry was intense and focused—on Willow. Willow, who adored them, and had already learned to manipulate them both.

"Shall we start once more?" the minister asked.

Devlin's shoes squished with water and sand as he joined Meadow under the arbor and took her hand. He smiled into her eyes.

The minister began the ceremony all over again.

Meadow wore a simple white dress. She had flowers in her red hair, carried a bouquet of orange blossoms, and, like her mother's, her feet were bare. Her nose was freckled, she had a burn on her finger from her latest glass project, and she watched him as if everything he did and was amazed her.

Meadow was the bride of his dreams—and this was the wedding of his dreams.

Although the other weddings had been, each in its way, an experience he would treasure. The first wedding, occurring within two weeks of those traumatic events in the attic at Waldemar, took place in the cedar grove outside Meadow's home in Washington, and involved not one, but two invalids. Sharon refused to start her radiation and bone-marrow transplant until after the ceremony, but although she'd welcomed Devlin with open arms, she'd been wan and quiet, and leaned hard on the much-warier River.

Devlin's leg had supported him long enough for him to stand up with Meadow while the woo-woo holy woman (as his mother called her) had intoned a blessing and waved a crystal over the happy couple. Luckily, the pain helped him keep a straight face when he glanced at Grace, immaculate in her mother-of-the-groom dress with the matching pillbox hat, and standing lopsided with her Prada slingback heels sunk into the forest floor.

And at Four, equally immaculate in his idea of spring-wedding casual—a Dolce & Gabbana goatskin blazer and striped poplin pants.

And at Bradley Benjamin, dressed like a proper Southern gentleman and torn between horror at the other guests, who consisted of artists and distressingly casual locals, and worry and affection for a daughter he'd barely met and from whom he desperately wanted to win acceptance.

But his bone marrow had matched Sharon's on all six points, and his willingness—no, his need—to donate for Sharon and help her with her cure had begun the healing between father and daughter.

An interesting couple had crashed the wedding in Washington—a tall, broad-shouldered, Italian-looking man with a tall, gorgeous blond on his arm. Devlin had recognized them right away; his brother Roberto Bartolini and his new wife, Brandi. That had been an interesting, potentially uncomfortable meeting made easy by Meadow's openhearted welcome and Roberto's Italian enthusiasm for family.

Now there were periodic phone calls and the occasional visits between the couples, and the idea of having brothers no longer seemed so alien to Devlin.

After that first wedding, Devlin and Meadow had lived in Washington. Meadow had cared for the artists' colony and grown ever more pregnant. While commuting between the two coasts, Devlin had gotten to know all her friends, especially the Hunters, the Russian grape-growing family up the road.

Sharon received her father's bone marrow—and damn near died. Devlin still broke a sweat when he remembered the look on Meadow's face the day he walked in to find Sharon had checked herself out of the hospital and gone home to live out her days.

She'd survived, but it had been a near thing, and Devlin didn't know whether Willow's birth or Sharon's stubborn determination to survive longer than Grace had contributed more to her continued existence.

A few months after Willow's birth, he and Meadow celebrated their wedding and Willow's christening at the Secret Garden *in* the secret garden by the waterfall. It had been, his mother announced with satisfaction, a real wedding with an ordained Methodist minister, Meadow trussed into a formal wedding gown, Devlin in a tux, and the guests, including Sharon and River, suitably if uncomfortably attired in dresses and suits.

Eddy hadn't been able to return from Europe in time for the first wedding in Washington, but this time he did indeed make a radiant maid of honor.

The first two weddings had been for their parents.

This wedding on the beach on Majorca at sunset was for them.

When Devlin and Meadow finished their vows and faced the smiling crowd, he knew he had truly given his heart and soul into Meadow's safekeeping.

And she knew he nurtured her heart and soul with equal care.

She looked around at her family and friends.

At her mother, cancer-free at last. At her father, quietly pleased for his daughter, but even more than that, ecstatic at the chance to visit the famous glassblowing centers of Europe. At Grace, wrinkled, disheveled, and thoroughly in love with her granddaughter. At Willow, wearing Grandmother's hat and teething on Grandmother's Christian Dior sunglasses. At Four, fidgeting because he'd given up his cigarettes. And at Bradley Benjamin, who, God help him, had tried for casual and managed old-guy absurd in a flowered shirt, shorts, and sandals with socks.

And at Devlin, still too rugged to be handsome, still tall and dark, still hers . . . and still alive. She had nightmares about that scene in the attic, about the amount of blood he'd lost before the paramedics got the bleeding stopped, about the damage done by the bullet to the muscle. He had survived both the hospital and rehab without incident, but when she woke at night and snuggled close and kissed him, he always kissed her back.

He'd been too close to death for her to take his existence for granted.

Now he lifted her hand in his and announced, "The party's set up in my yard right above the beach. Let's go up and celebrate our wedding!"

"Again!" Four raised his sweating glass to them.

"We're well married," Meadow answered.

"Third time's a charm," Devlin said cheerfully.

On the fringe of the crowd, an uninvited guest caught her eye. He removed his sunglasses and nodded once.

She gripped Devlin's arm. "Look. It's Sam!"

The day he rode away in the ambulance with Mr. Hopkins was the last time they'd seen him. The ambulance had been found empty except for the frightened driver and his dead assistant. Mr. Hopkins had disappeared completely. And repeated inquiries about Sam to the government and other officials had yielded no information.

The Rembrandt had gone to auction and brought in twenty-nine million American dollars. Judith had plea-bargained for a lesser sentence, and with her testimony and Four's, the feds had put a price on Mr. Hopkins's head.

The $56 million was rightfully Devlin's, but he had declared he was no fool. He'd turned the fortune over to Meadow, who had paid her mother's bills, given Bradley Benjamin a generous finder's fee, set up a small trust fund for Four—because, as she told Devlin, how else was he going to survive? He wasn't good for anything except entertainment— and used the rest for art scholarships in her grandmother's name.

Now Sam appeared, apparently hale and healthy. He watched their guests trudge up the path to Devlin's estate; then, as solemn as ever, he walked toward them. "Congratulations on your marriage."

"Oh, Sam!" Meadow threw her arms around him. "We hoped you were alive!"

Sam suffered her embrace without yielding an inch.

When she let him go, Devlin shook his hand. "Good to see you again, Sam."

"Good to see you, too, Mr. Fitzwilliam. And thank you for asking about me. At the time I wasn't able to respond to your inquiries."

"We suspected you were in deep cover." It was so good to see his pleasure at meeting them. At least, Meadow thought it was pleasure—with Sam, pleasure looked pretty much like indifference or anger or relaxation.

"I wanted to thank you both for your assistance with my investigation last year. In my line of employment I work for a lot of people, and Mr. Fitzwilliam, your organizational abilities and astute eye made my task easier." Sam replaced his sunglasses. "If you ever would like a job with the government—"

"What? No!" Indignant and incensed, Meadow stepped between Sam and Devlin. "He does *not* want a job with the government, and if I ever caught wind of him taking a job with the government—and I'm just as astute as he is—I would hunt you down and hurt you, Sam Whoever-you-are!"

Devlin caught her arm and pulled her toward him. "I believe I just declined, Sam."

"So I see." Something that might pass for a smile on anyone else tugged at Sam's lips.

"Would you like to come to the party?" Devlin gestured up the path.

"No, actually, I'm leaving the island as soon as possible." Yet Sam lingered, scrutinizing them as if looking for a flaw. Abruptly he said, "The investigation into your father and the disappearance of his fortune is reaching a climax, and soon there'll be closure for you and your brothers."

"How many brothers?" Meadow asked.

"What kind of closure?" Devlin took a step toward him.

"I can't say. I just wanted you to know." With a peculiarly Sam-like nod of farewell, he strode off down the beach until the setting sun swallowed him.

"That is a seriously weird guy," Meadow said. "I thought so the first time I opened my eyes and saw him, and I think so now."

"Hmm. Yes. I remember. You took one look at me and fell at my feet."

"Who has amnesia now?" *Smart-ass.*

Devlin tugged her toward him. "What did you think the first time you opened your eyes and saw me?"

She sniffed. "I thought you were rude and scary."

"And?"

"And sexy. And you smelled good."

"That's better."

From the party above them, the music started. People were laughing. Someone was singing. They heard the popping of corks and the clinking of glasses.

But here on the beach they were alone with the sea and the sunset—and each other.

He smiled down at her. "I thank God for the night you broke into my house and fell on your head hard enough to declare you had amnesia."

"And I thank God you saw my resemblance to Isabelle and said we were married."

"I don't know what wild hair got into me to make me say that." He shook his head, as if his own behavior bewildered him.

"I don't either, but every time you made up one of those fantasies about Majorca, I fell deeper under your spell." She kissed his chin.

"Have you ever wondered . . . ?" But it was such a silly thing to say.

"Have I ever wondered . . . what?"

He wanted to hold her, but he didn't want her looking at him while he offered his idea, so he wrapped his arms around her and brought her close, her back to his chest. "Have you ever wondered if your grandmother Isabelle sent you to Waldemar because she loved Bradley and wanted to give him another shot at happiness?"

"What a nice idea." Meadow leaned her head back against his chest. "You do realize my family's woo-woo quotient is rubbing off on you?"

"Don't be ridiculous." He looked over her head and across the water, where the last rays of the sun tipped the waves with gold. "I'm Southern, and while Washington state was still primal forest, we had ghosts haunting our houses."

"You and I aren't so different after all."

He hooted. "Are you kidding? Did you see our guests? Our families? And look at us!" He indicated her bare feet and his ruined leather shoes. "We've got nothing in common."

She twisted in his arms. "What are we going to do about it?"

"Celebrate the difference, my dear." He gathered her close to kiss her. "Celebrate the difference."